# Avenging Angel

Her lips moved and he yearned for their touch. Slowly she drifted toward him, long, pale hair streaming behind her. His eyes locked on hers—eyes so deep they could hold oceans. Her face was inches from his before she began to change.

The skin peeled away from her face. Fangs protruded from her once perfect lips. The flesh and cartilage of her nose disappeared, leaving a hole in the middle of her face. He began to scream as her mouth opened—wide, wider, jaws unhinged like a serpent's as they spread. Inches from his face, the horror floated, dead gaze locked on his own, mouth alive with its writhing tongues.

And then she breathed on him.

It was fire.

He had time to lift one hand, to see the flesh and muscle and nerve tissue burn away to its skeletal marrow.

Then the fire burned his face away and his soul was torn loose to flee naked across the wasteland. . . .

# ANGEL OF DARKNESS

## SAMUEL M. KEY

JOVE BOOKS, NEW YORK

This novel is a work of fiction. All characters and events in this book are fictitious, and any resemblance to actual persons living or dead is purely coincidental.

ANGEL OF DARKNESS

A Jove Book / published by arrangement with the author

PRINTING HISTORY
Jove edition / October 1990



ISBN: 0-515-10422-1

Jove Books are published by The Berkley Publishing Group,
200 Madison Avenue, New York, New York 10016.
The name "JOVE" and the "J" logo
are trademarks belonging to Jove Publications, Inc.

PRINTED IN THE UNITED STATES OF AMERICA

10 9 8 7 6 5 4 3 2 1

for
Sean & Carole

and for those
men and women of the OPF
who give their all
and then give some more

No man is an island, entire of itself; every man is a piece of the continent, a part of the main . . . any man's death diminishes me. . . .

—John Donne

---

What's one less person on the face of the earth anyway?

—Ted Bundy

A WITCHES' BREW of sound.

The vocalization of every hurt, every pain that could be experienced, was digitally stored in the computer's memory banks, brought to a boil by fingers dancing across a keyboard. VU meters burning into the red. Disk drives humming. Software restructured from a hundred mistakes until it reached its final, perfect, almost occult program. The matrix taking shape inside the hardware, circuits brought into play, one after the other in ordered sequence.

The sounds that lay in wait, that needed only one flick of a switch to burst from the speakers, had never before existed in precisely this configuration. No one had dared to harness these pains, these cries of hurt and terror before. Their precise pattern, the matrix of their interrelationship to each other, should have remained impossible to uncover.

But he had.

And he knew it worked.

He was sure it would work this time.

It was a simple given that one reasoning individual,

unbound by the social restrictions fettering other experimenters, could conceive of how to use these sounds. Could undertake the labor to interface them with the correct programs. Could bring to fruition an experiment of which others could barely conceive.

There was power in sounds.

Sounds could heal.

Sounds could kill.

This time he was sure he'd succeeded.

The last girl had given him everything he'd needed, from her first screams of terror to her final burbling moan, as what remained of her life fled from between her skinned lips.

He leaned back in the swivel chair, turning from the array of computer and sound equipment. A flick of a switch set hydraulic motors working, and a section of wall rolled aside on oiled bearings to reveal an expanse of dark glass. Another switch brought the room behind that soundproofed glass into sharp focus. He put his hands behind his neck and leaned farther back in his chair, surveying his handiwork.

She'd lasted the better part of a day and a half.

It was her youth.

Youth's resilience.

She had come to him for experience, as others did from time to time. Most he never touched. He only played the kindly father figure for them. He was there when they needed someone. The other half of the basement—the genuine sound studio half—was where they congregated to practice, where he made their demo tapes for them and gave them the expertise of a lifetime spent in music.

The kindly father . . .

But sometimes he kept one. To feed the program. To

give the software a human voice. Play a high C on the keyboard, and it came forth from the speakers in a human voice, shrill with pain. Combine it with other notes, and chords of agony came forth. A music of terror. A music that could wake the dead. A music that could kill. A music that could enlighten. His music. Created with his program. From terror and pain.

Not all the collected sounds in the memory banks had come from those who had died in that small chamber. There was genuine singing built into the matrix—dozens of young voices that had sung out their hearts in his studio, hoping for the big break. He'd left them untouched, except for the tiny part of their souls that was digitally stored in the memory banks. There was the sound of mothers in childbirth, sounds acquired at the scenes of fires and accidents, sounds recorded in asylums and hospitals. Once he'd kept a madman screaming for a week in that small black room, screaming until his voice finally gave out.

But this last girl . . . surely she'd given him the most.

He looked at what was left of her, strapped to the metal operating table. Electrodes sprouted wires that ran to an EEG machine and various monitoring systems. IV tubes sank into her veins. Some carried nourishment, others dispersed drugs to heighten the sensitivity of her nerve endings. A microphone hung above her head. Others were attached to the muscles of her neck. Still more had been drilled into the bone near her ears.

It smelled like a slaughterhouse in there, but the stench was a sweet scent to him. The slightly metallic narcotic that was blood. It was true that at first she'd loosed all that her bowels and kidneys held. But that was easily cleaned. And then she was empty. Purified.

And then all that remained was the smell of her flesh. And her blood.

What lay on the surgical table resembled a human being only in its shape. A doctor would recognize the musculature, bared to the air by the removal of her skin. But most viewing that shape would see only some monstrous thing out of their darkest nightmare. While he . . . he saw the sweet completion of his work.

He flicked on display screens, one after another. Their computer-generated roiling swirl of colors was the closest he could personally come to experiencing his program without personal risk.

But if he was to engage this one switch . . .

(He needed a suitable subject.)

. . . the sound that would come from those speakers . . .

(There was only one suitable subject.)

But he didn't dare. The true scientist never experimented on himself. It simply wasn't . . . objective enough. The sound . . .

It might kill.

Or it might enlighten.

It would certainly irrevocably change the subject.

Forever.

Death was permanent. As was enlightenment.

He toyed with the switch, his gaze moving from the display screens, where his program pulsed as though to the rhythm of his own heartbeat, to the room where the girl had been slowly skinned.

He had lost count of how many had given him their all. Would it be fair to them, to the sacrifice they had made, for him to retreat from this moment?

He leaned closer to the glass separating the girl's body from his control room. Her sightless eyes, the eyelids cut away, appeared to mock him. He lacked courage, they told him. He could bring pain, but could he dare it himself? Knowing what he did—like a coin toss, madness leading to death on one side, enlightenment on the other—how could he not chance the final step himself?

Who was more deserving?

There was power in sound. A certain note could bring uneasiness, a series of them fear, others happiness. Or healing. Or peace. And somewhere, in that complex pattern between eighty-five and eleven hundred cycles per second that was man's range of emission reception, it was waiting for him. The final matrix of his program. He could feel the auditory cortexes on either side of his brain humming in anticipation.

Did he dare?

How could he not?

Amplitude, frequency, and wavelength, fine-tuned to perfection. Digital ghosts awaiting one simple movement of his fingers . . .

Thumb and index finger tightened on the switch. He gave the sightless eyes of his last victim a quick smile. He flicked the switch.

At first there was no change.

His gaze went to the swirling patterns still undulating across the display screens.

And then he heard it. A pure tone, simple and stark, that set up a sympathetic vibration in his skull. A harmony rippled across it and the ossicles of his middle ear vibrated to its rhythm, sending the sound to his inner ear. His vision grew unfocused. The room spun with the same pattern that moved across the displays. Then his eyes rolled upward and he saw only a void as the matrix spilled its brew throughout the room in a sudden flood of sound.

The pleasure centers of his mind ached with sensation.

Between his legs, his penis grew stiff as a steel rod, pressing painfully against his pants. He clawed at his fly to release it from confinement. Freed, his penis vibrated like a tuning fork. His testicles became two tiny, hard rocks as his scrotal sac drew up tight against the base of his penis.

He was aware of every object in the room and his relationship to it by a sense of echolocation that made his entire body a receptor of sound. The sounds . . .

A woman in labor.

A madman's howling.

A child's pain as the skin was cut from her, piece by bloody piece.

Made into a music that had no known counterpart.

His back arched in the chair and he was allowed one brief lucid moment. He saw the room through a smoky haze. He smelled the acrid stench of frying circuitry, melting cables, burning plastic. He saw the skinless face of his last victim while the displays pulsed in his peripheral vision.

Then something began to take shape between the glass that separated his victim from him and the chair in which he sat. It coalesced slowly, from a bewildering spin of shapeless mist into a young woman's face. She floated on the air before him—a vision as perfect as the music, clothed in filmy white cloth as tattered as a child's helpless cries.

She was an angel of sound.

The soul of the music given a moment of human form.

Her lips moved and he yearned for their touch. Slowly she drifted toward him, long, pale hair streaming behind her. His gaze locked on hers—eyes so deep, they could hold oceans. Her face was inches from his before she began to change.

The skin peeled away from her face. Fangs protruded from her once perfect lips. The flesh and cartilage of her nose disappeared, leaving a hole in the middle of her face. He began to scream as her mouth opened—wide, wider, jaws unhinged like a serpent's as they spread. A multitude of tongues wriggled in that dark hole.

She was no angel now—unless it was an avenging angel.

A fury.

The music swelled and swallowed his scream. The control room disappeared and he found himself on a vast plain. A gray wasteland of unending bleak vistas spread in every direction. The skies were smog yellow, heavy with an unpleasant salty stench. Leafless trees reached with limbs like fingers to claw at the sky. Inches from his face, the horror still floated, dead gaze locked on his own, mouth alive with its writhing tongues.

And then she breathed on him.

It was fire.

He had time to lift one hand, to see the flesh and muscle and nerve tissue burn away to its skeletal marrow.

Then the fire burned his face away and his soul was torn loose to flee naked across the wasteland.

In the control room he was dying.

He was dead before his body crumpled from the

chair. But he lived on in the wasteland. A part of the horror; apart from it.

In the control room the figure spun slowly in place in the center of the room, her shape dimming as one by one the various speakers continued to melt. She floated over the corpse he'd left behind with its head and right hand burned away to the bone. The screen displays exploded, shattering with such force that glass shards were embedded in the walls. The computers smoked. The window between the control room and where the body of the young girl lay developed a webwork of cracks, then it, too, exploded. Acrid smoke lay thick and heavy in the room.

And still the figure spun.

Until the last of the music died in the last speaker.

Then she drifted away. Toward a wall. Passing through the molecules of solid matter as only sound can.

And then she was gone.

All that remained in the control room was the crackle of bare wires as they hissed and spat against each other before they burned out.

And then there was silence.

In the wasteland he screamed, still running naked across the plain, feet bloody, mind a ruin.

But that wasn't a sound that carried beyond its borders.

# ONE

## 1

JANET ROWE.

Pulling up in front of the house in his Toyota pickup, Jack Keller repeated the name to himself as though it were a charm. He'd never met her, but it was because of her that he was here. Killing the engine, he stared at the house. Unwelcome fears whispered in the back of his mind as he sat and studied the structure.

(He was already too late.)

Janet Rowe. Fourteen years old. Caught in that delusion of feeling mature beyond her years. Her mind told her she was an adult and knew exactly what she was doing. Family and social constraints told her otherwise. They explained, in less than understanding terms, that she had to wait for the magic ages. Sixteen, and suddenly she would be capable of driving a car. Eighteen, and she could leave home, vote, go into a bar and order a drink. Until then she had no status. She was to do what she was told, end of discussion.

Through his work Jack had come to the realization that all kids went through that period of confusion and questioning to some degree or another. The only thing that ever surprised him was why more of them didn't hit the streets the way the few nervy ones did. But the problem with the streets was that there were no answers there, either. His years in plainclothes and uniform had taught him that long before he took this job.

All that happened was that the kid's choices narrowed. They had to walk a tightrope, scrounging for a living, every choice driving them deeper into the mire, not out of it. There weren't many jobs on the legal side of the law for an underage kid. So they had to be found and brought home before they took a step too far. Before it was—

(too late)

Janet Rowe.

When her parents contacted him, he went looking. Not just because it was his job but because he didn't want to read about her getting picked up for hooking or B&Es. He didn't want to see her being pulled out of a river on the six o'clock news. He wanted her to have a chance.

What the parents didn't know when they hired him was that he was willing to give the kid the opportunity to tell her own side of the story. If it was just too weird at home—say her old man was coming on to her, or her old lady was a lush and beating on her—he'd let her know the options she had. There were other places these kids could go, and he was willing to show them what they were. He just wanted them off the street.

Because the ones he never found were each a personal failure. They lay in wait in his mind—elusive, slightly mocking faces that could pop into his mind at any time of the day. Wanting to know why he'd let them down.

But worse were the ones he found—

(too late)

—because they wouldn't let him sleep. They haunted his dreams. Twelve-year-old hookers. Thirteen-year-old junkies. Pale corpses, thin with malnutrition, dug out of shallow graves, floating in rivers. . . . Every city had them. The ones for whom it would always be—

(too late)

Jack rubbed his face, wishing he could forget, knowing that he never would. Not just because of the horrors he ran across, but because if he didn't remember those kids, then who would?

Take Janet Rowe.

She already had a lot of strikes going against her. Sure, her parents had hired him to track her down. Big investment on their part. Put out a little money and then sit back and wait for someone else to clean up their mess. Because what they hadn't told him—what he'd had to find out from her friends as he was tracking her down—was that there was a long history of abuse in the home.

The only real question in cases like this was: Why hadn't she run away a lot sooner?

Janet's friends hadn't come right out and told him that her old man beat on her, or that her mother had engaged in a campaign of mental warfare against her ever since she was out of her diapers, but Jack didn't need Janet's friends to lay it out for him. At this point in his career he was used to reading between the lines. What he wanted now was to hear it from Janet herself. If she confirmed what he'd already intuited, there was no way she'd be going back to her parents.

Just to run away again.

And maybe get in too deep. . . .

The house loomed in Jack's sight. He couldn't shake the feeling that she was already in way over her head.

(too late)

Getting out of the pickup, he walked over to Chad Baker's house. He'd known—just *known*—when he'd first tracked down word on the street that Janet Rowe had been seen with him that something bad was going down, but he never could have said why. After a while you got a feel for it. Standing on the porch—leaning on the bell, no answer—that earlier premonition crystallized into a sudden fear for the girl that was so sharp, it hurt his chest.

He knew then that he couldn't go in. Not now. Not on his own. This wasn't going to be a matter of just freeing some kid from a bad situation. This one needed cops to make sure the investigation went just right.

He left the porch, then stopped to look back at the house, the skin crawling all up and down his back. There was a sound in the air that lifted goose bumps on his arms and the hairs at the nape of his neck. He took a step back toward the house, and then he saw something that left its afterimage burned into his retinas, long after it was physically gone.

If it had ever existed.

If he hadn't just imagined it.

A mist coming out of the side of the house, riding that faint, eerie music. A figure in the mist that had the face of an angel and the body of a showgirl, long streaming hair flowing behind her. A look in her eyes that froze the blood in his veins because there was something behind that gaze that was merciless. . . .

A fury. . . .

A sense of vertigo made him stagger and then everything he knew was gone. A vast plain lay all around him, spreading out for as far as he could see. Dead reaches of wasteland, grey and empty under a sickly sky. A salty, metallic odor stung his nostrils. That faint trace of hellish music that had heralded the angel's arrival. . . .

The figure floated there, watching him. He wanted to run and hide from her. He wanted to embrace that showgirl body, he wanted the taste of those angel lips on his own. . . .

Slowly the city came back around him, though it still wasn't right. Buildings and trees returned first—the houses all ruined and falling in on themselves, dark holes where the lit windows should be. The trees were bare of all vegetation. The walkway underfoot was cracked and uneven. Then the cracks began to join. Foliage appeared on the trees and hedges. Lights flared in the windows of the houses, which were no longer ruins. And there was sound again. True sound. Traffic on Bank Street, a couple of blocks over. Wind in the trees. The hum of a city's residential area.

But that music was gone.

He wasn't sure how long he stood there, unable to move. The figure, the wasteland—if he hadn't just imagined them—had been gone for a while. He knew that much. Suddenly he gasped for air, lungs pumping, chest sore. He hadn't been aware of holding his breath. Hadn't been aware of anything except that . . . that vision. . . .

You're losing it, Jack, he told himself.

He turned again and this time he didn't look back, heading for his sister's house, a block away on Harvard Avenue, to use the phone, then stopped. He couldn't involve Anna. Not in this. Christ, she *knew* this Baker. Everybody in the Ottawa music scene did. He was half guru, half saint, to who knew how many of the local bands and players.

(And he had something coming out of the side of his house that looked like an angel, and she could take you to a dead place where nothing lived. . . .)

Don't think about it, Jack told himself.

He went on to Bank Street, looking for a pay phone, and lucked out when a patrol car came by. He flagged it down and spent five wasted minutes trying to convince the uniforms that this was a serious situation. It wasn't until he'd told them that he'd been a cop himself—worked the same field patrol that they were on right now, for Christ's sake—that they drove back to Baker's with him.

He said nothing about what he thought he'd seen.

Things had changed in the few minutes he was gone. There was a smell in the air now like burning plastic. The house had a dead look to it—as though it was still partially in that . . . other place. . . .

He didn't go in. He left that to the uniforms—it was their job. He just sat down on the steps while they tried the door. Unlocked. They went in. Jack didn't know exactly what they were going to find, but he knew it'd be bad. When the younger of the two uniforms came out and threw up in the bushes on the other side of the steps, he knew it was even worse than he'd imagined.

What did I see? he wondered as a yellow traffic cruiser pulled up.

The flashing lights strobed in his eyes, giving him a headache. He went to sit in the back of the first cruiser, slouching in his seat, fingers kneading his temples. He saw the unmarked car arrive, a pair of plainclothes get out. He knew both men, but he didn't recognize either of them at that moment. He was remembering an angel and a wasteland.

A fury. . . .

What the hell did I see?

He wasn't sure he ever wanted to find out. But that sense of premonition returned and he knew that he wasn't going to be given any choice in the matter.

## 2

NED MEEHAN SLOWED the unmarked sedan beside one of the blue-and-white patrol cars that blocked either end of Wendover Avenue, between Chesley and Warrington. Their rotating lights, combined with those of a yellow traffic cruiser, lent an unavoidable air of drama to the scene. He and his partner reached for their badges as a uniform approached and bent down to look into the open window of the Buick. Ned let his ID fall back into the inside breast pocket of his suit coat when he recognized the patrolman. Patrick Nichols was a constable in B Platoon—the same platoon Ned had worked on his last uniform tour.

"Figures, doesn't it?" Nichols said to the detectives. "Ten minutes to go on the shift and something like this comes up."

Ned's partner, Ernie Grier, leaned across him from the passenger's seat to talk to the uniform.

"How's it look, Pat?"

"Messy. We're going to be here all night."

Grier settled back into his seat. "And you said it was going to be a quiet shift," he complained to Ned.

The uniform stepped aside. Ned shifted into first and eased the Buick ahead. Pulling up to the curb, he shut off the engine. Before getting out, the two detectives sat and looked at the house from which the call had originated. A possible 10-11 was the first they'd heard of it back at the station—the catch-all code that ranged from an assault to any kind of a disturbance. Scratch the possible, Ned thought, remembering the uniform's comment.

The house was an attractive two-story brick bungalow, the first house but one from Warrington Drive, on the east side of Wendover. Beyond Warrington, the Rideau River moved slowly, its brownish waters glinting from the lights. The area was part of Ottawa South, a residential area that usually called in nothing more serious than a B&E. Ned knew the neighborhood well. He'd driven it while on field patrol, and he had friends living just one block over on Harvard Avenue.

Getting out of the car, he joined his partner on the pavement. At six-one and a hundred and eighty pounds, he seemed hefty only when he wasn't standing next to Grier, who topped him by two inches and weighed in at an extra thirty pounds, none of it flab. Both men had short-cropped hair and mustaches.

"Why do I get the feeling we're going to regret catching this call?" Grief asked. He shook a low-tar cigarette out of its pack—his one concession to the dangers of his one-and-a-half pack a day habit—and lit up. Blue-gray smoke haloed his face like frosty breath, but the May night was warm.

Ned just shrugged, knowing that his partner wasn't expecting an answer. Grier was a pessimist. Even in a city as quiet as the Nation's Capital, he always expected the worst on every call.

"It's not like I can't use the overtime," Grier went on as they started up the walk to the front porch where another uniform waited for them. "Christ knows I got bills coming out of my ears. It's just . . . messy, Nichols says. I don't need messy. I go home after one of these and I look at my kid, but I don't see him. All I can see is the blood. I mean, who needs it?"

Ned knew the uniform's face, but he couldn't put a name to it. "Meehan and Grier," he said to him. "We caught the call."

The uniform's face looked washed out, even taking into account the bright porch light. That, Ned thought, didn't bode at all well for whatever was waiting for them inside. Messy. Ernie was right. Who needed it? He wondered about the sharp smell in the air. It was like burned rubber or plastic.

"You okay?" Ned asked. The uniform was young. It was probably his first bad one.

"I . . . I'm getting there."

"We'll take you through it quick," Ned said. Grier fished out his duty book and pen to make notes. "What's your name?"

"Ron Coffey." Grier squinted for a moment at the man's badge, then took down its number.

"Were you and Nichols the first on the scene?" Ned asked.

Coffey nodded. "We were flagged down by a civilian on Bank Street at eleven forty-six. We called in our position, made a quick recon, then had Dispatch send you down."

"You got a body in there?"

Coffey's face went pastier in the bright light. An approaching siren heralded the arrival of an ambulance from the General Hospital.

"Are you okay?" Ned asked again.

Coffey took a deep breath, then gave a quick nod. "There's a couple of bodies—at least what's left of them."

Ned let that one pass, though he didn't miss the I-told-you-so look that his partner shot him. "What about the guy who flagged you down?" Ned went on. "Where's he?"

"In the patrol car."

Coffey made a quick motion with his chin to where one of the older blue-and-white models was parked, blocking off the other end of Wendover where it met Warrington. The detectives glanced in its direction. In the light thrown from the ambulance's headlights, they could easily make out the features of the man slouched in the backseat of the blue-and-white.

"Shit," Ned said.

"You know him?" Grier asked.

"It's Jack."

Jack Keller had been Ned's partner for two years, before Jack quit the force and Ned was teamed up with Grier.

"You want to go talk to him?" Grier asked.

Ned shook his head. "He can wait. Let's go inside." As he turned back to the door he noticed a small white card beside the doorbell that read BAKER STUDIO. "What's that?" he asked Coffey.

"Guy who owned the place had some kind of a recording studio in the basement."

"Anybody inside right now?"

"Constables Dwyer and Paige."

Ned nodded to himself. That was good. Benny Dwyer was a fourteen-year veteran. He didn't know

Paige, so he assumed that the yellow traffic cruiser was his.

"You don't have to come in," he told Coffey. The man looked relieved. "Just keep the medics out until we ask for them and put in a call to Dispatch. We need"—he began to tick the items off on his fingers—"the area sealed off. We need a coroner—whoever's on call. We need Inspector Fournier down here. If he's already gone off duty, then we need—" He looked at his partner.

"Ryerson," Grier offered.

"We'll need Inspector Ryerson down here," Ned continued. "Get the ID unit. . . ." He gave Coffey a quick smile. "Well, you know the drill." When Coffey left the porch to put in the call, he turned to his partner. "Ready?"

"No."

"Then let's go."

They moved down a short hallway. The smell of burned plastic was stronger inside. A living room led off to the left. On the right was what looked like an office. It had a large desk with a chair behind it, another pair in front of the desk, a wall of bookshelves. There appeared to be some diplomas on another wall. A half dozen or so framed gold records. A third uniform met them in the kitchen.

"Constable Paige?" Ned asked.

He looked to be in better shape than Coffey but still a little queasy.

"Meehan and Grier," Ned said when the patrolman nodded. "Where's Benny?"

"Downstairs with the body. Listen, you'd better steel yourself. It's not pretty."

"Time we found out for ourselves," Ned said.

But there was no way they could have prepared themselves for what they found below.

## 3

GIRLS' NIGHT OUT.

Anna liked the Rainbow. The dance floor was small, and when the band was good, it could get crowded, but it was the right kind of crowded. Everybody jostling and having a good time, moving to the music. Too bad Beth was working tonight, she thought as the band kicked into an old Motown number, "Mr. Big Stuff."

The Midnight Hour was one of her favorite bands—partly because she knew them personally but mostly because they were just so good. They were a five-piece—sax, guitar, bass, drums, and keyboards—fronted by Lisa da Costa, whose voice ranged anywhere from a husky growl to a pure soprano, depending on the song. Anna and Lisa used to live together until Lisa fell in love with a sax player and moved in with him, which left Anna looking for a new housemate. But then she'd found Beth. . . .

"I'm beat," Janice moaned when the song came to an end.

It was just the three of them out on the town tonight—Janice, Cathy, and Anna. Janice leaned heavily against Anna, five feet four inches of exaggerated limp muscles. Her brown hair was cut fashionably short, giving her a perky look.

Anna grinned. "Too bad. Someone's had his eye on

you all night—just waiting to get up the nerve to ask you for a dance, if you ask me."

"Where?"

"Over by the bar—the tall guy in the jean jacket."

"Dreamy," Cathy said, giving him a quick glance.

"Knowing my luck," Janice said, "he'll be gay."

"Want me to find out?" Anna asked.

"Don't you *dare.*"

The band started up a slow version of "Love Potion No. 9."

"Here's our cue to bow out," Cathy said.

She gave Anna's arm a quick tug, and the two of them were off the dance floor before Janice caught on to what they were up to. She moved to catch up to them, but the man by the bar was suddenly in front of her.

"Dance?" he asked.

Janice gave her companions a quick shrug, then smiled at the stranger. "Sure. What's your name?"

"Dave. What's yours?"

Anna and Cathy returned to their table on the edge of the dance floor and watched the pair dance. Janice had a happy look on her face, and Anna had to agree with Cathy about the stranger. He *was* dreamy. He and Janice worked their way closer to the stage, slow dancing. Checking each other out, or at least as much as they could over the sound of the band.

"So much for our girls' night out," Cathy said as she topped her glass with more beer. She leaned forward, pulling her long red hair free from behind her back and the chair. She wore it in a ponytail tonight.

"And if he'd asked you?"

Cathy laughed. "I'd be gone like a shot."

Anna laughed with her. Leaning back in her chair,

she stretched out her legs where they wouldn't get tromped on by a particularly romantic pair of dancers too caught up with the business at hand to watch where they put their feet. She drank some of her own beer.

She was a small attractive woman of twenty-eight with a dark complexion and medium-length black hair cut in long bangs that she was constantly brushing back from her eyes. She worked hard, taking contract proofreading jobs and working for a temporary secretary service, but mostly she liked to spend her time making things. She'd tried her hand at everything from weaving to painting to carpentry. Her current project was sculpting with fabric maché. She was working on a series of life-size old men and women. The sculptures, in various states of completion, were threatening to fill the back porch where she worked. The only thing she liked better than making things was singing, but somehow she could never find the time to make the commitment a band needed from its members. The only singing she did, besides serenading her sculptures, was some backup work in the local studios and occasionally onstage with the Midnight Hour.

"I'm glad he chose Janice," Cathy said.

"Why's that?"

"Oh, you know how's she's been since she broke up with Tom. The guy ended up being a total jerk, but they *were* together for how long? Three years?"

"Something like that."

"Well, you get used to being a couple. She hasn't been seeing anybody since."

"Not like you," Anna teased.

"Don't I wish. But I tell you, Anna, if there's a weirdo in the house, you can bet he'll hit on me. I swear—it's like I draw them out of the woodwork or something."

"It's that hair."

"Hair, nothing. It's short skirts and tight jeans."

"Not to mention no bra."

"Not to mention."

"So tell our viewers, Ms. Cole," Anna asked, holding a beer bottle up to Cathy as though it were a microphone. "To what do you owe your tartish behavior?"

"Strict parents, natch, but of course society's to blame."

The waitress came by to take their order. Since Janice had remained on the dance floor for the next number as well, they ordered another round just for themselves.

"Are you still seeing Kevin?" Cathy asked when the waitress was gone.

"When he's got the time. Mind you, I've been pretty busy working on that set design for Charlie's play."

"And baby-sitting your roommate."

Anna frowned. "That's not very nice, Cathy. If you'd been through half of what she has—"

Cathy held up her hands. "I know, I know. And I like Beth, don't get me wrong. But I don't think it's healthy the way she hangs on to you like you're some kind of lifeline."

"I *am* her lifeline," Anna said. "I'm all she's got right now."

Cathy gave her a long, considering look, then nodded. She wanted to say something about how she also didn't think it was healthy for Anna to be putting as much as she was into helping Beth. Sure, people like Beth needed help, but they never seemed to want to help themselves. It was all take, no give. They were like leeches. Psychic vampires.

Cathy didn't like seeing what it was doing to her friend. It was closing down Anna's own chances for a lot of happiness. She was always staying in with Beth, except for the few occasions that Beth could be coaxed out of the house. Cathy was surprised that Beth had stuck out her latest job as long as she had. Going on two weeks now. But this wasn't the time to get into any of that. At least Anna *was* out tonight.

"Want to see Janice freak?" she said suddenly.

"Cathy, don't. Whatever it is you're planning . . ."

"I'm just going to cut in, that's all. Guys do it all the time."

Anna caught up with her before she reached Janice. "Dance with me," she said.

"Or what?"

"Or I'll bop you one."

Cathy gave her a look of mock fear. "Okay, okay. I'm dancing, already."

# 4

THE STAIRS GOING DOWN into the basement were wider than usual for a house this old. In fact, Ned thought as he led the way down, the whole place had the look of renovation about it, from the oversize living room that had engulfed what must once have been the dining room, to the kitchen, which appeared to have been widened by an addition on the back of the house.

The burning smell grew stronger as they descended.

"I'm surprised no one's called in the fire department," Grier said from behind him.

Ned grunted a meaningless reply. There was something in the air—more than just the stink—that had the flesh crawling up his back. It was like walking into an old, low-rent tenement when you just *knew* someone was waiting in the dark for you, shotgun trained at your gut.

Benny Dwyer met them at the bottom of the stairs. "Whatever kind of fire they had here," he said, "it's long out now."

Dwyer was in his late thirties, a bulky man with too much stomach and an ever-increasing bald spot on the crown of his head. He gave Ned a considering glance.

"You feel it too?"

Ned nodded.

"Feel what?" Grier asked.

Dwyer shrugged. "There's a . . . I don't know . . . lost feeling about this place." He looked embarrassed at having opened up that much. "Guess there's a good reason. The bodies are in here."

Two doors led off from the small hall at the bottom of the stairs. Through the open door on the right the detectives could see a furnace room and the usual accumulation of junk that was in any basement. Dwyer led them through the door on the left.

"Jesus H. Christ," Ned breathed.

The initial impression was too much to take in all at once. There were the banks of recording equipment, slagged and blackened. Broken glass was everywhere, some of it embedded right in the walls. There were the speakers, woofer cones burned out, tweeters half melted. Ned's gaze went to the corpse on the floor, took in the state it was in, slid away, returned again. The man's head and one hand were burned away to the bone. Staring at the corpse, trying to figure out just what the hell could have done that kind of localized damage, a strange sense of dislocation came over him.

For a moment it felt like his view of the room was doing a slow strobe. He saw the mess of the recording equipment, the dead man.

Flicker.

Now he saw some vast, empty wasteland that stretched in all directions for long, desolate miles.

Flicker.

The room was back again.

"Ned?" Grier asked. "You okay?"

Ned leaned against the doorjamb and nodded.

Grier stepped around him. "What the fuck went down here, anyway?"

"This isn't the worst," Dwyer said. He pointed toward a hole in the wall that had once been a window.

The detectives moved toward it, Grier first, Ned bringing up the rear. Ned shot a quick look at the other side of the control room where the recording and drum booths lay beyond another glassless window.

Flicker.

Those bleak plains were back. He turned his head.

Flicker.

They were gone. He looked over Grier's shoulder and the contents of his stomach did a heave.

He'd been on the scenes of a lot of bad accidents, pulled a body from the river that had been in the water for a couple of weeks, but he'd never seen anything like this. It wasn't a human being. It was just a lump of red meat in the shape of a human lying there on the table. Except it still had hair. And eyes . . .

"Skinned," Dwyer said from behind them, his voice hushed. "The fucker skinned her."

Flicker.

Now Ned saw the body in that other place, lying on a flat gray stone, the sickly yellow skies above. . . . And there was something in the air, a sound, some kind of moaning that was like music. . . .

Flicker.

Beside him, Grier staggered. "What the hell . . . ?"

They were all feeling it, Ned realized. All of them seeing . . . something. . . .

Grier reached out a hand to catch his balance and cut himself on a piece of glass still embedded in the frame. Seeing the fresh blood well up from his partner's hand was just what Ned needed to start making some sense out of all of this.

"Out," he said. "Everybody out of here."

He caught hold of Grier's shoulder and steered him toward the door.

"What . . . ?"

"There's a gas leak or something in here."

Ned waited until both Dwyer and Grier were out in the hall before he closed the door to the control room. As the door slammed shut, Ned had the sudden feeling that he'd closed in something more than just the carnage.

"Let's get that hand looked at," he said, ushering the two men up the stairs ahead of him.

Grier looked down at the blood seeping from the cut as though he were seeing it for the first time. Ned didn't relax until all three of them were out on the front porch again. He drew the night air into his lungs as though it were a drug. One deep breath after another.

"I had the weirdest feeling in there," Grier said. "It was like I was . . . somewhere else. Just for a moment."

"Lost," Dwyer said. "It's like you could just get lost. . . ."

We're all spooked, Ned thought.

"It's got to be some kind of gas," he said firmly, trying to bring things into perspective.

Gas. Right. But that didn't explain the condition of either of the bodies.

"I don't want anybody else going down there without a gas mask on," he added.

He saw that the IDent van had arrived, the ID unit unloading their gear. A little up the street, Inspector Fournier was getting out of a cruiser. There were more uniforms, another pair of plainclothes. Bystanders were arriving. They would need to put up barricades and seal the site.

Flicker.

The street was gone. Empty reaches stretched for as far as the eye could see, endlessly gray under smoggy skies.

Flicker.

He rubbed a hand across his temples. Jesus.

"Nobody down there without a mask," he repeated to Dwyer. "Ernie, why don't you fill Fournier in on what we know while you're getting that hand bandaged."

Grier shot him a worried look. "You're not going back down there, are you?"

Ned shook his head. He glanced over to the right where a dark-haired figure still slouched in the back of the patrol car.

"No," he said. "What I'm going to do is have a little talk with Jack and see if I can't find out just what the hell's going on around here."

# 5

DETECTIVE SERGEANT Greg "Hardass" Boucher arrived on the crime scene with Inspector Fournier. He'd just started his shift when the first reports about what was going down at the Baker residence came in. Bored, he'd tagged along with the inspector under the pretext of lending a helping hand. Truth was, he just wanted a look at the mess in that basement.

He was a fifteen-year veteran of the force—part of the old-boy's brigade that didn't approve of pussyfooting around with the perps he picked up. He'd recently been transferred from the Sexual Assault/Child Abuse Unit to General Assignment. There wasn't much speculation around the station as to why the beefy detective had been transferred—it was common knowledge that he liked to lean on women, and he especially liked to lean on teenage girls.

The Children's Aid Society got involved in his last case with his old unit; they were brought in after a fifteen-year-old rape victim complained about harassment. Turned out she wasn't the hooker Hardass had thought she was. The case didn't get far—the girl couldn't substantiate her complaint—but the subsequent inquiry brought enough bad press that the Chief had had to do something. With Hardass's connections to the old-guard brass, all that entailed was a slap on the wrist and a transfer.

"Fried to the bone, huh?" he asked as Grier gave his report to the inspector.

Grier nodded.

"Be something to see," Hardass said.

The medic working on Grier shot Hardass a quick glance, then looked away. "Got a problem?" was perpetually written in the set of the big man's features. Anyone working the police beat picked up on Hardass's rep real quick. If you messed him around, he didn't do anything right away. But he didn't forget. One night you might meet him in a bar somewhere, or out on an empty street, someplace where it was just the two of you, and he was happy to settle any wrongs done to him then—real or imagined.

Hardass grinned, enjoying the momentary rush of psyching the medic out.

"Back off," Fournier said, not even looking at him. "What about the other victim?" he asked Grier.

Hardass wandered off, bored again. He didn't want secondhand reports. He wanted to see the meat. A guy fried. Some kid skinned. It was just the kind of weird shit that gave him a buzz. Made him feel a little sick, sure, but it fascinated him at the same time. Once he'd overheard a rookie at a bad traffic accident call him a ghoul. He'd turned to the kid and laid it out for him.

"Everybody's interested in this kinda stuff," he'd told the kid, "but it doesn't look good, so they're real serious about reports and stats and shit while they're getting an eyeful. Me, I'm just honest about my interest. I like to see what's going down. Better them than me—you know?"

Rookie or not, the kid had enough smarts to keep his mouth shut after that.

Hardass drifted up the walkway. When he got to the door of the house, Constable Dwyer stopped him.

"Ned says we've got to wait for gas masks."

Hardass sniffed the air near the doorway. "You smell gas?"

"No, but—"

"You let me worry about my own health, okay?"

Dwyer hesitated, then moved aside as Hardass pushed forward.

Fucking wimps, Hardass thought as he headed down the hall. 'Course that's what you got when you lowered your standards. Used to be you had to be a man to get on the force. You had to have some meat on your bones, some backbone. Now they were letting anybody join. Women, blacks—a goddamned chink, for chrissake! Next thing you knew, fag haircuts and pink suits were going to be regulation uniform.

He registered the stink in the air as he headed down the basement stairs. Burned plastic and metal. A faint underlying odor of cooked meat.

He looked at the body of the burned man. Je-sus. Now this was a mess.

His stomach did a little flip, but he ignored the queasiness he was feeling and deliberately bent closer to the corpse's bared skull. Whoever'd wasted this sucker had fried him good. Cooked his brains until all there was left was gumbo.

He stood slowly as a slight dizziness touched him. He smelled the air again, nervous, but there was no gassy odor. Just the acrid sting of the plastic and wiring. And the cooked meat . . .

The other half of the basement called to him.

Stepping carefully across the mess on the floor, he peered into the room at the body on the table in there. His eyes widened as his gaze settled on the second corpse.

Now this was bona fide sicko—no question about it. Christ, you could see every muscle just lying out—

Flicker.

And the room was gone.

He was standing on a wide, desolate plain. A wind came up, filling his nostrils with the smell of dust and decay. As far as he could see, there was nothing but an unending bleak vista, broken only by the haunted ghosts of dead trees.

What the fu—

Flicker.

And that wasteland was gone.

Hardass rubbed a hand against his sweaty brow and backed quickly out of the basement. Meehan hadn't been shitting them, after all. There really was some kind of gas leak down here, something that made you see things that just weren't there.

That *couldn't* be there.

He paused in the doorway, the stairs at his back.

Flicker.

The wasteland returned.

He turned slowly, but there was nothing behind him anymore. No stairs leading up out of the basement. He put his hand out to where the doorjamb should have been. No frigging basement.

He could hear a faint sound on the wind now. It was like singing. Or maybe screaming. It was too distant really to make out, but it put a knot in his stomach and made him grind his teeth together.

He got the sudden feeling that there was something out there in the wasteland, something that wanted him. . . .

"Okay," he said, his voice echoing emptily in the dead air. "Enough of this bullshit."

As he squeezed his eyes shut he could feel the—

Flicker.

He opened his eyes to find the basement back. Before the strobing effect could return, he was up the stairs and out of the building, so fast that his pulse was drumming by the time he reached the outside porch where Dwyer was still standing watch. The constable gave him an odd look, and Hardass knew just what he was thinking.

Hardass Boucher's finally been grossed out.

Well, fuck him. Fuck 'em all.

It wasn't the bodies. Christ, he'd seen worse. He'd just never had that feeling of being . . . *nowhere* before. Nowhere, yeah, but with something out there in the middle of it, looking for him. . . .

It was just craziness, he told himself. Brought on by the gas leak.

But he could feel something different inside himself. It took him a long moment to figure out just what it was: Fear.

No way. No way he was some chickenshit rookie, freaking at the first sight of some psycho's handiwork.

Oh, yeah? Then why was it that he knew he didn't want to go back down in that basement—didn't matter *what* someone'd pay him? If he closed his eyes, he knew he'd see that desolate landscape once more, hear that weird crying sound on the wind. . . .

He just couldn't face going down those stairs again.

"You okay, Hardass?" Dwyer asked.

No, he thought. No way I'm okay. But he had a rep. Right now the only person to know what he was feeling was himself, and that was just the way he was going to keep it.

"What do you think?" he said gruffly.

He left the porch before Dwyer could respond.

# 6

WALTER HAWKINS FELT like a TV private eye as he slouched in his old Chevy, waiting for the restaurant to close. A tough guy. Somebody you didn't mess with. Somebody who paid back what was owed to him, who didn't take shit from nobody, especially not some two-bit little tramp who thought a piece of paper could dissolve their marriage vows. Christ, she'd gotten into this women's lib shit like she'd found God or something. But nothing had changed. To have and to hold, baby. For better or for worse. And he'd show her worse. Nobody walked out on Walter Hawkins. *He* called the shots. Not Beth or her new Lesbian friends. Not the law laid down by some senile old fart of a judge who wouldn't remember where to put it if he ever did get a hard-on again.

It was funny how it all came together. Hanging around with the boys in the Barefax after work last night, putting back a few brews, watching the girls strut their stuff, Ted mentioning that he'd seen Walt's ex working in Mexicali Rosa's down in the Glebe. . . . It figured that that was where Beth'd end up. Nothing but smartass yuppies, old hippies, and fags'd live in the Glebe.

But he had her number now. He'd play it nice and easy. No big public scenes. He'd just follow her home tonight, get her someplace nice and private where he could explain a couple of things to her. Like what Walter Hawkins did with those who fucked him around. Like how what he owned was his until *he* threw it away.

So he sat in his car, humming to himself, watching the people come and go through the restaurant's front door. It was getting late now. She'd be in there, cleaning up, going around the tables, last call. What the hell did people do in places like this? There was no entertainment. The drinks were all overpriced—just because all the rich fags and yuppies who came to places like this could afford to pay through their teeth. Stupid fucks.

He lifted the Pepsi bottle from the seat beside him and took a long swig. The rum mixed with the pop went down smooth, settling warm in his stomach. You wouldn't catch him in a place like that. He'd had a look in this afternoon, just checking it out. Sure, it looked down-home. Ranch-style decor—oh, yeah. Battered tables and chairs, antiques hanging from the walls, everybody dressed casual. But you'd probably catch AIDS sitting next to some fag, and you'd go broke before you got a decent buzz on. Still, he'd bet the tips were good.

Wonder how much Beth had stashed away by now. Whatever she had, it belonged to him. No question.

He sat there nursing his rum and Pepsi until the place finally closed. Cleanup time now. Make everything look just the right kind of rustic. Assholes.

Around one-thirty he slouched a little lower in his seat, eyes glittering as he finally spotted Beth coming out. All *right.* But the big grin on his face faded as he saw her get into an old Honda hatchback with some tall brown-haired dude.

Images of the guy humping Beth strobed before his eyes. Beth going down on him, head bobbing. Beth letting the guy come all over her face, laughing—

A red haze like blood-soaked gauze stained the images.

"You're dead, fucker," he muttered. "You don't know it yet, but you're dead."

Nobody took anything that belonged to him—not without paying for it. *No*body.

He let them pull out onto Bank Street, then started up the Chevy and followed, keeping his distance. His fingers drummed a monotonous tattoo on the steering wheel. The look on his face was one Beth knew all too well.

As it turned out, the trip wasn't long. The Honda continued south on Bank, past the Civic Center and over the Lansdowne Bridge, then through the lights at Sunnyside. Just after Cameron Avenue, at the bottom of the hill, the Honda's brake lights flashed red, then the vehicle turned right on Chesley Street. Following it, Walt had a moment of sudden panic. Not two blocks from Bank, the street was crawling with police cars, cherry lights flashing.

Trap. They were just setting me up for a—

But the Honda turned left on Harvard Avenue, the street in between Bank and where the police action was going down.

Got to watch those nerves, Walt told himself. He slowed right down, taking his time making the corner at Harvard. The Honda was parked by the curb up ahead and Beth was getting out. Walt pulled over to the curb himself, killing the Chevy's lights and engine.

He watched Beth wave to the driver of the car, then his gaze settled on the way her ass moved in those tight jeans as she headed up the walk of a brown brick house. His fingers tightened on the steering wheel. Soon, baby. You'll be back with the best thing you ever had.

The guy in the Honda waited until Beth had unlocked her front door and gone inside before he pulled away. Neither he nor Beth appeared to have noticed the Chevy.

The red haze that had grabbed Walt outside the restaurant was dulling to a headache. He was still a little high from all the booze he'd been putting back while staking out the place but sober enough by now to know that tonight was a no-go. Not with cops crawling all over the street just a block away.

But that's okay, he thought. I know where the bitch lives now. And I can find out who her boyfriend is and where he lives, no problem. Plenty of time.

There was a momentary flash of their bodies entwined—Beth's and the stranger's. A flood of red half blinded him. His knuckles went white where they squeezed the steering wheel. Then he let out a long breath and the fire eased inside. The headache stayed, dull between his temples. The anger was a red core, hot in his chest. But he was okay. No problem.

He drove on home, fingers drumming their monotonous tattoo on the steering wheel again, keeping time to the throb of his headache.

## 7

NED GOT INTO the front of the patrol car. He stared out through its windshield for long moments, watching the bustle of the crime scene. Barricades were going up. Inspector Fournier and Hardass Boucher stood by the ambulance as a medic worked on Ernie's hand. Uniforms and plainclothes stood around, waiting for someone to bring some semblance of order to the proceedings. When Ned saw the first television crew arrive, the bright blue and orange CBC symbol on the side of the van, he turned to the back of the car, leaning on the back of the seat.

"What were you doing here, Jack?"

Jack Keller lifted his gaze slowly until it met Ned's. Instead of replying, he dug a creased color snapshot from his pocket and silently handed it over. Ned flicked on the overhead light and looked at the photograph. He held it close to the light, one finger tracing the crease. The girl was pretty—thirteen, fourteen tops. Short blond hair. Her small breasts just starting to push against her tank top.

Ned tried to compare the photo in hand to the corpse in the basement, skinned and wired up to God knew what kind of crap. He couldn't do it.

"Did you go inside?" he asked.

Jack shook his head.

"Why not?"

"I knew it was going to be bad." He paused, looking away. "Was she in there?"

Ned looked down at the photo again. "There was . . . something in there that could've been her."

"What the hell's that supposed to mean?" Jack's gaze had snapped back to Ned's face.

Ned sighed. "We found two bodies in there. One's a Caucasian male, maybe five-eleven, a hundred and sixty pounds. The other's a teenage girl. There's not a whole . . ."

Flicker.

He saw the skinned corpse, tubes from the IVs running directly into the raw flesh. All around it the grey plains. The dead skies . . .

Flicker.

Sweat popped out on his brow and stuck his shirt to his back. He took a thick breath.

"We haven't IDed either of them yet," he finished.

Jack's gaze was steady on his face. "What's the matter, Ned?"

"What's the matter?" Ned's rage at what he'd been forced to experience surfaced in a sudden rush. "It's a goddamn slaughterhouse down there—how's that for starters? That fucker had the girl wired up for sound. He wanted to record every noise she made while he skinned her. How's that for 'what's the matter'?"

"Ned . . ."

"What're you doing here, Jack? If you're so fucking set on playing cop, why the hell did you ever quit?"

He glared at his ex-partner, the old argument fueled to new depths by what lay inside the basement of the house.

Jack's gaze never wavered. "I wasn't making a difference," he said finally.

Ned tossed the snapshot back to him. "And now you are?"

If there'd been anger in Jack's eyes, Ned could have taken it. What he couldn't take was the hurt he saw there.

"I'm sorry, Jack," he said. "I was out of line."

Jack only nodded. He stowed the snapshot back in his pocket.

"You want to tell me what you found in there?" he asked.

"No," Ned said. But he told him, anyway. "You know the guy, Jack?" he asked when he was done.

"His name's Chad Baker." Jack waited for Ned to get out his duty book and pen before he went on. "He's from England originally. He had a few big hits back in the sixties—'We Can't Lose,' 'Got to Drop You Outta My Heart,' 'Heartbreak Heaven.' Do you remember any of those?"

Ned nodded, still writing.

"He makes a fair buck off his royalties," Jack went on, "especially with all the cover versions that've been coming out in the last few years. A few of the pieces made it onto a couple of recent sound tracks. The guy had money."

"What was he doing here?"

Jack shrugged. "Who knows why he picked Ottawa? Anyway, he moved here in the mid-seventies, and ever since then he's been kind of a guru to anybody trying to make it in the local music scene. He's got a recording studio in his basement—twenty-four channel, digital, the works. A lot of the local talent got their first breaks with his demos. He's promoted concerts and shows, backed a couple of clubs. He's got money to burn."

Ned looked up from his duty book. "You sound like you've been doing some digging on this guy."

Jack looked away.

"Don't hold back on me, Jack."

"Anna knows him."

"Oh, shit."

Ned had been chasing Jack's younger sister for as long as they'd all known each other, which was running on to nine or ten years by now. It was his job that kept them from being anything more than just good friends.

Cops tended to socialize with cops—they had to. Civilians just didn't understand what went into the job, how you had to carry it around with you night and day.

Ned knew Anna liked him, but she didn't feel comfortable spending weekend nights just going to Russell's—the Police Association's private club up on the third floor of the old Delco Building. She didn't feel comfortable with his friends, who were mostly other cops, just like he didn't feel comfortable with hers, who were all in rock bands or theater or the arts.

"When you say Anna knows him . . ." he began.

"I mean, she's hung out at the studio," Jack said. "Like I said, most of the people on the local music scene have been there at one time or another. You know how Anna likes to sing."

Thinking of her being involved in what they'd found in Baker's basement woke a sick feeling in the pit of Ned's stomach. Don't think about it, he told himself. He looked down at his notes.

"What's Baker's connection with runaways?" he asked.

"I didn't know he had one. I was just looking . . . looking for this Rowe girl. I got a tip she'd been seen with Baker a couple of times, so I came down to talk to him."

"Who tipped you?"

"Kids on the street. I don't have any names."

"I'm going to need them."

Jack sighed. "Nobody's going to talk to you, Ned. You know that. And I can't afford to lose my connections. There's other kids I can still help, so I don't want to throw away—"

"You want me take you down there and show you what a guy like Baker can do with a kid?"

"No. I . . . It's not that, Ned."

"This is serious shit you're in, Jack," Ned said. "You start holding back now . . ."

Flicker.

They were still in the patrol car, but it was sitting in that wasteland now. Its flashing lights spat against the dead limbs of a nearby tree. The dead yellow skies hung down on them like a shroud. Ned looked at Jack to see a mirror there of the shock he knew was on his own features.

"Jesus Christ," he said softly. "Are you seeing it too?"

# 8

AFTER BETH GREEN carefully locked the door behind her, she stood there in the hallway, looking out at the street through the door's leaded windows. She watched Alan's Honda turn the corner. An older American car passed by after it. Looking at that second car gave her a chill, so she turned away. She didn't like being in the house by herself. Any little thing was liable to set her off.

She was a slight woman in her mid-twenties, attractive but frail. Her blond hair hung straight, curling under where it touched her shoulders. She wore clothes well—a Mexican-style peasant blouse and jeans tonight—but she could never see any of the attractiveness in herself that others did. All she saw was one of the walking wounded. Someone who'd just barely made it through another day.

Ever since she'd left her husband—

(*ex*-husband)

—she felt as though she'd regressed back to her

childhood. She was always nervous, starting at shadows, so sure that the bogeyman was just waiting to get her alone, watching her at work, following her around. When she got home, she imagined him hiding in her bedroom, under the bed, in the closet.

All those police cars down on Wendover tonight didn't help. It just meant someone was in trouble. In pain. Like the hurting times when Walt just hit her and hit her until she gave up trying to block the blows. It was only then that he would stop.

Caught in those haunted memories, she hugged herself to stop from shaking and stared at the haunted reflection that looked back at her from the mirror. Was it ever going to get any better?

Walt would find her again, and court order notwithstanding, he'd do what he wanted to her until they finally locked him away. Like they should have a long time ago, only she'd been too scared to step forward. It took a news report on the TV dealing with homes for battered women to allow her to make the first step, the first call for help. It was only knowing that she wasn't alone that had given her the courage to act. The women at the center had taken care of her, helped her deal with the police, first getting the restraining order, then filing the charges when he found her and brought her home again—

(to that dark place filled with pain)

—where she'd still be if it hadn't been for Anna.

"Stop looking like a victim," Anna told her more than once. "It's putting out that kind of impression that lets the crazies know who to hit on."

Easy for her to say. Words were always easy. Beth knew all the ones that described Walt. She could repeat the words over and over. "I won't ever let him hurt me again," but it didn't make any difference. She knew he was out there, looking for her. And when he found her, he'd take her back—

(to that dark place)

—and how was she supposed to stop him? She saw his face in every man's face. She even dreamed about him. He'd become her bogeyman. He'd joined forces with her childhood fears to stalk her night and day.

All that kept her sane was Anna and her job. It wasn't much of a job, slinging drinks in a bar, but without any marketable skills it was all she could get. And at least it was *something.* At least she was earning her own way. And the people she worked with were good to her—especially the bartender, Alan Haines, who made sure that nobody bothered her and even gave her a lift home when she worked nights. She couldn't afford to lose it. It was the best possible proof she had that she *was* good for something. She *could* make it on her own.

She was going to save enough this year to take some courses at the community college and make something of herself. Right now she might be dependent on the kindness of strangers—

("Walt works hard," her mother said. "He's under a lot of pressure."

"But he hurts me, Mom."

"Keeps you in line, you mean," her mother's current boyfriend said with a smirk.)

—but she was going to make it on her own. It was hard when what family you had turned their backs on you and you found out you didn't have any friends because you had been too ashamed of your bruises and failed marriage to go out and meet anybody. It was hard when only strangers like Anna were there for you instead.

Though at least she had someone, Beth thought. She remembered being in the center with all those other women, their bruises like a uniform. Some of them didn't even have strangers. Just the social workers who ran the center, and they had such big caseloads.

Beth shook her head. Think positively, she told herself. That was Anna's constant reminder. Be strong. Don't worry about dreams and bogeyman fears. Get on with your life.

But it was hard to be strong.

She left the hallway to walk aimlessly through the living and dining rooms, turning on a trail of lights behind her to banish the shadows. In the kitchen she paused, then looked out the window of the kitchen door to where Anna's latest fabric maché sculptures filled the back porch. The various forms, mostly still little more than wire frames covered with newspaper, gave her a creepy feeling. They looked like half-made ghosts out there, almost alive for all their unfinished state.

She was mildly envious of Anna.

Anna knew how to be strong. It didn't seem to be anything she'd had to learn, either. She just was. She wasn't desperately trying to put her life together, with no real knowledge yet of who she even wanted to be—

Beth froze as she heard sounds on the front porch. She took a few quick steps across the kitchen to where she could see the front door, heartbeat accelerating, then felt a hot flush of embarrassment begin to spread up from her neck as the lock was disengaged and the door opened on Anna and Cathy Cole. The two of them were talking in excited, slightly slurred voices.

"They're right near the studio."

"*At* the studio, I'd say."

"Well, I still think we should go over and—"

Cathy broke off when they saw Beth standing there at the far end of the hall. Anna's quick smile didn't quite hide the worry in her eyes.

"Hello, Beth!" she called cheerily. "Are you all right?"

Even after an obviously tipsy night on the town Anna's first concern was for her. It was something that was hard for Beth to accept, but gratifying to know at the same time. She wasn't alone anymore.

"I'm fine," she said quickly. At least now I am. All it took was Anna's presence to turn the house from a place of possible threat into a cozy home. "Did you have fun?"

"Not as much fun as Janice," Anna said.

"Who's being escorted home—"

"By a dreamboat in a jean jacket."

The two started to giggle.

"What's going on out there?" Cathy asked.

Beth joined them by the door. "I don't know. It was like that when Alan dropped me off."

"Shall we go see what's going on?" Cathy said.

Anna moved back out onto the porch. "Oh, I don't know if that's such a good idea."

Out on the porch now herself, Beth looked down the street and saw more lights on in the various houses than there ever were at this time of night. The warning flashers of the police cars and ambulance, reflecting from the street corner and above the roof of the buildings across the street, gave the impression that there was a fairground back there, hidden from view.

(Where the rides bring only despair and pain. . . .)

As she suppressed a shiver she caught Anna looking at her.

Anna gave her another quick smile, then turned to Cathy. "I thought you said you wanted a coffee."

"I do, I do."

"I'll go put the kettle on," Beth offered.

The other two stayed on the porch for a few moments longer, looking at the lights, before they closed the door on the night's excitement and followed Beth into the kitchen.

## 9

NED WASN'T SURE exactly what Jack was seeing—if it was the same dead landscape that his own eyes were telling him lay outside the cruiser—but he knew Jack had to be seeing something. Something weird . . .

"I had a bad feeling," Jack said softly, not looking at Ned. His gaze was fixed on whatever he saw beyond the windows. "I was just standing there, looking at Baker's house, when this . . . thing came drifting out of the wall."

"Thing?"

"It was the most beautiful woman I've ever seen, Ned." There was an odd note that Ned couldn't recognize in Jack's voice. "An angel. Just floating out the side of the house, her hair streaming behind her. And when she looked at me . . ." Jack's gaze left the wasteland beyond the patrol car to settle on Ned's face. "I heard a kind of sound. It was like music . . . a kind of music I've never heard before. And then I was here."

Ned swallowed thickly. As Jack spoke of the music he thought he could hear it too. But it wasn't a sound that could come from any instruments that he knew. It sounded more like people crying—or screaming. Softly. The music was their pain. . . .

"What . . . what're you seeing, Jack?"

Jack looked away again, out past the windows. Ned followed his gaze. There were dust devils stirring out in the dead lands. They caught the spinning light thrown from the cruiser's warning flashers, strobing in and out of view whenever the light hit them.

"Jack?"

"I . . ."

Flicker.

The street was back. But empty. Theirs was the only vehicle on its deserted length. The houses were dark, falling in on themselves. There was a buzzing in the air, like bees or flies caught against glass. Ned thought he saw a flutter of movement at the far end of the empty street. A figure dodging out of sight.

Flicker.

The sudden return of the real world—flashing lights, headlights burning into their eyes—left them both half blinded. Ned looked away from the numbing brightness. He turned to Jack.

"A dead place," Jack said. "That's what I saw. First a wasteland, then this street, but it was dead. The houses empty . . ." Ned knew that the confusion he was seeing in Jack's eyes was no different from what he was feeling himself. "It's not possible," Jack went on. "I *know* that, Ned. But I still saw it."

Ned took a steadying breath. The beginnings of a headache tapped behind his temples.

"Fumes," he said. "There's some kind of fumes in

the air, a gas leak or something coming out of that basement. It's making us see things."

"Things that real?"

"Christ, Jack. What do I know? The equipment in Baker's studio was mostly slag when we got down there. Maybe he had some kind of dope that got burned up with it. Stuff got into the air . . ."

Jack nodded in slow agreement. "But I still can't shake the sense that somewhere that place is real."

Ned didn't want to let that thought take root in his own mind, but he knew exactly what Jack meant. He'd never done any dope stronger than a couple of hits of hashish himself—and that was only to see what it was like. He'd never touched hallucinogens. Maybe what they had both just experienced was what the dope heads got every time they got happy. Ned didn't want to know about it.

"I've got to go tell the others to be careful—even outside the house," he said. "Maybe we should even clear the area. There's no telling how far those fumes are spreading."

"I don't think it's that simple," Jack said.

"I've still got to make the effort."

Jack caught Ned's arm as he started to leave the patrol car. "Careful how you tell them," he said.

"What the hell's that supposed to mean? Jack, if you know something that you're not telling me, you'd better just—"

"Will you think about it for a minute? Look out there. You see anybody else affected?"

"Ernie and Benny Dwyer felt something in the basement."

"Will you *look*?"

At the urgency in Jack's voice Ned did just that. Outside, it looked like business as usual. A major crime investigation. Uniforms and plainclothes. ID Unit getting their gear out of their van. Medics and coroner standing around the ambulance. A red fire chief's car pulling up. Two TV crews—CJOH had joined the CBC now—filming the proceedings. It all looked so normal that Ned was wondering what the hell he'd even thought he'd seen himself. But then he remembered, not just the weirdness inside the basement but out here. Both he and Jack wired into the same hallucination.

"I'll just warn them," Ned said, "without getting specific." He glanced back at Jack. "Why don't you get yourself out of here? We can get your statement tomorrow."

"Sure."

"Think you can drive yourself?"

"I'll stay with Anna."

"Think you'll be able to—"

"I can make it that far, Ned." He cracked a weak smile. "But thanks for the thought."

Ned nodded. "You might tell Anna I'll be talking to her tomorrow. About Baker."

"Sure."

Ned got out of the patrol car, stopping long enough to let Jack out of the back—there were no interior handles on the doors in the rear of the cruiser—then headed over to where Ernie was making his report to the inspector. Ernie's right hand was wrapped in white gauze now, but there was a small pink stain in the middle of the white where the blood was still seeping through. Ned was sure that the cut was going to need stitches. He glanced back at where he'd left Jack by the cruiser and saw that Jack had started off down the short block to Warrington.

"Who was that?" Inspector Fournier asked when Ned joined the two men by the ambulance.

Fournier was a stocky Frenchman who at first glance gave the impression that he was almost as wide as he was tall. But there was no flab on that weight, never mind Fournier's desk job. Ned had worked out with him in the weight room back at the station often enough to be assured of that.

"Jack Keller," Ned replied. "He called it in. He's a bit shook up, so I sent him over to his sister's. We'll get his statement tomorrow."

Fournier nodded. "He was a good man—used to be your partner, didn't he?"

"Up until he quit."

"What's his connection with this?"

"He was tracking down a runaway and the trail led him here. I think the kid he's looking for is the girl we found . . . downstairs." An image of the skinned corpse rose up in Ned's mind. He forced it out of his thoughts before the flickering took him away again. "Did Ernie fill you in on what we found in the basement?"

"What little he knew."

"So he told you that there might be some kind of a problem with fumes down there?"

Fournier glanced at his watch. "The masks should be arriving anytime now."

"Good." Ned turned to his partner. "How're you feeling, Ernie? You look a little punchy. You want we should get a uniform to run you over to the General and get that hand sewn up?"

"I'm okay," Grier said. "It looks worse than it is. Medic said it won't even need stitches."

Another blue-and-white van arrived just then, stilling further conversation.

"That'll be the masks," Fournier said.

Ned nodded. "So let's get this show on the road."

## 10

JACK'S LEGS FELT SHAKY as he walked down Wendover to Warrington. Instead of turning right toward Anna's he crossed the street, shoes clicking on the pavement. Then the grass verge on the far side swallowed the sound. He stood and looked at the slow-moving waters of the Rideau River. His headache was worse. He thought about what he thought he'd seen coming out of Baker's house, then that long moment in the patrol car when the wasteland returned—only this time Ned had seen it too.

Christ, he was losing it. Came with the territory, he supposed. So many cops lost it. He'd turned in his badge, but the work he did was the same. Playing the cop, Ned never tired of telling him. Looking for the lost. It was hard to tell who was more screwed up. Sometimes the parents of the kids he was looking for seemed more lost than the kids themselves. Sometimes he felt like he, himself, was just—

Flicker.

The flashing lights behind him disappeared. Billings Bridge Shopping Centre, across the river, went dead. The buildings were still there, but they were dark now, with gaps in the long structure where parts of it had fallen in on itself. All the lights in its acres of parking lot were blacked out as though there'd been a power failure. His gaze was dragged to the river. Swollen white corpses drifted by in its brown waters. They spun slowly in the current, puffy features turning toward him, the white flesh of their faces swelling to make dark holes where their eyes should be.

A faint music reached his ears, coming to him as from a great distance. He recognized the sound. It made his skin crawl.

Janet Rowe.

He was hardly surprised to see her body drift by, not quite so swollen, a faintly accusing look on her face.

(Why didn't you help me?)

Then the white skin was stripped away and the waters bore her freshly skinned body slowly downstream. He took a step toward the riverbank—

Flicker.

Lights blossomed across the river in the shopping center's parking lot. His shadow was thrown onto the dark water by the flashing lights of the patrol cars behind him.

He rubbed at his face and turned away, steering his feet toward Anna's house. There were lights on when he arrived. He heard the sound of her stereo spilling out of an open window as he came up the walk. It sounded like k.d. lang—the cowpunk singer from the Prairies who claimed to be a reincarnation of Patsy Cline—but he didn't recognize the song. Maybe she had a new album out. He leaned on the doorbell, too beat to dig out his key.

The door opened the eight inches that the security chain would allow it to show him his sister's face through the crack.

"Jack!" she cried delightedly.

The door closed. He could hear her fiddling with the chain. On the stereo, k.d. lang started a new song. Behind him, the night was lit up by the streetlights and the cast-off red flashes of the cruisers one street over. But he could feel the darkness closing in on him all the same. Dead eyes in swollen faces searching for him. He concentrated on keeping the flickering appearance of that wasteland at bay.

The door swung open to its full width. "Hi, Jack," his sister said. "What's shaking?"

Anna's face was so buoyant—she was always so full of the sheer joy of living—that it made him want to weep. He wanted to pull her against him, to feel the life in her chest beat against his own. Instead he stood numbly on the porch, staring at her. It was like there was a wall rising up between them.

"Jack . . . ?" Anna said, her voice faltering. "Are you all right?"

"I need a place to lie down," he said.

She looked past him to where the police lights stabbed the sky behind her neighbors' houses across the street. Her hand was light but comfortingly firm on his arm as she pulled him inside.

## 11

"YOU'D NEED A FLAMETHROWER to do that kind of damage," Detective Sergeant Louis Duchaine said, looking down at what they supposed was Baker's body.

Duchaine worked Arson. He was a thin, wiry man wearing jeans, a T-shirt, and a windbreaker. Unshaven and still slightly disheveled, he looked like he'd come to the crime scene straight from his bed, which he had.

He hunched down beside the corpse to peer closer, careful not to touch anything. There was still skin on the back of its skull, singed hair attached to it. Grey matter oozed from the eye sockets and from between the maxilla and mandible bones.

"Cooked his fucking brains," Duchaine added as he stood up.

Officers in gas masks from the ID Unit had tested the air and found it clean, but Ned had still experienced one flicker of dislocation coming back into the room. The wasteland. Here for a moment, then gone again. He hadn't bothered to say anything about it this time. Had to be in his head.

(Sure. And that was why Jack had seen it too.)

His partner had left after a couple of minutes—to keep out of the way, he told Ned—but Ned marked the haunted look in Grier's eyes before he went back upstairs. Dwyer and the other uniforms first on the scene hadn't come down at all. But then, it wasn't their job to.

Strangest of all, Ned thought, was how Hardass Boucher—always in the thick of the bloodiest investigation—had stayed outside as well. Normally he'd be down here getting into everybody's way.

"So what are you saying?" Ned asked Duchaine. "Somebody came down here and offed him with a flamethrower? Is that what caused the rest of this damage?"

Duchaine shook his head. "That," he said, indicating the destroyed equipment, "just burned itself out. Overloaded circuits or something. We'll know more after we sift through it."

"Could it have blown up in the guy's face?"

"Maybe. But it's not likely. The wounds are too focused. See, it's just the front of his head and the one hand—that'll be a defense wound. I'd guess he raised the hand just before whatever hit him did the job. If that equipment blew on him, he'd be a mess all over. Chest, shoulders . . . If he was standing, his whole torso. Probably even his legs. No, he got hit by a concentrated, *focused* blast. Problem is"—Duchaine turned slowly around the crowed control room—"you can't aim a flamethrower that narrowly. There'd have to be more fire damage. On the walls. Or the equipment."

"Lovely."

"You got yourself a real freak show here," Duchaine said. "What you need is Sherlock Holmes, Ned."

Ned gave him a weak smile. "I'd call in the fucking Pope if I thought it'd help."

He followed Duchaine up the stairs to make his report to the inspector, leaving the murder scene to the men from the ID Unit and the coroner.

## 12

"I STILL CAN'T believe it," Cathy said. "*Chad* Baker."

She sat on one end of the couch, knees pulled up to her chest, toying with her long red hair. Her eyes sparkled with the look of someonc coming across a particularly juicy bit of gossip in *People* magazine. Jack almost expected her to come out with the clichéd "He was always such a quiet guy—kept to himself, you know?"

"They haven't made any positive IDs yet," he warned.

"Sure, but it's still *his* house. I really can't believe it."

"Oh, I don't know," Anna said. "Sometimes he'd get a look in his eyes that'd give me the creeps."

She was sitting in the middle of the couch, plainly unhappy. Part of that, Jack knew, had to do with the fact that she didn't like knowing she'd been associating with someone capable of what the police had found in Baker's basement. Jack could tell that she was worrying about him, too—he was too close to his sister not to know sibling concern when he saw it. If he looked half as bad as he felt, she had something to worry about.

Beside Anna, on the other end of the couch from Cathy, Beth had withdrawn into herself, her already pale skin washed out and drawn tight across her features. Jack wished there was some way he could have spared her having to hear all of this, but both Cathy and Anna had insisted on knowing what all the excitement on Wendover was about. Beth didn't need to hear about this kind of thing right now—not when she was just coming out of herself. By the time Anna realized what it was doing to her, it was already too late.

"Have . . . have you told the girl's parents yet?" Beth asked in her soft voice.

Jack shook his head. "I'll hold off on that until I'm sure that it was . . . that she's the one Ned found in there. Depending on how things go, they'll probably tell her folks first, anyway."

Would they care? Would their daughter's death be a relief, or would it just give them something else to blame Janet for—dying with such notoriety that they would have no peace for weeks? Jack didn't much care about that right now. All he could think of was Janet Rowe, alone in that basement.

He made an effort not to think about it, turning his attention instead to the stereo where one of Anna's musical discoveries was playing—an album by the East Texas singer Michelle Shocked. It had been recorded around a campfire at a folk festival, complete with the incessant chirping of crickets and the occasional rumble of an eighteen-wheeler going by. Shocked's voice, backed only with an acoustic guitar and the ambient background sounds, gave the conversation in Anna's living room the feel of a yarn-swapping session around a campfire. All that was needed was the smell of the wood smoke and some ghost stories to accompany the lurid story he'd already told.

Ghost stories . . .

He hadn't said anything about the angel or her wasteland, but he thought he could still sense her eyes on him, prickling the skin at the nape of his neck. From time to time the room wavered slightly, but the flickering jump to the angel's dead lands remained at bay. He rubbed his face—ever since that moment he'd first seen the angel coming out of Baker's house he'd felt as though he had cobwebs clinging to his skin. Clogging up the workings of his mind.

The image reminded him of a drugged-out pharmacist's sketch on one of the late-night comedy shows a few years ago—the guy was always seeing giants bats or trying to wipe cobwebs from his face. Anna had the thing on videotape and it always made them laugh, but there didn't seem anything funny about it now.

"You look beat, Jack," Anna said.

"I feel a little out of it. Mind if I sleep over?"

Cathy gave him a quick smile. "I'm staying over, too—do you want to share the guest room with me?"

Jack was never quite sure what Cathy would do if he ever took her up on one of her invitations, but tonight wasn't a time to find out.

"I'll be okay on the couch," he said.

Cathy's lips made a moue, but he knew she wasn't serious. "I was even going to call in sick tomorrow."

"You were going to call in sick, anyway," Anna said, standing up. "It's time we were all hitting the sack. I'll get some bedding for you, Jack."

The Michelle Shocked album ended as the three women made their way upstairs. Jack took it from the turntable and returned it to its jacket, gazing a little bemusedly at the photo of the singer. She looked a little like a hardcore punk with her sleeveless T-shirt and her hair so short at the sides and back, sticking up in spikes on top. It made him wonder why Anna had never got one of these punky haircuts herself.

"Pretty neat record, isn't it?" Anna said.

Jack turned to see her coming down the stairs, arms loaded with sheets, a blanket, and a fat puffy pillow.

"It's . . . interesting."

Anna laughed. "Coming from you, Jack, that's almost a compliment." She shooed him away as he went to help her make up the couch. "I just got it in the mail this morning. She's a U.S. singer, but I had to order her album from England—go figure it."

She removed the back pillows from the couch, then made up the bed, quickly and neatly, without a wasted motion. It always amused Jack to see that his sister, who could be so spaced and funky, was such a little homemaker at the same time. After fluffing the pillow she sat down on the newly made bed to give him a long, considering look.

"How are you feeling—really?" she asked.

"Low," Jack admitted. Outside the windows, he could feel the night pressing in closer. "I let her down, Anna. The poor kid. I . . ."

(I'm going crazy. I'm seeing shit like you wouldn't believe.)

"You did your best, didn't you?"

"Yeah—but in this game it's results that count. Not the points you scored on style."

He wanted to tell her about the angel, about that place she'd taken him to, the wasteland that both he and Ned had seen from the patrol car later, but he couldn't find the words. Anna was the one in the family that had all the curiosity about things out of the norm. All he ever felt about that kind of thing was that it was crazy. Harmless crazy, some of it; right out wacko, the rest. He didn't have the vocabulary to talk about it.

"I wish you'd get into a line of work that didn't leave you running on empty like this, Jack."

He shrugged. "When this kind of thing comes up, I just try to remember the times I did some good."

"Does it help?"

"Not a whole hell of a lot."

Anna sighed. She looked like she wanted to get into it some more but then thought better of it. "Well, don't sit up brooding about it all night," she said finally. "Try to get some sleep."

Jack nodded. "Anna?" he added as his sister rose from the couch. She paused to look at him. "Ned asked me to tell you he'd be by tomorrow."

A tired look came into her eyes. Jack knew she was

thinking of Baker—not so much feeling bad for him as sick at what he'd done.

"I take it that it won't be a social call," she said.

"Not this time," Jack admitted. "But that doesn't mean the door's closed on it."

"Don't push, Jack. I like Ned. It's just . . ."

"A big part of what makes Ned click is his being a cop, Anna. If you like him—well, that's part of what made him somebody you could like."

"It's not just Ned. It's thinking of him and me together. It's his friends and my friends—they're miles apart. I can't see myself hanging out at Russell's, just going to cop functions and stuff like that. And you know what he's like around my friends."

A little like he was himself, Jack thought. "Cops don't just hang out with each other," he said.

"No. But they don't relax unless they're with their own. I *know,* Jack. I've been around you and Ned long enough to know." She rose from the couch, unwilling to continue what was just an old argument, anyway. There was never going to be a solution to it. "Get some sleep, Jack. I'll see you in the morning."

Jack stood up. "Thanks for your ear—and a place to lay my head."

"You just take care of yourself," Anna said. "And I don't mean just physically, either."

She gave him a good-night kiss, then went about shutting off lights. Jack waited until she'd gone up the stairs, then turned off the last light in the living room himself and sat down on the couch. He could sense the darkness watching him but shook off the feeling.

What the Christ? he asked himself. I'm going to crawl into bed with my sister, maybe because I can't sleep in the dark alone anymore? Maybe not. But there was always Cathy. . . .

He shook that thought away as well.

He lay down on top of the bed Anna had made for him on the couch, not bothering to undress yet. Hands behind his head, he listened to the three women get ready for bed upstairs. Footsteps in the hall. Faucets running in the bathroom. Toilet flushing. Bedsprings settling.

Sleep seemed impossible. There were too many ghosts lying in wait for him to close his eyes and drift off—not to mention the angel.

He drifted off all the same.

When he woke, he wasn't sure how long he'd been asleep. The silence that lay over the house was so complete that the small sounds he made sitting up seemed oddly magnified. He started to get undressed—who could sleep properly in their clothes?—and smiled, knowing that Cathy would be making an effort to get downstairs early enough tomorrow morning to catch him in his skivvies.

The smile faded as the utter silence of his surroundings hit home. Where was the hum of the fridge? The annoying buzz of Anna's old Molsen's clock that came from something loose inside that neither of them had ever been able to track down? There was a smell in the air too. Moldy and a bit sour. Like being in a dump. He reached for the light, but nothing happened when he worked the switch.

Oh, shit.

He stood up quickly. Gradually his eyes had been growing accustomed to the poor lighting. By now he could see enough to know that while this was still Anna's living room, it wasn't in the same state it had been when he'd drifted off. The couch he'd been lying on was a moldering ruin. The shadowed furniture that began to take shape was in the same, or worse, repair. Garbage crackled underfoot as he stepped away from the couch.

Graffiti on the wall where Anna's prized *Kaleidoscope,* by the Swiss-born Hey Frey, used to hang drew his gaze. The bright paper collage with its primal acrylic colors and funky designs, handmade with some machine stitchery, was crumpled in a corner—home to rodents, Jack assumed, when something rustled under it at his approach. The graffiti had been applied with bold, uneven strokes. It read, I ATE HER TITS—JODY GOT THE BRAINS and was signed KIRK. Beside the words was a crude drawing of a woman with Anna's pageboy haircut.

A dull rage started up in Jack's chest as he stared at the scrawl.

A dream, he told himself. It's just a fucking dream. All you've got to do is wake up.

Only what if it wasn't a dream?

What if he was really in that ruined city this time?

Then he remembered an article in *Omni* on lucid dreaming that Anna had him read once. It said that the way you could test if you were dreaming or not was to read something, look away, then read it again. If you were dreaming, it'd change every time you looked back at it.

He looked away.

When he read the words again, they hadn't changed.

This is bullshit, he told himself. At any other time of his life he'd have had no trouble agreeing with that. But after the night he'd just had—the angel, the flickers of dislocation, that wasteland, and the ruined city . . . all so real. . . .

He went up the stairs at a trot, slowing down when his foot went through a rotted-out step. He saved himself from a fall by grabbing the banister. Moments after he straightened, the banister toppled over with a crash to the ground floor. He tested each step after that, keeping close to the wall on the stairs, and then went down the hall.

The bedrooms were all deserted. They stunk of urine and excrement, of dried blood. In Beth's room he thought he saw movement out of the corner of his eye. A flash of something pale by her closet door. He started across the room, but a warning crack from the floor froze him, breath held in. Slowly he edged back to the door. Just before he reached it, the floor gave way in a thundering cloud of plaster dust.

He jumped for the door as the floor fell away below his feet, catching hold of the doorjamb and dragging himself to the relative safety of the hallway. Plaster dust filled his lungs, making him cough. When he could stand again, he gave his clothes a perfunctory brushing but gave up as that set up new clouds of dust to trouble his lungs and throat.

He leaned his head against the wall, staring back into Beth's room. It all seemed so fucking real.

His ears were still ringing from the falling of the floor, so it took him a while to notice the faint, familiar sound coming from outside the house. That music again.

I'm dreaming.

I'm asleep on Anna's couch.

At the same time he was here—wherever the hell "here" was. Listening to the music—if that arrhythmic, discordant sound could be called music—he decided to go with the flow of the dream. He'd just wake up when it was over.

Back on the couch.

And none of this would have happened.

He was still careful making his way down the hall and out of the house. Outside, there was a different smell in the air. Metallic. Salty. He could taste it on his tongue. The music was louder. Above him, the sky was like that of the wasteland, a putrid smog, more yellow than grey. The houses leaned against each other, beaten and worn. Roofs had caved in on some. Huge holes gaped in the walls of others. The trees were all dead, their limbs bare. The grass on the lawns was dry underfoot.

(just a dream—no problem)

He saw movement down the street—a figure in diaphanous robes with long pale hair, drifting ghostlike toward the river. By the swing of her walk he knew it was a woman. The music seemed to follow her. It had to be the angel.

He started after her, keeping to the grass so that the click of his shoes on the road wouldn't warn her of his presence. She kept on, giving no sign of knowing that he was in pursuit, crossing Warrington Drive to the grass verge that ran along the river. At the riverbank she paused and Jack slowed down. He kept to the left side of Harvard, cutting from a lawn to the small park that took up the quadrangle formed by the last house, Bank Street, the river, and the corner where Harvard met Warrington.

The music swelled, and now Jack could plainly hear the cries of pain and hurt that made up its tones. Synthesized voices blending into musical notes. He was halfway across the grass square when the figure turned.

It wasn't the angel.

It was Janet Rowe, wearing her skin again. Staring at him. Waiting for him.

(just a dream)

There was a buzzing in the air, overriding the music that had begun to grow fainter. Jack stepped toward the girl. Her hair was longer than in the photo her parents had given him, her body fuller. She was older. But it was the same girl, no question about it. As he moved closer, he could see tubes and wires dangling from her head and arms.

*Fucker had the girl wired up for sound,* he could hear Ned saying. *He wanted to hear every noise she made while he skinned her.*

The music, composed of agonized voices.

The recording studio in the basement.

The buzzing sound was growing louder, the closer he approached.

Jesus Christ, Jack thought. What the hell—

(just a dream)

—was going on here?

Six paces away and she stopped. There was something wrong with her eyes, Jack saw. There was too much movement in the eye sockets. There was—

With a sound like cloth tearing, the girl's upper torso split open and a stream of insects came flying out. The buzzing drone had the volume of a jet taking off. Bile rose in Jack's throat and he staggered back. The flies clouded the air, making it hard to see—

(he didn't *want* to see)

—the girl's body falling in on itself like a dropped coat . . . lying in the dead grass . . . a puddle of skin on a puddle of filmy cloth . . . the flies buzzing . . . the stink of decay in the air . . . the hair on top of the skin and cloth puddle like a discarded wig . . . the skin falling in just such a way that he could still make out a face lying there . . . flat . . . the darkness behind the eyeholes staring at him.

Jack dropped to his knees and lost the contents of his stomach. The flies buzzed around him, hitting him in the face, rasping against his clothes. Frantically he brushed away at them, a scream building in his throat. Then the world tilted under his knees. Vertigo spilled him the rest of the way to the ground. And he lay staring up into a lit streetlight, the glare blinding him.

"Uh . . . uh . . ."

His throat worked convulsively as he turned over to look at where the remains of the girl had puddled on the grass. Nothing. No music in the air now, just the sound of the city. No flies. No smell but that of the green grass into which he pressed his face, colored by a slightly sour smell. He'd thrown up. He remembered that. But it had all been—

(just a dream)

—that's all. He was going to be okay. He was—

Slowly he sat up and looked around. Was it still going on? Christ, was he *still* dreaming?

Because he wasn't on the couch back at Anna's. He was lying by the river, down from her house. Beside a pool of his own vomit. Then he looked down at his clothes. They were covered in plaster dust. He looked at his hands. They were dirty, as though he'd been scrabbling about in some broken-down old house.

Oh, Jesus.

He was really losing it.

He got to his feet on weak legs and started slowly

back to Anna's house, then paused. He didn't know if he could face going in there right now. He turned and headed up Warrington, pausing at the corner of Wendover where his pickup was parked. Looking down the street, he could see that the IDent van was still parked in front of Baker's place. The barricades were still up, too, though the crowd they'd been holding back was long gone. A couple of police cruisers and the IDent van were all that remained to show that the investigation was still in progress.

This is real, he thought. I'm not dreaming now. I was just sleepwalking—that's how I got to be outside, away from the couch. That's why I'm here, instead of—

He touched the plaster dust on his clothes. Then where the hell did this come from?

(losing it)

He couldn't think about it. He couldn't clear his thoughts. He considered going back to Anna's again, then dug in his pockets for the keys to his pickup. The Toyota started at the first crack. He let the engine warm up for a few moments, then slowly pulled away from the curb and headed for home.

## 13

WALT HAWKINS AND his buddy, Ted, were sitting in Ted's apartment in Vanier watching some porn flick called *Firebox* that Ted had picked up in the same place from which he'd boosted the TV and VCR. The broad on the screen right now was one of those punky types, her blond hair short at the back and sides like a guy's, long and spiky on top. Her head was bobbing up and down in some greaseball's crotch, and Walt wondered if the greaseball thought he had some guy giving him the old sixty-nine. 'Course, with tits like hers, it'd be kind of hard to make that kind of a mistake. Now, if she was Walt's, he'd never let her wear her hair like—

"So you tracked her down, huh?" Ted asked.

Walt blinked, his mind still on the woman in the flick. Then he made the connection.

"Right where you said she'd be," he said as he reached for his beer.

"Toldja. There's one thing I never forget, Walt, my man—and that's a piece of ass. And your little wifey, she's sure got some—"

"Can it, okay?"

"Hey, hey. Lighten up, why dontcha? What do ya think I'm gonna do—hump her or something?"

"You don't talk about a man's wife that way."

"So sue me."

Walt started to frown, but then he saw that Ted was only ragging him. "And get what?" he asked. "You've got nothing worth suing you for."

"Tout-chay," Ted replied, mangling the expression he'd heard on some late show.

He was a thin little weasel of a guy, black hair slicked back, skin pockmarked from a bad case of acne he'd had as a kid. But he was a stand-up kind of a guy, Walt thought. No question. You wanted a guy you could trust at your back, then Teddy Rimmer was your man.

"So whatcha gonna do with her?" Ted wanted to know.

"I'm thinking about it. First thing is, I want to know all the people that've been helping her out—just so's I can have a little talk with them and convince them that maybe it wouldn't be such a good thing to do if she fucks off on me again."

"And then?" Ted asked when Walt fell silent.

"Then I'm going to bring old Beth home and teach her all about pain."

"If you need any, you know, help—"

"We're talking about my fucking *wife,* Teddy!"

"Hey, hey—relax, buddy. I'm just talking about these stiffs you wanna mess up a little."

"I'll let you know." Walt took a swig of his beer. "Thanks for the offer, though."

"No problem."

Walt looked back at the screen. "Aw, shit. I missed the part where the guy shoots his load. You want to rewind that thing?"

He got up to get them each another beer while Ted fiddled with the machine. Tonight was celebration time. He'd finally tracked down the long lost tramp. He wasn't even going to go in to work tomorrow. He was going to be too busy with a different kind of job for the next few days.

## 14

HARDASS BOUCHER CAUGHT a call from Dispatch—patched through to the inspector's car in front of the Baker residence—and met his partner, Jimmy Glover, at the scene of a Mac's Milk that had just been held up. Afterward he sat back at his desk, trying to get his paperwork up-to-date, but he couldn't concentrate on his work. He kept thinking of what he'd seen in Baker's basement.

Not the bodies. They'd been in bad-news shape, no question about it, but he'd seen worse.

No, he was thinking about those hallucinatory flashes that had hit him from out of nowhere. And about the weird feeling of being afraid. Christ, he couldn't have turned into a wimp all of a sudden, so what the hell was going on?

Even stranger was the roll call that had chosen tonight to go marching through his head, a parade of faces he didn't particularly want to remember.

The rape victim he'd felt up in the cruiser while they were waiting for the ambulance to arrive.

The teenage hooker he'd forced to sixty-nine him in a Harvey's restaurant; she under the table, head between his legs, he and his partner just shooting the breeze over a coffee while she did her mouth magic.

The drug dealer whom, when he found out she was a Lesbian, he let some of the boys gang-bang for a night, because it was either that or he was turning her in.

And others . . .

All too many others . . .

Each clamoring for his attention. Each pointing a finger at him and saying, "You fucked us up. Now it's your turn, Hardass. Now it's coming for you."

Coming for him.

He could feel it. Something. In that haunted wasteland. Riding that weird music he'd heard. Waiting for him out in the night beyond the station's walls. Right now.

Something.

Didn't matter that he knew it was all just bullshit.

That it had been just a flash of never-was, brought on by inhaling some bad fumes.

In his gut he knew it was real—whatever it was.

And it was out there.

Somewhere.

Waiting for him.

# TWO

## 1

THE PHONE WOKE HIM. He didn't pick it up until the fifth ring.

"Jack?"

"Yeah."

"It's Anna."

"I know. I kind of recognized your voice."

"Why'd you leave so early?"

"I needed a little time on my own. Just to think things through a bit."

(What do *you* do when you think you're losing it, sis?)

"Have you called the girl's parents yet?"

"No. I want to tell them in person . . ."

(I want to look in their eyes and have them tell me they didn't drive their kid out onto the street.)

". . . but I've got to talk to Ned first."

"He hasn't called me yet."

"He's probably busy, Anna. You'll be hearing from him."

"You sound so distant."

(That's because I'm on another fucking planet.)

"Must be the connection."

"Are you sure you're okay, Jack?"

"I'm not exactly okay, but I'm working on it."

"It wasn't your fault—what happened, I mean."

"I know."

(It's never anybody's fault, is it?)

There was a moment's pause.

"I love you, Jack."

"I know you do. It's what keeps me going sometimes."

"Just don't close me out of your life."

There was a soft click, then the hum of a dial tone. He nestled the receiver into its cradle and stared up at the wall of his bedroom. He was a little surprised to find himself still at home. In his own bed.

But then, he hadn't dreamed.

After that first one.

Not that he could remember.

He turned his head. Beside the phone and his digital alarm clock—it had come free with a half-year's subscription to *Newsweek*—was a small Fimo clay sculpture of Anna. A self-portrait. A present on his last birthday.

"I love you too," he said softly.

Then he got up and started his day.

## 2

POLICE WORK.

Ninety-nine percent of it was routine, and every cop bitched about it. The paperwork. The calls. Maybe it'd be a domestic, or a gas bar getting hit. A B&E. They still all ran together. The faces changed but the complainants and perps all looked the same after a while. The cases all ran together. Making for more paperwork. More of the same routine.

You did your job. Maybe you'd work out in the gym or the weight room on the other side of the floor after your shift was over. Pump a few. Or see who was on break in Fuzzie's. Maybe you'd head over to the Delco Building and shoot a little pool with a couple of the other guys, grab a couple of beers in Russell's. Maybe a lot of beers. Shoot the shit. Finish the late shift, pick up the early. Try to adjust. Shoot off a few rounds in the gun room and pretend the paper target you were filling full of holes was the same perp some candy-assed judge had let off on a technicality the week before.

Routine.

But no matter how much you bitched, you didn't want to get wired into a freak show. Times like this, Ned thought, all you wanted was that routine back again.

They'd finished up at Baker's house around three-thirty, though the ID Unit was still going through the place when he and Ernie left. They had an appointment with the coroner at the General for the autopsy. Funny thing about the hospital. The same horror-show corpses you wanted to puke over at the scene of the crime didn't look half so bad lying on a shiny metal table under the bright lights. It was like they weren't human anymore—not the bodies of dead people. Just bodies on a table. And you stood by while the coroner did his bit. It wasn't the same as when you found them. Then you *knew* these were people you were looking at. Dead people. Who'd died hard.

The girl had been a long time dying. The coroner just confirmed what they'd all already known from seeing that little meat factory in Baker's basement. The tubes going into her had been feeding crap into her system to keep her aware. To fire up her nerves so that she felt every little thing the sick bastard did to her. There was no fading away for her. She'd had to take it all, on her own, with no one to turn to but the freak who was peeling back her skin, inch by fucking inch.

The coroner read off a list of the shit Baker had been feeding her when the sample slides came back from the lab, but the medical terms just went over Ned's head.

Nobody could come up with an explanation of what had taken Baker down. It *was* Baker—they were sure of that much. His prints were on file from when he'd done some government work and needed security clearance. Research into noise pollution—wasn't that a kicker?

At his desk in the squad room, making out his report, Ned found himself sitting back and staring at the wall, his fists clenched, just wanting to hit somebody. Trouble was, somebody'd already done the job on the only likely candidate. And now it was up to him and Ernie to track down who did him in. What they should do, when they found this guy, was pin a fucking medal on him. No question about it. There ought to be a special award for people who took down slime like Baker. Ned wondered if he should bring it up at the next Police Association meeting.

Routine.

Jesus, Ned thought. Give me routine over this any day.

Because the real trouble was—never mind Baker and his sicko games—the *real* kicker was Ned wasn't so sure that he was playing with a full deck himself anymore. He kept seeing shit. . . .

"How's it going, Ned?"

Ned started. For one moment the squad room blurred, and those dead lands were rolling in—

(keep the fuck away from me!)

—then he focused on Ernie, pulling up a chair to his desk.

"You okay?" Grier asked. He shook out a cigarette and lit it with a bright orange Bic lighter—one of the new, smaller models.

"Feeling a little punchy, that's all," Ned said. It was going on thirty hours since he'd first gotten out of bed yesterday morning. "It's been a long shift."

"And it just keeps getting longer." Grier paused to take a drag off his smoke. He'd had the bandage on his hand replaced. There was no telltale trace of blood on this one. "We've got a meeting in the briefing room in fifteen minutes," he added.

"Wonderful."

Grier sat and smoked for a few moments. Ned could tell he had something on his mind, but he knew from experience that he'd hear it quicker if he just waited Ernie out.

"Let me ask you something, Ned," Grier said finally. "Have I got B.O. or something?"

Ned blinked. "What are you talking about?"

"Well, I get this feeling that no one wants to be around me this morning—like people are avoiding me. So I was wondering, maybe I need a new deodorant."

"What you need is a shave."

Grier rubbed the stubble on his cheek. "I'm going for that *Miami Vice* look—what do you think?"

"Well," Ned said, pretending to consider it. "If you

get yourself a nice baggy white suit and shades and stop wearing socks . . ."

"How do you suppose Crockett keeps those pants of his clean, crawling around in the dirt looking for evidence? Christ, all he's got to do is sit in one of our squad cars and it's game over for those cotton whites."

"That's the beauty of TV, Ernie. You get to look a little rough, but you never have to get dirty doing it. They just keep changing your clothes in between scenes."

Grier lit another cigarette. "I was serious, though, Ned. About this feeling I've got. Maybe I'm getting a bug—I don't know. You feel weird around me?"

"No weirder than usual," Ned began, but then he thought about something.

Going up to Fuzzie's for a coffee an hour or so ago. Thinking about sitting down at a table with a couple of the guys and taking a little break, shooting the shit for the ten minutes it'd take him to drink it down. But he'd felt a coldness in the cafeteria—like he didn't know anybody, even though they were all guys he saw every day—so he'd come back down to the squad room to work on his report while he drank it instead.

He hadn't really given it much thought, because coming down the stairs, he'd had another one of those flashes. . . .

Flicker.

The stairs were gone. And he was back there. In that place. The dead plains stretching for as far as he could see.

Flicker.

And it was gone again.

But he wasn't going crazy.

Jack had seen it too.

And unless they were both losing it . . .

"Back there in Baker's basement," he said, looking at Grier, "when you cut your hand. What did you see?"

"See?"

"Something made you stumble, Ernie, and it wasn't just looking at that kid."

"I . . . well, it was fumes—right?"

"That's what I thought."

"Except they tested the air and there wasn't anything there, was there? No fumes. Nothing."

"That's what the machines said."

"Unless maybe it drifted away before they got things set up . . . ?"

"What did you see, Ernie?"

Grier stubbed out his cigarette and lit another. He looked down at the butt as he spoke, watching the smoke curl up from its end, not looking at his partner.

"It was like—just for a moment, Ned—it was like the room wasn't there anymore. It was like I was standing out on . . . I don't know, the Prairies, except everything was dead. There was nothing growing. Nothing alive. It was just this flash—there and gone—but even after I cut myself I felt like it was still sitting there inside me. That place. Waiting for me, maybe."

Finally he looked up at Ned. "I really think I'm getting a bug, Ned. I was talking to Bernie just before I went on shift yesterday, and he says there's this flu going around."

"I saw it, too, Ernie."

It took a moment for his words to register. "You saw . . . ?"

"That place, Ernie. I saw it too. A couple of times. And Jack saw it when I was talking to him in the cruiser."

"What the fuck's going on, Ned?"

"I don't know. But you know what I'm going to do? I think I'll track some of the other guys who were there last night—the uniforms who got there first. Talk to them."

"They're going to think you're ready to eat your gun, Ned."

"Not if they saw it too."

Grier nodded slowly. "The guy on the porch—Coffey. He was really spooked."

"And Dwyer."

"Hardass went down too," Grier added. "Went down once and came up fast—at least that's what Dwyer told me—and he didn't go back down again."

"Not like him," Ned said.

"Yeah," Grier agreed glumly.

Duchaine from Arson stuck his head in the squad room, ending further speculation. "You guys waiting for a written invitation or what?"

Ned recovered first. "Just wanted to see your pretty face, Lou—to see how bad you missed us."

Duchaine gave him the finger with a grin. Grabbing their report files, they followed him down the hall to the briefing room. There was a definite chill in the air. They both felt it.

## 3

BETH WAS UP EARLY after a restless night. She lay awake for a long while, waiting to hear some sound from downstairs to let her know that Jack was up. Finally she washed, put on a pair of light blue cotton trousers and a dark blue cotton-knit sweater, and went down only to find Jack gone. All that remained of his presence was the unmade bed on the couch and his jacket, which was slung over the back of the fat easy chair by the window. She put on a pot of coffee and folded up the bedding on the couch while she waited for the coffee. By the time she was on her second cup Anna had come down, ready for work in an old Kate Bush "Lionheart Tour" sweatshirt and a pair of faded jeans.

"Morning," Anna said brightly. "Where's Jack?"

"He was already gone when I got up."

Anna showed no signs of either the late night or the at least one too many beers she'd had the night before. But then she never did. Sometimes Beth wondered if she ever slept at all.

"Cathy must have scared him off," Anna decided.

"I suppose."

"Or maybe it was you."

Beth blushed and started to protest.

"Just kidding." Anna helped herself to the coffee and sat down at the kitchen table with Beth. She pulled the phone closer. "I'd better give him a call. He didn't seem to be in very good shape yesterday."

Beth listened to Anna's side of the conversation when the connection was made and wondered why the world had to be the way it was, things going wrong far more often than going right.

"So how'd you sleep last night?" Anna asked as she cradled the receiver.

"Not very well. I couldn't stop dreaming."

Concern rose in Anna's eyes. "Were they . . . ?"

She didn't have to finish. They'd discussed it only once, but after that they never put it into words again. Never talked about—

(that dark place)

—what had happened the last time Walt had dragged her home. Locking her in the basement, the windows hammered shut, the door going up to the kitchen locked. Walt had the only key. He let her out to cook and clean. Under his supervision. She used a pail for a toilet that she was only allowed to empty upstairs once a day. She slept down there, on an old mattress. The same mattress on which he fucked her. When he could get it up. He had to hit her to get it up. Because it was her fault that it wouldn't get hard. But once he got it up . . . his grip painful on her bruised skin, each lunging thrust of his hips an agony.

She was there for weeks—

(in that dark place filled with pain)

—in the dark. And the damp. Nursing her bruises like a hurt animal.

"Beth . . . ?"

She looked up, eyes bright with unshed tears.

"I'm sorry," Anna said. "I didn't mean to bring it all up again. Shit. What a way for me to start your day."

"It . . . it's not your fault, Anna. Besides, Dr. Hansen

says I'm not supposed to hide it . . . what happened. . . . I'm not supposed to hide it from myself. I've got to learn to face it."

Anna reached across the table and took her hand. "I know, Beth. And it makes sense. I just hate to see you feeling this way."

Beth looked for and managed to find a small smile. Anna gave her hand a squeeze, then reached for her coffee.

"Anyway," Beth said, "I wasn't dreaming about . . . about *that.* But it was almost as bad. I was here in the house, but everything was broken down and decrepit. Like no one had lived here for years. I was lying in my bed in the dream. I woke there—in my bed. But it was, like, all moldy-smelling. The plaster was hanging down from the ceiling, the wallpaper curling back from the walls."

She noticed an odd expression on Anna's face.

"Anna?"

"Go on."

"Well, then I heard something coming up the stairs, sort of dragging itself. I thought it was Walt—and I was ready to die. I heard him put his foot through a step, then it sounded like the banister gave way. There was this big crash.

"I just lay there in my bed, skin crawling because it was so filthy, but I was too scared to move. I kept listening, hoping Walt had gone down with the banister, but then I heard him again, still coming up the stairs. I wanted to scream but I couldn't move a muscle. It wasn't until he was in the hall right by what was left of the door that I finally jumped up and hid in the closet.

"I found an old blanket and covered myself with it,

hoping he'd think I was just some pile of clothes or something, but I didn't really think it was going to work. I crouched in there, hearing him come into the room. I knew he was going to get me any second. Then the floor in my room gave way. You should've heard the sound—the whole house shook when it fell.

"Well, I just stayed there in the closet, hugging the wall, wrapped in my blanket from head to toe. He must've just gotten to the hallway in time because I could hear him on the stairs again. I waited until he'd gone outside, then I crept to the edge of the closet and looked downstairs through the hole where my floor had been. And then . . ."

She gave Anna a quick smile.

"It was the weirdest thing. Suddenly I wasn't wearing my nightie anymore. I was dressed in this long, shimmery robe. My hair was down to here"—she touched her waist—"and I just knew that all I had to do was step out into the air and I'd be able to just fly away."

"Did . . ." Anna cleared her throat. "And did you?"

Beth nodded. "It was wonderful . . . at first. I just floated around my room, then downstairs. The window in the dining room was broken, so I just drifted out of it into the night. Everywhere I looked, the city was dark, the houses broken-down. Then I heard a sound—like the wind, only it was more like voices. Not chanting—but sighing, maybe. Rhythmical. I started to get a real creepy feeling then. The city sort of faded away—you know the way that happens in dreams?—and I was zooming along this huge empty landscape. Everything was dead—trees, grass, whatever—for as far as I could see. And the music . . .

"It was still there, but now I could hear it better and

knew that it was made up of people crying. Sad people, hurt people, scared people. And everything around me felt like that. Like it was a place where those who've got no more hope end up or something. And I was still just zooming along, going nowhere fast, because everything looked the same."

A small shiver traveled up her spine as she remembered.

"And then?" Anna asked.

"Then I woke up." She gave a nervous laugh. "Pretty weird stuff, don't you think?" She looked up at Anna, startled by the very odd look on her friend's face. "Anna?"

"It's not half as weird as you think," Anna replied.

"What do you mean?"

"Beth, I dreamed about those same places last night. Our house, all a ruin. I woke up in my bed, and it was the same as yours—like something you'd find in a junkyard. I didn't stay in the house, didn't look around at all to see if anybody else was around. I just went outside to find the city, run-down and empty. I saw you—or I saw someone with blond hair in a filmy white gown—come floating out of the house.

"I called after her but she wouldn't stop. Maybe she didn't hear me. So I started to run. I just kept running, and the city faded away around me, and then I found myself in the same wasteland that you just described to me."

"You . . . you're just saying this, aren't you?" Beth said nervously.

"I swear I'm not making it up."

"You're scaring me, Anna."

Anna reached out and caught her hand again. "I

*swear* I'm not making it up. I wouldn't do that to you, Beth."

"But then . . ." Something like a rock formed in the pit of Beth's stomach. "What . . . what does it mean?"

"I don't know," Anna said softly. She let go of Beth's hand to rub her face—a habit both she and Jack shared when they were worried or thinking. "It doesn't make any sense. How can two people—"

Cathy chose that moment to come downstairs. Her hair was pulled back in a ponytail and all she was wearing was one of Anna's oversize T-shirts.

"Rats," she said, coming into the kitchen. "He's already gone." She glanced at the two of them, sitting at the table. "Hey, chums—why so glum?"

"We were talking about our dreams," Anna began.

"Dreams! Let me tell you about dreams. I had one of those after-the-bomb-drops kind of Armageddon dreams—you know, where the city's all empty except for you, and you're just wandering around looking for someone to talk to, thinking 'Armageddon outa here,' only there's no place to be 'geddon' to?"

Anna and Beth exchanged worried looks.

"Will someone tell me what's going on around here?"

"I think you'd better sit down, Cathy," Anna said.

# 4

THE BRIEFING ROOM was crowded by the time Ned and his partner arrived. Duchaine took a chair beside Gilles Ouellette, the Staff Sergeant from Arson. Representing the General Investigations section was their own Staff Sergeant, Andy Coe, and Inspector Fournier, who'd be handling the statements for the press. Also present were Detective Vicki Watson from the Sexual Assault/Child Abuse section; Dr. Barrett Kiers, the coroner on call last night when the report first came in; Constables Benoit Petrin and Lisa Lachance and Staff Sergeant Gord Ferris from the ID Unit; and Superintendent of Staff Operations Jacques Mondoux.

Fournier got up to speak as Ned and Grier took their chairs. Briefly and concisely he gave a general rundown on what they had so far, then asked for more detailed reports, starting with Dr. Kiers. Ned was already familiar with the results, having been present when Kiers conducted the autopsies. The only new piece of business was that with the name Jack had given Ned, they'd been able to obtain Janet Rowe's dental records and make a positive ID of her body.

Ned doodled on the pad in front of him as various postulations on how Baker'd bought it were raised and discarded, not really returning his attention to the proceedings again until Fournier called on Detective Watson from Sexual Assault/Child Abuse. She was a handsome woman in her late thirties, beginning to take on a mature look that probably would help her on the job, Ned thought, but she wasn't quite there yet. She glanced at him as she began her report but didn't return his smile. They'd worked together before Ned had been transferred to General Assignment and kept up a good working relationship since, so her snub surprised Ned. Then he remembered what Ernie'd been saying earlier: *I get this feeling that no one wants to be around me this morning. . . .*

Watson's section didn't have a file on Baker—not even any rumors.

"But that's not really surprising," she said, "when you consider the sheer volume of incidents that exist. What we actually get to investigate is only the tip of the iceberg. Even more so than rape victims, these kids take the guilt on themselves. They end up believing that it's all their fault, and they hide what's happened from everybody. This isn't helped by the threats of what will happen—not so much to them but to a parent, or a pet, or even a favorite cartoon character in the case of some of the very young victims—that the offenders level at them.

"What's surprising in this case is not so much what Baker had been up to but that we found out at all."

"Come on, Vicki," Duchaine said. "The guy wasn't just diddling kids, he was butchering them."

Watson nodded. "This is an extreme case, I'll grant you that, but Baker's motives boil down to the same thing that motivates them all—a need for power. These offenders do what they do to children only for the feeling of omnipotence that it gives them. What Baker did with the Rowe girl was a radical departure from most sexual offenders—raising the ratio of his power over his victim to insane levels—but it still grew out of his need to be the one in control."

"The guy was slime," somebody muttered down the table.

"I've checked with Youth Intervention," Watson went on, "and Baker was clean there, although he was in their files. Runaways often gravitate to the music scene—clubs and the like—and it seems Baker's recording studio was quite the hangout for more than just hopeful musicians. Lots of kids went there as well. There's been no indication before this, however, that Baker was anything more than what he appeared to be: a philanthropic patron of the music scene who was willing to put his money where his mouth was. He's actually on record as having brought in runaways. Youth Services have nothing but good to say of him—had, I should say."

"Is there any chance that whoever killed Baker was also responsible for the girl's death?"

The question came from the Superintendent of Staff Operations, Jacques Mondoux, a grey-haired veteran of thirty-five years with the force. Typical brass worry, Ned thought. The street slime were capable of anything, but let's bend over backward for Joe Citizen. The ID Unit's Staff Sergeant answered.

"Not when you consider the very nature of the room we found her in," Ferris said. "Obviously Baker had had it constructed expressly for the purpose to which he put it to use. There's a section of wall that closes to make the room impossible to detect. It's built farther back under the yard, so you'd have to actually know it existed before you could even go looking for it."

"What about prints?" Fournier asked.

Ferris nodded. He was getting some grey hairs among the red, Ned noted. Christ, they were all getting old.

"I was getting to that," Ferris said. "We lifted dozens of latent prints from all over the house, but the only ones in that room were Baker's and the girl's."

Baker hadn't disposed of her skin yet, Ned remembered. They'd found it in a green garbage bag under the metal table on which the corpse had been found. The ID Unit had gotten the girl's prints to make the match from the pads of her fingertips that were found in the bag's gruesome contents.

"So unless there was a third or fourth party wearing surgical gloves," Fournier went on, "we have to assume the girl was Baker's victim."

"His first?" the Superintendent asked.

"We've no way of telling that at this point," Fournier said. "But from the setup of that room—the renovations were completed ten years ago, according to the building permits that were filed with City Hall—I'd have to say that I doubt she was his first. We've just started checking the grounds of the house this morning."

Ferris completed the ID Unit's report. Photographs and sketches of the crime scene, and lists of relevant evidence collected there, were passed around the table.

"I don't have to tell you," Superintendent Mondoux said, "just how much the press is going to be all over us on this one. We need a quick solution. Inspector Fournier will continue to coordinate the investigation and make any necessary statements to the press. If anyone has any—"

The phone by Fournier's elbow rang just then, making more than one of them start. Watching Fournier's face tighten as he took the call, Ned got a nervous flutter in the pit of his stomach.

Somewhere, something bad was going down. . . .

"You're sure . . . ?" Fournier was saying. "Yes, but . . ." Confusion was apparent in his features, mixed with something that Ned couldn't quite pinpoint. "No," Fournier said before he rang off. "Don't touch a thing. We'll be right down."

He cradled the phone and looked down the table. "We're wanted on the gun range," he said.

## 5

SHEILA COFFEY LOOKED in on her husband at mid-morning to find Ron turning fretfully in their bed. She hesitated, wanting to go comfort him, but then quietly closed the bedroom door.

Let him sleep, she thought as she moved down the hall to where the wash was waiting to be folded and put away in the linen closet. He hadn't said much when he'd come in this morning—late off his shift, his features drawn—and that in itself had been unusual. From the subsequent news bulletins on W1310, which had come in between the goldie oldies that Gary Michaels was spinning, she'd learned more details of the last call that Ron had taken before he went off shift. She'd never heard of this Chad Baker before, but from what the announcer had to say during his newsbreaks, Baker had been completely twisted. And from the look of Ron when he'd come home last night, whatever he'd seen there had been very bad.

"Get used to it," her mother had warned her when Sheila and Ron first got engaged. "The life of a policeman's wife isn't an easy one . . ." her mother had begun, and then she'd proceeded to run through a list of divorce, failed marriage, and suicide statistics until Sheila had simply shut out the flow of her mother's words.

Sure there were problems. The shifts were hard to get used to. The worry about what Ron might have to confront in his work—there seemed to be more and more cops hurt on the job recently. The way she'd just drifted away from most of her old friends until the only people she saw much of anymore were the wives of other policemen. But what marriage didn't have its share of problems? She loved Ron, and in the end that was all that counted. She loved him and he loved her.

So what am I doing putting away the laundry when I could be giving him the comfort he needs right now? she asked herself.

She let a stack of towels drop back into the laundry basket and stood up to stretch a kink out of her neck. Then she walked down the short hallway back to the bedroom, unbuttoning her blouse as she went. A warm feeling stirred in her stomach, but her smile faded as she opened the bedroom door.

The bed was empty.

"Ron?" she called.

Her first thought was that he'd gone to the bathroom, but she'd been out in the hall and he couldn't have come out of the bedroom without her seeing him. The only other way out of the room was through the window, and since their apartment was on the twelfth floor . . .

"Ron?"

Feeling a little silly, she crossed the room to the closet and looked in. Only their clothes were hanging there. No mysterious, disappearing husband.

"Okay, Ron," she said. "A joke's a joke."

But he wasn't under the bed, either. Nor anywhere in the apartment. Sometime in between her looking in on him ten minutes ago when he lay naked in their bed, sleeping restlessly, and now, he'd vanished. Only he *couldn't* have come out of the bedroom, because she'd been right there in the hallway the whole time.

She'd heard it said among their friends on the force that a cop's wife developed a certain intuition. Right now there was something humming inside her like a taut wire, plucked and reverberating. She hesitated a few moments longer, then sat down on the bed, drew the phone toward her, and dialed Pat Nichols's number.

For a patrolman in Field Operations, Pat was the closest Ron had to a partner. Although the officers usually worked solo, when Ron was teamed up with another, it was with Pat that he patrolled in the two-man cruiser. She hoped to God Pat would know what to do. Somehow Ron had dressed and left the house without making a sound. He'd sneaked by her, passing within inches of her in the hallway, and she'd never noticed. Why had he done it? Where had he gone?

She listened to the phone ring on the other end and tried to keep her voice from trembling when the connection was finally made.

# 6

THERE WAS NO place Ron Coffey would rather have been than in his wife's arms. Unfortunately he was miles away from her at the moment and didn't seem to have much choice in the matter.

He'd never had a dream like this before.

It started with him thinking he was awake. A dull light came through the window, letting him believe that it was late in the afternoon and he'd slept through the day, but then the smell hit him. The room smelled like a sewer. He sat up to find himself lying naked on a moldering old mattress in the middle of a mound of trash. The stink came from the garbage. The smell of stale urine made him think of how the patrol car stank when they pulled in a wino. Mostly the walls were smeared with long streaks of old dried feces, but there was graffiti there as well, written in shit: STICK THE PIG'S WIFE; COP SOWS GIVE THE BEST HEAD.

"Sheila . . . ?" he asked softly.

There was no answer. Just the silence. Not even the hum of the fridge.

He got off the mattress, but there was no place to stand that wasn't covered with trash. He slid on something slimy and fell back onto the mattress. A few inches from his face, a dead rat stared back at him, ants crawling out of its ears and mouth. Bile came up Coffey's throat and he turned away, heaving up the contents of his stomach on his hands and knees until there was nothing more to come up. The stink of fresh vomit cut across the room's other odors.

He lurched to his feet, spitting to try to get the taste out of his mouth. This room . . . ?

The familiarity of it got to him. It was just like his apartment—like it would look if nobody'd lived in it for a few years and the place just went to the dogs. His gaze settled on the graffiti again. Sheila. The fuckers were talking about Sheila.

He started out of the room, still a little unsteady, then looked down at himself. Jay-naked. What a picture. He checked the room again, training taking over after the initial shock of the situation. There was a heap of cloth on the floor of the closet. Rooting through it, he came up with a pair of jeans and a stained white shirt, missing all the buttons and one arm. The clothing smelled, but at this point Coffey wasn't feeling particular. Everything smelled in here.

He stepped out into the hall and followed it past a bathroom and kitchen until it opened onto a living/dining room. Again the sense of déjà vu hit him. The layout was exactly the same as the apartment he and Sheila had. There was more graffiti here—spray-painted this time. A dog chewing out the crotch of a nude woman with a pig's face. PAIN RULES under it. A crudely sketched but recognizable cop, drawn and quartered. But what caught his gaze like a magnet was a macramé hanging that lay in the middle of the floor beside some broken bottles and other trash.

He spread it out on the floor as best he could to have a better look at it. An owl. Sheila'd made one just like this, hung it over there where the TV used to . . .

He looked over to see a TV smashed on the floor—a twin to the Zenith they'd bought a month ago. Their wedding photo lay beside it, the glass cracked. Christ, Sheila'd looked so good that day.

He stood up quickly and headed for the front door, careful not to step on any glass in his bare feet. The carpet was damp, slick with mold. When he swung the door open and looked down the hall, the sound of the door hitting the wall inside the apartment sent an echoing boom down the hall. He heard a baby cry. Had to be the Wilsons' kid, just around the corner. Kid was always crying.

He started down the carpeted hall, which was littered with trash as well. A sense of competency had returned to him. The moment in the bedroom was forgotten, except for the sickly taste in his mouth. But then he turned the corner and saw—

The kid was howling. Cherub face red with the effort. The kid was—

Coffey's footsteps slowed.

His first impression was that someone had tied—

(nailed)

—her to the door. But as he got closer, feet dragging on the slimy carpet, he could see that the kid was attached to—

(growing out of)

—the door.

Coffey froze, unable to move. He stared at the eight-month-old baby girl, her eyes shut, mouth open, wailing. She was like a bas-relief come to life. He could see where the flesh joined—

(became)

—the wood of the door. More graffiti. Over the kid's head. SUCKS THE BIG ONE. Red spray paint. Some of it had dripped like blood onto the kid's head. The kid. Attached to the door like it was growing out of it.

"Jesus . . ." Coffey moaned, backing away.

It was sick. It wasn't real.

He got around the corner and pressed the side of his head against the wall. He banged his head hard against the plaster. Once, twice. Again.

"Wake the fuck up," he told himself.

Nothing changed.

The baby's cries followed him around the corner. He fled down the hall, back to his own apartment, slamming the door on the sound. Leaning against the door, he tried to quiet the frantic thumping of his pulse. His gaze settled on the graffiti.

Sheila. Jesus, where was Sheila?

Back into the bedroom now. He threw everything out of the closet, looking for shoes, boots, anything he could put on his feet. He couldn't stand that slime touching his feet anymore. The stink of the room clogged in his lungs. He found one of his uniforms, shredded. He found the holster for his handgun, but the .38 itself was gone. He found his billy club, only something had chewed off and taken the greater part of its length.

He remembered that show he and Sheila'd watched on the tube last year—about what it'd be like when they dropped the bomb. Was that it? Had he slept through a fucking nuclear war? Where *was* everybody?

His hands were shaking so hard, he had to grip his knees.

Okay, think, he told himself. What do I do now?

(Sheila)

He combed his sweaty hair with his fingers. If anybody else had survived, they'd be at the station. He didn't know about civilians, but that's where the cops would go. He didn't have anything to protect his feet.

He didn't have a weapon. But he was going to have to make it there, anyway.

He bound his feet with the rags of his uniform. From the dining room he took a discarded chair leg and hefted it. There were going to be things out there. Maybe just looters, maybe people looking for help. But there were going to be things too. Like that kid on—

(growing out of)

—the door. He suppressed a shudder. Things like her. Maybe worse. But he couldn't stay here. He had to know what was going on. He had to find Sheila.

When he cracked the door to the hallway, the baby was still howling. He didn't figure the elevators would be working, so he took to the stairs straightaway. The upper sections weren't so bad, but the stairs began to get clogged as he got to the last couple of floors. He found himself crawling over furniture and all kinds of crap that someone had just tossed down the stairwell. There was more graffiti on the walls, but it wasn't so personal now. All of it sexual or violent. Some more PAIN RULES.

There was only a foot and a half to spare between the piled junk and the top of the door leading into the apartment's foyer. If someone hadn't trashed the door itself, he might never have gotten out. As it was, he was cautious in the foyer and heading out the front door, watching his surroundings with a continuous sweeping motion of his head, trying not to focus on any one thing for too long. But once he hit the street, all he could do was stop and stare.

The skies above were a dirty yellow, as though a high smog bank were hovering over the city. The streets themselves seemed empty. He checked behind the apartment building, but while his car was in the lot, he didn't have a key for it. And somebody'd stripped the wheels from it, anyway.

Where the hell was everybody?

(Sheila)

Maybe more to the point, where was whoever was vandalizing the empty buildings and cars?

He'd get no answer standing here, he told himself. He set off on foot from the apartment building on Bronson Avenue, straight across the downtown core for the eight long blocks across and five or so blocks down to the station on Elgin Street. Ottawa's downtown core looked like photos he'd seen of the South Bronx. Half the buildings were rubble. Gutted cars and buses littered the street. There was trash everywhere. From time to time he caught glimpses of dogs in the ruined buildings but no people. It wasn't until he was a block away from the station, just cutting through the grounds of the National Museum of Natural History, that he saw a human figure.

It had its back to him and didn't turn, even when he called out. He hurried by the museum, noting that its castlelike walls were the least damaged of any he'd seen on his trek so far. His feet were sore and he couldn't move fast. But neither did the figure. He chased it down Metcalfe to where it turned left on Catherine Street. He could see the station now. The figure disappeared around the front of the squat utilitarian building. Coffey picked up his pace, wincing whenever a piece of stone came between his bandaged feet and the pavement.

The figure waited for him by the big glass doors of the station, its back still turned. All the glass was missing from the door. As Coffey hurried to close the gap between them, the figure began to shuffle off again.

"Hey!" Coffey cried. "You there. Stop!"

The figure turned and all of Coffey's hard-won rationalizations fled screaming from his mind. The thing coming for him now was the corpse they'd found in the basement of that house last night. Chad Baker. Face burned away to the skull, hair and skin hanging from its back. One hand a skeletal ruin, held close to its chest. The other reaching for Coffey like some ghoul from a late-night horror flick.

He was dead, Coffey told himself.

He'd seen the corpse, for chrissake. The guy was dead.

Yeah, and so was the city now.

What the *fuck* was going on?

He turned from the creature's shuffling advance. He ran straight for the doors, jumping through the frames, glass crunching underfoot. He staggered as a jagged edge cut into the sole of his left foot but limped on. He was heading for the first basement. There'd be weapons down there. The shotguns you signed out on patrol. Maybe in the gun range. There had to be something. It looked like he was all alone in the city except for a baby growing out of a door, some wild dogs, and a fucking walking corpse. Well, he wasn't going down alone. He didn't know what the hell was going on anymore, but he wasn't going down alone.

He got down to the first basement, hobbling heavily now. He couldn't put any weight on his left foot. Every time he did, it was like his whole leg was on fire.

There was nothing he could use at the Staff Sergeant's desk. Somebody'd already cleaned it out. He could hear the creature still shuffling toward him in the stairwell. He went down the hall. At the next station he could see a tangled mess of trashed walkie-talkies, radar, and other crap, but no weapons. That left the gun range, but it had nothing, either. As he turned to leave, the creature was there, filling the doorway.

Coffey backed away from it. He'd found no better weapon than the chair leg he'd left the apartment with. He raised it, wincing as his hurt foot bumped against the floor. He was right in the actual target area of the range now, the creature following him through the portals holding the controls that moved the targets.

He had no place left to go, Coffey realized. He had to make his stand here.

But then the creature stopped. It was hard to tell with just a skull to go by, but its attention seemed to be focused on something behind Coffey and to his left. Coffey moved slightly to one side so that he could check out his rear while still keeping his eye on the creature. He almost dropped his makeshift weapon.

Drifting out of the wall—right *through* the wall—was the most beautiful woman Coffey had ever seen. Looking at her was like the first time he'd seen Sheila—when everything was still new between them and the world had a sparkly cast to it. The floating woman brought it all to mind. Just looking at her eased the tension that had been knotting Coffey's muscles.

He barely noticed the dead creature flee the woman's presence. His arms went limply to his side as she drifted closer to him. Her feet touched the ground, light as feathers. She went to her knees, moving like smoke. Her hair was so bright—especially after the dullness outside—that it hurt his eyes. He could see right through the filmy robes she was wearing. Her body was a perfect shape.

She looked up at him with her angel's face. She pressed her breasts against his knees—a cool, soft pressure. Her hands, fingers as delicate as butterflies, rose to tug at the fastenings of his jeans.

"I . . ." Coffey cleared his throat. "I don't think we should . . . uh . . . you know . . ."

Because he was thinking of—

(Sheila)

The woman made a soft growling sound, deep in her throat. She leaned a little away from him, fingers tearing at the material of his jeans. One of her nails caught in the sturdy material and ripped right through it, drawing blood from the flesh underneath. Coffey stumbled out of her reach. Hot red pain fired up from his left foot as he put pressure on it.

Coffey lifted the chair leg. "Get back. . . ."

There was something different in her eyes now—nothing soft. He saw with a shock that her canines protruded a quarter of an inch from her lips.

She's a fucking vampire, he thought. Some kind of mutant—

The woman lunged at him. Without even thinking, Coffey swung the chair leg. It broke against the woman's head, not even fazing her. Her jaws opened—wide enough to swallow his head. From the darkness of her throat emerged dozens of wriggling tongues.

"Oh, Jesus," Coffey moaned, trying to get away.

Her breath hit him in the lower torso like a concentrated blast of liquid fire. It boiled away skin, muscle, intestines, major organs, leaving a hole the size of a watermelon. Coffey had long enough to smell the stink of his own burned body, and then he was dying. His last thought was that he'd never see—

(Sheila)

—again.

# 7

IT WAS CHAOS in the gun range. Ned stood over Coffey's body, staring down at the corpse for long, silent moments while a babble of conversation rang all around him. Ned gave the body a careful study. Whoever had killed Coffey had had access to the same weaponry that had killed Baker. The hole in Coffey's lower torso looked like someone had just taken a blowtorch to him. A *big* blowtorch. Coffey also had a bullet wound in his shoulder from where one of the officers on the range had shot him. Supposedly Coffey had just *appeared* on the range, popping in out of nowhere, just as the officer was firing.

When Constables Petrin and Lachance wheeled in the equipment from the IDent van, Ned moved away and went to talk to the officer who'd shot Coffey. Constable Gilles Myre was a first-year rookie, a brawny dark-haired man who stood just over six feet. Right now he looked badly shook up. He sat in Sergeant Alec Shouldice's office, slouched in a chair. Shouldice was in charge of the gun range.

"He was just there," Myre was saying. "Jesus, I don't know where he came from. I was already firing, and then he . . . he . . ."

Shouldice touched his shoulder. "There was nothing you could do, Gilles," he said. "The man was dead before you ever hit him."

"His eyes . . ." Myre looked up at Ned's approach. "I could see him looking at me. I was already firing, and it was too late to do anything." He pushed his face into his hands. "Where the fuck did he come from?"

Ned crouched by his chair. He glanced at Shouldice, got a nod that said okay, then laid a hand on one of Myre's arms, gently pulling the man's hand from his face.

"Think you can backtrack for me?" he asked.

"I . . ."

"Take your time." Ned glanced at Shouldice.

"Gilles Myre," Shouldice said.

"It's okay, Gilles," Ned went on. "There was nothing you could do." And even if there had been, Ned wasn't about to bring it up right now. "Just run through it for me, would you? And take your time."

Myre swallowed thickly and nodded. He was pale from shock, but Ned was pretty sure he'd pull through okay. It'd take some time. Maybe he wouldn't sleep too well for a while. . . . Sleep. Adrenaline was burning through Ned's body right now, but he could feel his lack of sleep lying under it like a deadweight. There just didn't seem to be enough time for anything.

"I . . . I was taking my six-month," Myre began.

Ned nodded encouragingly. Twice a year every officer had to be tested on the gun range. No exceptions.

"Alec had set up the target," Myre went on. "We did the seven-foot, I reloaded, then Alec set up another target. He got it into position. When I was ready, he hit the switch. The target swung around and I was pulling the trigger and then . . . then he just . . . the guy just *appeared* in between me and . . . and the target."

"Appeared?" Ned asked.

Myre nodded. His gaze fixed on Ned's. "One minute I had my sights on the target, the next the guy was stumbling in front of it. It was like . . . like he was stepping out of nowhere. I saw his head and shoulders first, then my bullet hit him, spinning him back, and the rest of him appeared. Christ, I didn't have a chance to stop. I was *already* firing."

"It's okay," Ned said. He glanced up at Shouldice. "You saw all this, Alec?"

"It's like he said, Ned. Sucker just stepped in out of nowhere."

"No chance he came in behind you?"

Shouldice shook his head. "We were both looking at the target and Coffey just *appeared* there. I never saw anything like it. Did you see the way he was dressed?"

Ned nodded. Like a rubbie. Bloody rags on his feet like he'd walked across town in them. Old clothes that smelled like a wino's. A broken chair leg lying just beyond the reach of one hand.

"What do you figure?" Ned asked.

"It's a fucking *Twilight Zone,*" Shouldice said simply. "No ifs, ands, or buts about it."

"Anybody else down here at the time?"

"Just me and Gilles."

And they'd already checked with the Staff Sergeant's desk. Coffey hadn't come in that way. Nor through the main doors upstairs. Looking like he had, there was no way anyone would have missed seeing him.

"You about finished, Ned?" Shouldice asked.

"Sure." Ned looked at Myre. "You can make your report later, Gilles. Right now, why don't you get away from all of this"—he waved a hand behind him to the range where the investigation was under way—"maybe grab yourself a coffee up in Fuzzie's. We'll talk to you later when you've had a chance to come down a little."

"I'll get someone to go up with him," Shouldice said.

Myre just shook his head. "Jesus. He was just *there,* you know?"

"I hear you," Ned said. "Just take it easy, Gilles."

He got to his feet and waited while Shouldice found an officer to go upstairs with Myre. The Sergeant returned to stand beside Ned, the two of them looking out at the gun range.

"The burns on Coffey," he said. "It's the same deal as that case you caught last night, right?"

"Pretty much. Only Baker took it in the head. He also had a defense wound on one hand."

Defense wound. Right. Would you believe no hand left, period?

"What the hell are we dealing with here?"

Ned sighed. "Looney tunes," he said. "That's all I can figure, Alec. We're going looney tunes."

"I saw it go down," Shouldice said. "No bullshit here, Ned. It happened fast, but I *saw* that guy step in out of nowhere."

Ned nodded. "No one's saying you didn't—it just doesn't make a whole lot of sense."

Before Shouldice could reply, Ned went to rejoin his partner out in the gun range. Earlier, people'd been thinking that whoever had killed Baker had done them a favor. But nobody would be thinking that now, Ned thought. Not with a cop dead. Only where the hell were they supposed to turn now?

# 8

"THIS IS SO CREEPY," Cathy said. "It's just like that movie, you know? 'Freddy's back.' "

When Cathy got excited, she had a way of raising the pitch of her voice so that her sentences ended on a higher note than the rest of the words. Normally Cathy's enthusiasm made Anna smile, but today it just seemed to add to the headache that was developing behind Anna's left temple.

"What do you mean?" Beth asked.

"That movie, *Nightmare on Elm Street.* Didn't you ever see it?"

Beth shook her head. "I don't like that kind of thing."

"Too spooky," Anna agreed.

Cathy smiled. "And no redeeming social value, right?"

"Well . . ."

"You want to talk about spooky," Cathy went on, "what about real life? What about this dream we all had?"

"Synchronicity—" Anna began.

"Pardon me, but bullshit," Cathy interrupted. "Maybe if we'd all just watched some disaster flick together, okay. But not out of the blue like this. This is just spooky. And that place gave me the creeps."

Anna nodded. She knew just what Cathy meant. She'd never experienced such a feeling of desolation—

and loss—before. It was as though everything good had died and all that was left was pain. And loneliness.

"I started out feeling scared," Beth said, "but then I got . . . I don't know. It was like all of a sudden I was in control. Of everything. For the first time *I* was the one in charge. I never felt like that before."

"Wish fulfillment," Cathy said. Anna shot her a dirty look but Cathy only shrugged. "I'm sorry, but it's true. Why else would anybody like a place like that?"

"It wasn't the place," Beth said. "It was the feeling in me."

"Besides," Anna added, "dreams are supposed to be where we work out the stuff that bothers us during the day."

Cathy's eyebrows went up. "More dream psychology? Well, then, what was I supposed to be working out? And how come we were all in the same place—right down to the graffiti on the living room wall?"

"I didn't see any graffiti," Beth said.

"No, but Anna and I did."

Anna shivered, remembering. The crude drawing beside the words had looked too much like a caricature of herself for her to feel comfortable thinking about it.

"I did that dreaming test," she said. "You know, where you look away from writing and then look back? If the writing's changed, you're dreaming. If it doesn't . . ."

"And did it? Oh, please!" Cathy cried when Anna shook her head. "Don't get me thinking that place really exists somewhere."

A wistful look touched Beth's features. "Maybe that wouldn't be so bad," she said. When the other two gave her strange looks, she went on. "Well, not for me, at least." Her gaze settled on Cathy. "You don't know what it's like being me. Or somebody like me. Everybody's always hitting on me, using me. It was different in the dream. *I* was the one in control there. I felt like nobody could hurt me—nobody could even touch me."

Cathy shook her head. "If that place *was* real, you wouldn't catch me wanting to go back." She gave Anna a look. "Imagine meeting the jerks responsible for that graffiti? Jody and Kirk. Wouldn't you love to run into *them* some dark night?"

Beth went chalk white.

"But that place *isn't* real," Anna said quickly. "And those feelings you had there, Beth . . . it can be like that here too."

"It's not that easy."

"I know. But you've got to try. *Here* is where the real world is, where we've all got to deal with whatever comes our way. Dreams are just . . . well, dreams."

When she saw Beth withdrawing into herself, Anna wished she could take her words back. Why did she always feel that everything had to be a lesson? Beth had things tough enough as it was, without being lectured every time she sounded a little unsure of herself.

Cathy stood up from the table. "So are we still going shopping?" she asked. "The sales wait for no woman."

"Do you want to go?" Anna asked Beth.

"No. You two go on ahead. I'm trying to save some money."

Anna had to bite back a "Are you sure you'll be all right?" Give the lady some slack, she told herself.

"You know what I wonder?" Cathy said as they went upstairs to get dressed.

Anna shook her head. "What?"

"I wonder what kind of dreams Jack had last night."

# 9

AT EIGHT-THIRTY that morning Julie Clark had only been asleep for three hours when the pounding came at the door of her apartment on Clarence Street in the Market. Eyes puffy, she dragged her gaze over to her alarm clock.

It couldn't be that early, she thought.

The front door shook under again as someone thumped their fist heavily against it.

Couldn't be Reggie, she thought. A bomb going off wouldn't wake him before noon. But if it wasn't her pimp, then who was it?

"Open the fuck up," a too familiar voice shouted through the door, "or I'll bust my way in."

Oh, shit. It was that frigging cop again.

She'd first run into Hardass Boucher when she almost got picked up for soliciting on a hooker sweep of the Market a couple of months ago. Boucher saw that she didn't get taken in, but now he came by at least a couple of times a week for freebies. He told her later that he didn't even work the Enforcement Unit; he just liked to tag along with the guys on his off hours to have a little fun. It had been her bad luck to have him pick her to hit on.

It was all a game to him. That night he had her backed up against the wall of an alleyway, big meaty hands fondling her chest.

"Kinda young, aren't you?" he'd asked her.

She was young, all right, but at fifteen she'd already

been working the streets for two years. It wasn't something she'd aimed for when she'd run away from home to live with Reggie. Back then Reggie treated her like a queen. Like an adult. Got her nice clothes. Dope. Took her places. She thought living with him'd be everything she didn't have at home.

When she found out he was a pimp, when she found out she had to hustle her body to keep his loving, it hadn't been such a hard decision. Not at first. Why not get paid for it, when living at home her old man took it for free?

And it wasn't so bad. Reggie still took good care of her. She only had to do this until they got a stake, and then they were going away together. To California. Reggie had some connections there, maybe he could get her into pictures or something. But first they needed some cash.

By the time she wised up—Christ, only the dumbass kid she'd been could have been so stupid as to have believed that line of crap—and realized that she wasn't Reggie's only girl, it was too late to get out. Calmly, sorrowfully, Reggie explained how, if she tried to take off from him, he was going to have to break her face. He wasn't like her parents, see? He cared about her. Really cared. So it didn't matter where she went—he'd find her. They were family now, see?

Two years later she no longer pretended she was anything but what she was: a fifteen-year-old junkie hooker. There wasn't going to be any trip to California. There weren't going to be any movies except for the porn flick Reggie'd made her do last year. There wasn't going to be any loving except what she got from Reggie. And her johns. And the dirty cop who was hammering at her door right now. The cop who'd told her, that first night he'd grabbed her, "But that's okay, kid. I like 'em young."

What he didn't know was that Julie was an old woman by now. An old junkie hooker trapped in some kid's body that was getting worn out way before its time. Hardass couldn't know, but he wouldn't care, either. Just so long as he got his.

The hammering continued on her front door.

"Open up this goddamned thing!" Hardass was shouting.

Wishing she could call a cop—

(yeah, right—and make it a gang bang)

—Julie headed for the door. "Don't make trouble with him," Reggie had said when she'd told him about Hardass. Make nice, Jools. You never know when a cop could come in handy.

Hardass's fist was raised to hit the door again when she opened it on him.

"You doped up again?" he demanded.

She shook her head.

"Then what the fuck kept you?"

"I was sleeping."

"Well, sleep on your own time, kid. I got needs for you to look after."

As he pushed by her, Julie felt a stronger repugnance toward him than ever before—if that was even possible. It was like there was a stink about him, except you didn't smell it with your nose, you smelled it with your soul.

She stared at him, wanting to run, but she couldn't move.

"Jesus Christ," Hardass said. "You *are* doped out."

He slammed the door, then, grabbing her by the arm, dragged her off to the bedroom.

# 10

JACK FELT STRANGE sitting in the squad room of the General Assignment Unit again. It had nothing to do with the detectives. Most of the men treated him like he'd never left the force. Like nothing had changed. Except he *had* changed. The large dark blue visitor's pass clipped to his windbreaker in place of the small light-blue plastic ID badge with a photo on it said it all.

He was a visitor here. He'd quit the force. He didn't belong here anymore. And listening to Ned describe what had happened down in the gun room earlier today made him wonder if he belonged anywhere anymore.

"Could anything be salvaged from Baker's equipment?" he asked when Ned was done.

"What do you mean?"

"What was he working on? What kind of stuff did he have in those computers? What was he doing with what he was recording?"

"How come I get the feeling you know something I don't?"

Jack shook his head. "Anything I've got, you can have."

"Okay." Ned leaned back in his chair. "The ID boys couldn't find anything that hadn't been slagged by the heat."

"I'm not just talking about what was in the machines at the time Baker died."

"Neither am I. It's all gone—master tapes, computer

discs, cassettes, the works. *Nada.* Nothing left. Why, Jack?"

"I . . ." Jack hesitated.

Flicker.

Last night's dream returned, and for a moment he was there again, in that other place. Not the wasteland but the station. This squad room. Deserted. Trashed. Graffiti on the walls. Litter everywhere.

"Jack?"

Flicker.

It was gone.

"Did you—did you just see anything, Ned?"

"You mean, like last night?"

Jack nodded.

"No. But I could feel it there, just for a moment. That weird sensation of something else pressing in on me. Something I couldn't see but could *feel.*"

"I don't know where to begin with this, Ned. It's going to sound so off-the-wall."

Ned leaned forward. "Off-the-wall? Have you been listening to me or what? We had a guy just pop in from nowhere, right in the middle of the station, Jack. Basement level. You know how tight the security is here. There's no way Coffey could have gotten in without being spotted. But he showed up all the same, just like"—Ned snapped his fingers—"that. So don't talk to me about off-the-wall."

"I had this dream last night, Ned. It took me to—I was still in Ottawa, but the place was a ruin. Like nobody'd lived here for years. And I saw that figure I'd seen coming out of Baker's house before."

"Jack . . ."

"The thing is, there was this music you could hear when you were near her. Synthesized stuff. Voices—not singing so much as being used as instruments. You know about digital samplers, Ned? How they can record any sound now and use it to play a whole keyboard range?"

Ned nodded.

"The music was like that. Voices, played like instruments. And they were in agony, Ned. Really hurting." Jack's gaze settled on Ned's and held. "I think that Baker did something to open a . . . I don't know . . . a door to somewhere else. To that place we saw in the squad car last night, Ned. To the ruined city I was in last night."

"You mean someplace real?"

Jack nodded slowly. "Someplace that lies side by side with our own world, only we just can't see it."

"Jack, this is beginning to sound a little—"

"See the really weird thing is, I woke up in that dream—I guess you could say I dreamed I woke up—and then I wandered around for a while in it. Through Anna's house. The floor fell out of one of the rooms I went in and I just about went with it. I managed to jump free, but I was covered in plaster dust and got a bit banged up for my efforts. Then I went outside, down to the river at the end of Harvard, and I woke up."

"Jack—"

"I woke up *there,* Ned. By the river at the end of Harvard. In the real world. This world." He rubbed his face. "Unless I'm dreaming this too." He held up a hand before Ned could speak. "Do you understand what I'm saying, Ned? I woke up and I was standing outside of Anna's house, down the block from it."

"Do you ever . . . you know, sleepwalk?"

"Ned, I was covered in plaster dust."

Ned studied him for a long moment. Finally he asked, "What are you saying, Jack?"

"You were telling me about Coffey—just popping in out of nowhere in the middle of the gun range? Well, maybe he dreamed himself into the station."

"That . . . that's not possible, Jack."

"I know that. You know that. But I know where I woke up this morning. I washed that plaster dust off me. And you've got a couple of cops downstairs who'll swear that they saw Coffey appear out of nowhere. Did you figure they were lying?"

Ned shook his head. "They believed they saw what they saw."

"This is one weird fucking mess, Ned."

"Tell me about it." Ned hesitated as if he didn't know where to take the conversation next. "This guy, Baker," he said finally. "You think he was . . . what? Making some kind of a doorway to another world, is that it? Like he was planning to do it, or maybe it just happened—like an accident?"

"We're probably never going to know."

"And the . . . things that are happening to us . . . You figure we're going to move back and forth between that place and here?"

"Maybe it'll wear off, Ned. The way I see it, we got caught up in some residuals of whatever it was that Baker was up to. That's why we can see into it. Why Coffey and I were *in* it."

"How do we stop this from going on, Jack?"

"Christ if I know." Jack rubbed at his face again. He felt worn to the bone. "What did you dream last night, Ned?"

"I haven't slept yet."

"Well, just be careful when you do." He rose wearily

to his feet. He was just starting for the door when Ernie Grier came in the room.

"We're on," Grier said.

"What's up?" Ned asked.

Grier glanced at Jack, then back at Ned. When Ned nodded, he went on. "You think things weren't fucked enough, we just got a call from Pat Nichols. He's over at the Coffey place. Went over because Coffey's missus called him. Seems . . ." Grier shook his head. "Christ, I don't believe this. It seems Coffey vanished from the apartment about an hour or so before he showed up downstairs."

"Disappeared?"

"Yeah. He was sleeping in the bedroom. The missus looked in on him, then got to folding some laundry right outside the door. When she looked back in, he'd vanished. No way Coffey could have gotten by her—not without her seeing him go. That's what she told Pat."

"Ned?" Jack said quietly as Ned stood up and grabbed his sport jacket.

"Yeah?"

"Think about what I told you."

"I will."

"What's going on?" Grier wanted to know.

"I'll fill you in on the way to Coffey's, Ernie."

They rode the elevator together, Jack getting off at the main floor, the other two continuing down to the garage in the first basement.

"When you get some sleep," Jack said as he stepped out. "Hang on to your gun or something when you go to bed, Ned. You might need it."

"I'll be careful. You watch out for yourself, Jack."

"Always do. See you around, Ernie."

As Jack walked away he could hear Grier's voice coming from between the sliding doors of the elevator. "What the hell am I missing here, Ned?"

Everything, I hope, Jack thought as he turned in his visitor's pass at the desk and left the station. Maybe whatever Baker had set loose would be satisfied with what it had now, but Jack wasn't ready to make book on it. He had the feeling that things were just starting to heat up.

## 11

WALT HAWKINS AND Ted Rimmer slouched in the front seat of Walt's old Chevy, watching the front door of a semidetached in Sandy Hill, that area of Ottawa just south of the Market that was getting its turn at a face-lift as the yuppies continued their upgrading of the city's core. The half of the house in which they were interested belonged to a guy named Alan Haines—the bartender at Mexicali Rosa's.

The name had been easy to get. They waited until noon, then Ted went into the restaurant with a ten-spot and asked the daytime bartender what the name of the guy on the night shift was. When the guy behind the bar wanted to know why, Ted left the ten-spot on the bar.

"Because I owe him this. You wanna pass it on to him?"

"Sure. I'll give it to Alan."

"Alan?"

"Alan Haines."

"That's the guy," Ted said, and left with a breezy wave.

After that it was just a matter of looking the guy up in the phone book and cruising on out to his place. Piece of cake. A bit of fun. Except sitting in the car for forty-five minutes plus was getting to be a royal pain in the ass.

"You get your old lady back," Ted said, turning to look at Walt, "what's the deal then?"

"What do you mean?"

"Well, are you gonna keep her around, or are you gonna smack her around a little and dump her, or what?"

"She's my wife. She supposed to live with me."

"Okay. So tell me this. All these people you're gonna warn to keep away from her—what do you think they're gonna do, first thing, when she turns up missing? I'll tell you what. They're gonna go running to the man. You were gonna bring the little woman back to your house, right? Where's the first place the man's gonna come looking?"

Walt let a few moments tick by. "I see your point," he said finally.

"You know what I think you oughta do?"

Walt shook his head.

"You snatch the missus and take off somewhere for a while—a cabin or something. Someplace no one knows to come looking. I can keep watch on her for you while you spend a coupla days just going about your business. The man comes, you don't know nothing from nothing. You're clean. They go away and then you're home free. They won't come knocking twice. They got more important shit to take care of—like grabbing the guy who offed this Baker. You hear it on the radio this morning?" Ted shook his head. "I mean, can you figure it, Walt? Some guy does the man a favor, but they wanna run him down and put him away for it, anyway."

Walt looked at Alan Haines's house again. "I don't like the idea of him just doing what he likes with my woman and not having to pay for it."

"So where's the problem?" Ted asked. "Wait a coupla weeks, then we'll come around his place and play a little footsy on his face. Piece of cake, Walt. So whaddaya say? Are we gonna get serious and put the snatch on your little lady, or are we gonna end up being a coupla pussies about the whole deal?"

Walt started up the Chevy. "I like the way you think," he told his companion.

"Yeah, well, I'm kinda partial to it myself, you know." He tapped his head. "You gotta stay smart to stay on top—that's what my old man used to tell me."

Walt grinned. "When I'm on top this time," he said, "I'm never getting off."

"My old man woulda liked you," Ted said as the Chevy pulled away from the curb.

# THREE

## 1

JACK WAS WORN to the bone by the time he got home. He'd stopped by to talk with Janet Rowe's parents after leaving the station and to return his fee; Ned had already called the family. It was the first time Jack had seen either of Janet's parents since he first took their case. He'd studied them, trying to see what it was about them that let them treat their own flesh and blood so badly.

Whatever it was, he couldn't find it.

Ed Rowe refused to take back the retainer.

"You . . . you found her," he said. "You've earned it."

Rowe and his wife sat in the living room of their suburban bungalow, washed out with what appeared to be genuine grief. The man who'd beat his kid until she fled the family home wasn't there. The woman who hadn't given her daughter a moment's respite from verbal abuse didn't exist in the wan features of Rowe's wife, hunched beside him on their couch.

You could have done something, Jack wanted to tell

them. You could have done something long before it came to this.

And maybe they had. They'd hired him, hadn't they? Maybe Janet's friends—going through their own teen-age angst—had perceived the relationship to be more negative than it actually was.

Right then Jack just couldn't tell anymore.

The house had seemed empty the first time he'd come by to discuss the job. It was desolate now.

Like that wasteland.

Jack didn't stay long.

The twenty-minute drive from the West End back to his own apartment on Fourth Avenue in the Glebe drained the last of his energy. He parked the pickup in the lane and went wearily up the stairs of the small two-story brick building. His apartment took up all of the second floor. He shared the lane and had the use of the backyard along with his downstairs neighbor, a feisty young woman who was training to be a welder. She kept a German shepherd named Frank, who gave a few obligatory barks when Jack entered the building.

Jack was sure that by now the dog recognized the sound of his footsteps. He only barked to show how much he was on the ball.

That strange wasteland was still on his mind when he entered his own apartment—enough so that it gave his own place a disused feeling about it as well. There was a close, musty odor inside, as though it hadn't been used for weeks, even though Jack had just been in it this morning.

It felt too empty.

Too much like that other place.

Jack rubbed his face, then went about opening a cou-ple of windows to let in some air. He could feel the presence of the wasteland flickering just beyond his awareness, licking at his mind with its desolate reaches. Its music. Its angel.

Its fury.

He knew he'd be back there again—he doubted that he could avoid the place even if he wanted to—but this time it was going to be on *his* terms.

In the kitchen he got a can of Blue out of the fridge and popped the tab. The icy beer seemed to frost his throat as it went down. He drifted back into the living room and shucked off his windbreaker.

Okay. What was he going to need?

He made a list on the back of an unpaid phone bill as he finished his beer. Back in the kitchen, he popped the tab on a second can as he started to get his gear together.

First he changed. Fresh jeans, a flannel shirt, sturdy hiking boots, a brown leather bomber jacket. Fingerless leather gloves went into the right pocket of the jacket. He got an army canteen down from the top shelf of his closet and went into the kitchen, filling it and attaching it to his belt. A packet of beef jerky and a couple of chocolate bars joined the gloves in his jacket.

In the dining room he moved aside the antique pine cabinet that held his stereo. Removing a loose board that had been hidden by the cabinet, he took out a snub-nosed Smith and Wesson Centennial revolver, two holsters, and a box of .38 standard police cartridges. He weighed the two holsters—one was a clip-on that attached to your belt, the other a shoulder harness—and settled for the shoulder harness. Replacing the clip-on back into the cubbyhole, he set the floorboard on top once more and pushed the cabinet into place.

Back in the living room, the can of Blue at hand, he

checked over the revolver, then loaded it. Five shots. He didn't have a permit for it. Ex-cop or not, it was a bitch to get a handgun permit. He'd picked up the weapon on an undercover case while he was still on the force and simply kept it. A lot of cops—especially when they worked plainclothes—had a weapons cache. It wasn't something planned. It just seemed to happen.

He slipped the .38 into the shoulder holster, then put his jacket back on. The box of remaining shells went into its left pocket, along with a small brass compass. A hunting knife with a ten-inch blade joined the canteen on his belt. Finishing the beer, he checked his list again.

Phone.

He unplugged the phone by the couch, then went into the bedroom and did the same with the extension.

Sleeping pills.

There was a bottle in the medicine cabinet, left over from a prescription he'd gotten when he'd first quit the force. He shook out three and swallowed them with a mouthful of tap water.

Back to the list.

All done now.

I've got to be crazy, he thought lying down in the bedroom. Maybe he *was* crazy. But talking to Ned, hearing about Coffey disappearing from his home and then popping in out of thin air in the gun range . . . No way that was sleepwalking. He might have put his own experience down to that—Christ knew where he'd picked up the plaster dust that was covering him, but it was still possible that he'd been suffering from somnambulism. Put that together with Coffey, though, and you began to see a pattern emerging.

The wasteland.

The ruined city.

Close as a thought. Just a dream away. All you had to do was wait and they would reach out for you.

Or you could go to them.

He looked at Anna's self-portrait sculpture on the night table, then rolled onto his back, adjusting the canteen and knife so that neither was digging into him. He stared up at the ceiling.

Looney tunes.

He closed his eyes.

Here I come.

## 2

JODY AND KIRK.

"How could you *know*?" Beth had wanted to shriek at Cathy.

She'd never told anybody about them—not even Anna or her therapist. She sat on her bed, the house quiet around her now that Anna and Cathy had gone out shopping.

Jody and Kirk.

Just thinking of them made her skin go clammy with fear.

It had happened twelve years ago, when she was fourteen. She was in her second foster home, because Mr. Gregoire in the first had started coming into her bedroom when Mrs. Gregoire was out, just like Daddy had. He wanted the same things, he wanted to teach her about love, just like Daddy. Except what they did wasn't love. It had nothing to do with what love was supposed to be—good feelings between people who cared for each other. It just made her feel dirty. Made her scrub herself after each time until she couldn't take it anymore.

That last night she had run screaming from the Gregoires' house, out into the street. Collapsing on the neighbor's lawn in just her nightie. Head tilted back, tears streaming down her cheeks. Arms hugged tight around her chest. Cramps in her stomach. A painful fire spreading from between her legs. Her cheek still burning from where Mr. Gregoire had hit her.

The Children's Aid Society had taken her away. Weeks in the hospital followed. Then the second foster home.

And Jody and Kirk.

She'd been living with the Halpins for almost a year and a half by then. The past wasn't forgotten, but it could be wrapped in an old box and stored behind the slow build-up of better memories. The Halpins were good to her, not physically demonstrative—they'd been warned about how she'd react to any kind of physical contact—but still very kind.

They had a daughter of their own. Cassie was one year Beth's senior and, after some initial coolness, seemed to accept Beth as, if not a sister, then at least a confidante. Beth started to feel better about herself. She learned to hope again. Started to believe that there could be good things, even for someone like her.

Then the night of the prom came.

Jody and Kirk.

*Why* had she ever gone?

It was a double date, Beth and Jody, Cassie and Kirk, the two couples both riding in the new Oldsmobile that Kirk's father had loaned his son for the big night. After the prom they went for burgers, eating them in the car. And after the burgers they went parking. Out by the sand pits. And someone had the idea of going for a swim. They took a couple of blankets out of the trunk and brought them down to the edge of the water. The boys stripping down to their briefs. Cassie in her bra and panties. Only Beth still dressed. Not wanting to join them. Protesting the whole time, quietly, but trying to be firm.

The moon was out, not quite full but bright enough to show the scars on her back where Daddy had burned her with the glowing tips of his cigarettes. Cassie knew. She'd seen them. So why was she going along with the guys, egging them on? Why couldn't they just leave her alone? Why couldn't they just go have their stupid swim and let her sit on the blankets?

"Oh, don't be so prissy," Cassie said.

There was something different about her tonight, Beth realized. Something dark grinning at her from behind Cassie's eyes. Beth started to back away from this sudden stranger, but Cassie was too quick for her.

"No you don't, Little Miss Perfect."

Her grip was painful on Beth's arm. "Cassie, please . . ."

Cassie turned to the guys. "Cassie, *please,*" she mimicked. When she looked back at Beth, the transformation from familiar foster sister to stranger was complete. "I'm so *sick* of you," she said. "Always in on time, always doing what you're told. So fucking neat. Such good marks. Did you ever think of how that makes *me* look? Some little slut who was banging her father when she was—what? Seven? Six years old? You can't take off your pretty little prom dress because we might see too much of your hot little bod?"

"Cassie—"

Cassie spat in her face. "Take it off or I'll rip it off."

Beth tried to pull away again, tears brimming in her eyes.

"Jesus," Jody said. "Maybe we should just forget—"

Cassie turned sharply toward him. "I promised you guys a good time. Are you backing out on me now?"

"Yeah," Kirk said. "Lighten up, Jody. We're not going to hurt her—just fuck her brains out. For chrissake, it's not like she's a virgin or something."

Beth gave a desperate tug, but the grip on her arm was too firm. When she started to lift a hand, Cassie slapped her. Hard. And again. And Beth just folded in on herself, dropping to her knees on the blanket. It was just like with Daddy. Or with Mr. Gregoire. The same thing. That's all anybody wanted. . . .

She barely felt Cassie's fingers unbuttoning the back of her dress, the dress being pulled off over her head. It was Kirk who tore off her bra, then her panties. Who pulled off his own underwear, his hard penis standing at attention, and pushed her down on the blanket.

"Take it in your mouth," he told her.

He crouched on top of her, his penis pressed up against her lips, his rear end heavy on her breasts, the weight of him making it hard to breathe. When she opened her mouth, he thrust in. Hard. Choking her.

"The other end's yours, Jody, boy," he said.

Whatever doubts Jody might have had, had long since vanished. He got down between her legs and thrust his own swollen penis into her, arms on Kirk's shoulders as he started to pump.

Jody and Kirk.

And Cassie standing by, watching it through those stranger's eyes. As they did it to her, again and again. Getting rougher each time. Cassie egging them on.

It was a long time before the guys went down to the water to wash themselves off. Cassie knelt by Beth's head, stroking the hair from Beth's brow, grinning as Beth flinched at each touch.

"You tell," Cassie said softly, as though they were talking about homework, "and I'll kill you. Don't think I won't, you little slut."

The Halpins were already asleep by the time they got home, but they noticed the sudden change in their foster daughter the next day. The sunken eyes. The way Beth had drawn in on herself again—just as she'd been when she'd first arrived.

"Jody dumped her last night," Cassie explained. "I guess she's taking it pretty bad."

"Don't worry, honey," Mrs. Halpin had said. "There'll be other boys."

Never, Beth had thought then. Never again.

When Mrs. Halpin touched her shoulder, she flinched. She kept her eyes downcast. She didn't tell. At school her grades went down. As soon as she was legally able, she left the Halpins' home and moved to Ottawa. But she didn't tell. Because she knew then that she was just what Cassie had said she was. A slut. Why else would people treat her the way they did?

It took Walt to bring her out of it. Walt, who was so kind when they met, always looking out for her. Who changed after they married, just as Cassie had changed. Treating her like dirt. Because that was what she was. Dirt.

Walt.

Jody and Kirk.

Mr. Gregoire.

Her own daddy.

She wept against her pillow. When they were hidden away, she could pretend that the box of bad memories didn't exist. But the box was old and swollen with too much remembered pain. And when it broke open . . .

Last night's dream. She'd been feeling so good, remembering it. But then Cathy had to mention that graffiti. And those names.

Jody and Kirk.

Cathy had to go and open all those unhealed wounds again. Why couldn't the past just go away? Why couldn't everything and everybody just leave her alone? Why couldn't she be like she was in her dream last night?

Strong.

In control.

The memory of her flight across the dead plains helped to quiet the pain she felt. It was so peaceful there. She could have just flown there forever. And she knew . . . if that place was real, if Jody and Kirk were there . . . She'd know how to deal with them. She'd teach them all about pain.

She sat up slowly, hearing something, but not sure what it was. Then she realized that it was the front doorbell.

Go away, she thought.

She couldn't see anybody looking like this. Her eyes red and puffy from crying. Her throat so constricted, it was hard to breathe. But the doorbell kept ringing. Finally she got up and quickly ran some water, dabbing at her eyes. Throwing on a pair of jeans and a sweatshirt, she went downstairs. From a table in the living room she picked up a pair of Anna's sunglasses to hide her eyes. But first she looked through the peephole.

A deliveryman.

She put on the sunglasses and cracked open the door.

The delivery man looked up at her. "Ms.—" he glanced at a waybill in his hand "Green? Elizabeth Green?"

Beth nodded. By the man's feet was a large cardboard box. "I didn't order anything," she said.

The deliveryman looked down at his waybill again. "Elizabeth Green. Harvard Avenue. This's gotta be the place, lady. Want me to carry this in for you? It's kinda heavy."

"No. I . . . that is . . ."

"Suit yourself."

Beth suddenly realized how stupid she was being. It was broad daylight. What was he going to do? She opened the door a bit wider.

"I'm sorry," she said. "I'd appreciate the help."

The deliveryman bent down to pick up the package, grunting as he took up its weight. Beth stepped out of the way as he brought it in. A shadow fell across the sunlight coming through the door, and Beth looked over. Her heart seemed to stop in her chest. Walt.

"Hi, babe," he said. "I've come to bring you home."

## 3

FLICKER.

And Jack was there. In the ruined city. He wasn't sure if he'd fallen asleep and was dreaming the place, or if the flicker had just pushed him here—as it had a couple of times last night. All he knew was that he was back.

It was his apartment, but the place was a shambles. The air smelled bad. Garbage and crap. What was left of a curtain moved limply, a wind blowing in the strong, unpleasant metallic scent of the yellow skies that he could see through the smeared upper pane of the window. The lower pane was broken—just some shards sticking out of the casing to show that it had ever been there.

Jack sat up and checked his gear. Everything he'd been wearing had crossed over with him. Did that mean he was a good—a *lucid*—dreamer, or was he really here?

Don't think about it, he told himself. Just get to it.

His gaze shifted to the night table before he got up. Anna's sculpture was still there, only someone had stuck a nail in its mouth, another between its legs. The disfigurement struck too close to home for Jack right then. It was too real. Red paint around the entry point of each nail completed the illusion.

He pulled the nails out. Putting some saliva on a finger, he started to rub at the paint, then hurriedly set the sculpture down. It was too much like really putting a finger between his sister's legs.

He wiped his finger on his jeans and stood up, testing the floor as he crossed the room. There was no sound from the bottom apartment as he made his way down the stairs and outside. He stood for long moments on the porch, staring at the desolate city spread out before him. The sky seemed to hang low, swollen with sickly clouds. The metallic tang was sharper out here. He listened carefully—for the music, for any kind of a sound—but all he heard was the wind's mournful passage through the deserted houses.

There's the city, he thought. And then the wasteland. Are they separate places? Does this city stand in between the real world and the wasteland? Do you have to pass through the one to get to the other? Or would he find the wasteland lying outside this empty city's suburbs?

Well, he had time to find out. The sleeping pills should keep him under for a while. He felt alert here, though. Not at all dragged out as he had when he'd gotten home earlier.

Time to get moving.

He had two places he wanted to check out. Baker's house and the police station. He opted for the station first—that was the last place the killer had struck.

It was an eerie sensation, walking the deserted streets downtown. Abandoned cars and buses littered the streets. He saw movement from time to time—rats in a heap of garbage behind a restaurant on Bank Street once. Dogs looked at him from the shelter of dilapidated buildings. The only birds he'd seen were a pair of crows winging lazily south.

An odd memory came to mind as he worked his way north. He remembered sitting around a campfire when he was a teenager—a bunch of the guys just out for the weekend, putting back some brews, shooting the shit. And then someone asked, "What's the worst thing you ever did?"

Something about that night, sharing the fire under the cold vault of the night sky, awoke an honesty in the four of them. They were still pretty young then, innocent, really. Not like the kids of today. The evils they'd done were small-scale compared to what you read in the newspapers now, saw on the tube. But they were ugly things all the same.

Gaff—Tommy Gaffney—had doused a neighbor's dog with gasoline and then set it on fire. His voice broke as he told them about it, sitting there by the fire, poking at the coals with a stick.

"I didn't know what the fuck I was doing. It was me and Red—I don't know who thought of it first. But when the dog was howling . . . Jesus. Just running out into the street, *burning* . . . I wanted to stop it worse than anything I ever wanted to do in my life, but there was nothing anybody could do by then. That poor fucking dog. . . ."

What Jack had done was take Ellie Dugan on a date. She was the local fat girl—about as wide as she was tall. He took her out for a ride in the country, telling her spook stories, then he just left her out there to find her own way home. Big joke. He was halfway home before it sank in. Ellie out there. Alone. In the dark. Some joke.

He turned around right then and went back to get her, but she was gone. He spent hours touring up and down the back roads, looking for her, sick with imagining all the weird shit that could have happened to her. He got home just as the dawn was breaking and couldn't sleep. He sat by the phone, waiting for the day to get on enough so that he could call her house.

When she heard his voice, she slammed the phone down, but Jack had never been so relieved to have someone so pissed off at him before. Because at least she was okay.

(no thanks to him)

At least she was alive.

After that the talk around the campfire dwindled

until someone came up with a new zinger. What was the worst thing you could imagine happening to you? Jack's reply had surprised even himself at the time.

"If anything happened to Anna . . ." he'd said.

And no one laughed, though it was a pussy kind of a thing to say at that age.

Anna.

Walking down the streets of the deserted city, Jack couldn't stop thinking of her. The graffiti in her living room. The mutilated sculpture of her in his own bedroom. Losing Anna would still be the worst thing that could ever happen to him. And here, in this city—

(just a dream)

—in that wasteland—

(except it was real)

—he couldn't shake the feeling that something was going to take her away from him.

Forever.

And there'd be nothing he could do about it.

Just thinking about it made him feel a little sick. He tried to turn his thoughts to something else, something pleasant, but that was impossible in this place. And then he was getting close to the station. He could see the squat building looming up ahead, walls spray-painted with graffiti. He paused, looking at it, hand reaching in under his bomber jacket to touch the comforting presence of his .38.

And then he heard it.

The music.

The pain in it.

He searched the rubble-strewn area for its source.

# 4

PAT NICHOLS WAS at the Coffeys' apartment when Ned and Ernie Grier arrived. Sheila Coffey wasn't holding up well. The disappearance of her husband from their bedroom, coupled with the bizarre discovery of his body in the station's gun range, had left her grasping for meaning in a situation that held no logic. It was a losing battle, and the wounds showed in her swollen eyes and the deep lines etched in her face.

She appeared to drift in and out of a catatonic state as Ned gently questioned her. She'd speak for a few moments, then just drift off, eyes losing focus, until Ned asked her another question. She needed to be treated for shock, he realized. After getting the bare bones of the story from her, he left her with his partner and took Nichols aside.

"It's a bad business," he said.

Nichols nodded. The strain was showing on him as well. He and Coffey had been close.

"Yeah," he said. "One minute you're married, the next you're a widow. One day you've got a partner, the next he's pushing up the flowers. Jesus Christ. Sometimes you think about the worst that could happen to you, but you never think about how you're going to *feel*."

Ned steered Nichols to a chair in the kitchen. "I know it's a bad time, Pat, but I've got a couple of things I've got to ask you. Think you're up for it?"

"Sure. I'm not going anywhere."

"This business with Coffey disappearing from the bedroom—what do you make of it?"

"You mean, do I think Sheila imagined it?"

Ned shrugged. "Or maybe she was turned away long enough for him to get by, only she doesn't realize it."

"You've seen the size of this place," Nichols said. "The narrowness of the hall. If things happened like she said they did, there's no way he could have gotten by her without her knowing."

"Any chance they just had a fight and he walked out on her? Maybe she was too embarrassed to tell you about it when she phoned, and then this shit went down and she was caught in her lie?"

For a moment Ned thought Nichols was going to hit him, but then the patrolman sighed, calming down. "You know how civilians react when you tell them you're a cop? And all the stories about how the job breaks up relationships and marriages?"

"Tell me about it," Ned said.

Anna's features floated up in his mind with their usual accompanying pang.

"Well, Sheila was big on Ron being a cop. She was proud of him—no bullshit there. I think maybe it even . . . you know, turned her on?" He shook his head. "Christ, I feel weird talking about them like this."

"Look, we can just forget—"

"No, let me finish, Ned. They were tight. Really in love. Four and a half years down the road from tying the knot and they were still just as much in love as they were the day they got married. So no, I don't think this is something Sheila made up because they had a fight. And yes, I believe what she says."

"Then how'd he get out?"

"Jesus, Ned. I just can't figure it. I was talking to

Baxter just before you guys showed up. He said Ron was dressed like a bum." Nichols shook his head.

"You get any sleep yet?" Ned asked.

"A couple of hours."

"And?"

Nichols gave him a puzzled look.

"Did you have any . . . dreams?"

"What're you talking about?" Nichols asked.

"Remember back at Baker's place when we had them check the air? Well, I still think there was something in it, only it broke up before we had a chance to get the equipment down there to do the testing."

"So?"

"So I think whoever was early on the scene got a whiff of whatever the hell it was and it's . . . doing something to them."

"Like what?"

"Like giving them weird dreams. Everybody finding themselves in the same places. Either Ottawa looking like it's been abandoned for a few years—streets deserted, no one around—or in this huge wasteland. An empty plain like the prairie, where nothing's alive, going on for as far as you can see."

The look that came over Nichols's face told Ned that he'd hit home.

"Everybody's having these dreams?" Nichols asked. "Everybody who caught the call?"

"Ernie has. Jack Keller—remember him? He used to work GA before he quit. He's had them. I . . . I've been having flashes. I haven't talked to everybody yet, but I plan to."

"And you think it was due to some kind of gas?"

Ned nodded. "Fumes. Strong enough to affect Jack,

who never went inside, but it broke up and was gone before we had a chance to go down and test the air."

"Jesus." Nichols ran a hand through his short hair. "I dreamed of those same places, Ned. Not the wasteland but the empty city. Streets deserted. Gave me the creeps. It wasn't like any dream I'd ever had before. Sheila's call pulled me out of it, or I'd probably still be there."

"There's got to be a connection."

"Yeah, but everybody dreaming about the same place? That doesn't make sense."

"Not a whole hell of a lot of any of this does," Ned said. "But there've been group hallucinations before."

"Sure. Except the people are usually all together in the same place."

"We were . . . at Baker's."

"Yeah, but it didn't affect us until later."

Nichols got up and ran himself a glass of water. He drank it all down in one long chugalug, then filled the glass again and brought it back to the table.

"You figure Ron had a dream like that?"

"Stands to reason. He was there."

"Right." Nichols drank some more of his water. "But it doesn't explain what's going down."

"I don't have the answers," Ned said, "but I'm going to keep looking into it."

"You talk to your Staff Sergeant about this? Or to any brass?"

Ned shook his head.

"Well, don't. They're just going to give you a fast shift into some forced holidays because it sounds too fucking weird."

"What do you think?"

"I think it's too fucking weird," Nichols said, "but

you can count me in to help out. Just give me a chance to run Sheila over to the hospital. I think she needs something to bring her down."

"Do you know John Paige?"

"He's the guy from Traffic who was at Baker's last night."

"Maybe you could talk to him and Benny."

"Can do. What're you going to do?"

"I'll be heading back to the station with Ernie to file this report. I'll see what I can get out of some of the people from ID that were there. Lou Duchaine too. Then I'm heading for some sack time."

I just hope to hell I don't dream, Ned thought. He didn't speak, but he could see that Nichols knew just what was going through his head.

"One more thing," Ned said as he rose from the table. "Ernie pointed this out, and I've been picking up on it ever since. People seem to be uncomfortable around us. If you're around anyone who wasn't at Baker's last night, I'd like to know their reactions. I think it ties in—and don't ask me how."

"Weird."

Ned nodded. "You ever bitch about everything being too routine?"

"Sure. Who doesn't?"

"Well, right now that's all I can think of. I just wish we were back on our routines again—I don't care how much fucking paperwork I'd have to push around."

"The Chinese call it living in interesting times," Nichols said. "This kind of thing."

"Yeah. I heard that somewhere." Probably from Anna, he thought.

"I read it in a book," Nichols said.

Ned paused at the doorway. "You read too much,"

he said, then he went down the hall to collect his partner.

"Maybe I don't read enough," Nichols said to the empty room. "Maybe I should've gone on to be a lawyer like Dad always wanted me to. Then I wouldn't even be thinking about this kind of shit."

## 5

IT WAS THE sudden shift in the bedsprings that turned Julie around. Her eyes went wide. She knew the feel of someone getting out of her bed while she was lying in it, and that's just what had happened. The cop had gotten up. Except he wasn't standing by the bed. He wasn't anywhere in the room.

Weird, she thought. How'd he get out of the bedroom so fast?

She lay there listening to the sounds of her apartment, waiting to hear a footstep—the fridge door opening, maybe—or Hardass in the can, taking a leak.

Nothing.

Not a sound, except for the hum of the fridge and her alarm clock. Traffic outside. The sound of a radio coming from one of the other apartments in the building.

This was very weird.

She got up and padded out of the bedroom in her bare feet. A complete search of the apartment showed that the cop was gone. Except that his clothes were still in her bedroom.

What gives? she wondered, feeling a little creeped out. He's gone out on the street bare-assed?

Maybe that wasn't such a bad thing. Maybe he'd get picked up, and then, cop or no cop, they'd put him away and he wouldn't show up on her doorstep anymore.

When she returned to the bedroom, she went through his clothes, found his wallet, but didn't take any money out of it—three bucks and change, big-time spender—picked up his gun, still in its shoulder holster.

She hefted its weight in her hands.

Something like this could solve a lot of problems. She imagined having the cop in her sights. Or Reggie. Dead people didn't hit on you. If she had the nerve, she could just—

The sound of the bedsprings shifting made her drop the gun back onto Boucher's suit and turn nervously.

He was back.

Sitting up on the bed like he was just waking up.

Like he'd never been gone.

Hardass wiped at the sweat beading his face.

"Jesus fuck . . ." he muttered.

There was a wild look in his eyes that slowly faded as he took in his surroundings. Julie didn't say a word. She just stood there by the chair, staring at him, trying to understand what was going on. How could he just . . . *appear* like that? Out of nowhere. Because she knew—she *knew*—he hadn't been in that bed a second ago.

"How . . . how did you do that?" she finally managed to ask.

Hardass focused on her, his eyes narrowing. "Do what?"

"Disappear—I mean, you were *gone*—and then you just appeared again. . . ."

Her voice trailed off at the look he gave her.

"I told you," he said. "Lay off the fucking drugs, kid."

"But I'm . . ."

Not high, she thought. She hadn't hit up since a couple of hours before she finally collapsed in her bed this morning, drifting off as the high faded, before the downer blues set in.

"What're you staring at me for?" Hardass demanded.

"N-nothing."

"I just had a dream—that's all. A weird fucking dream, okay?"

She nodded. His eyes were haunted as he remembered whatever it was he'd seen before he'd woken up.

Dreaming. Right.

Maybe she *was* high.

"Get your ass over here," Hardass told her.

She scurried back to the bed, not wanting to even be in the same room with him, too scared to do anything but what he told her. As soon as she was close enough, he grabbed her and pushed her down on the bed, then climbed up on top of her.

"Gotta forget," he said. "That's all. Just gotta forget all the shit."

She closed her eyes at the pain as he entered her. She wasn't ready, she didn't want it, she was too dry, he didn't care, the feel of his body was like having a corpse rubbing up against her. . . .

Her hands gripped the sheets, convulsively knotting them as she tried not to scream.

## 6

JACK HAD TO cast around a bit before he could pinpoint the direction from which the music was coming. It was disconcerting to be in the city and to have it be so quiet. Just the wind, moving through the deserted streets, drifting through the broken windows and doors. And the music. Low but impossible to ignore. Seeming to come from everywhere at once.

He started north on Elgin Street, in the direction from which he felt it was the strongest. By the time he was a few blocks from the station, nearing Gladstone Avenue, he knew he'd made the right choice. He stopped at the corner, head cocked to listen.

It was stronger now. He could hear the voices that had been synthesized to sound like instruments. But there was no disguising the pain in them. Agony in each note. It lifted the hairs at the nape of his neck, and he drew the .38 from its shoulder holster, holding it down by his leg as he continued on.

A block and a half farther north, he knew he was almost upon its source. He thought about the angel—

(Janet Rowe's bloated body floating by in the river)

—about her turning—

(her skin bursting open and the cloud of bugs flying out)

—and he stopped. He looked around. He was getting used to the awful reek in the air, but his eyes were beginning to sting from whatever was in that layer of smog hanging over the city. It seemed to be a little darker now. Night coming? How long had he been here, anyway?

He checked his watch. It told him it was about a quarter past four. But the second hand wasn't moving. He held it to his ear. The watch was dead. It could be any time. He listened to the music and wondered if he could go through with it. Facing her again—

(her skin puddling on the ground where she'd been standing)

—didn't seem like the bright idea it had been before he'd gone to sleep. If this place was real, if people could be killed here, their bodies pushed back through whatever membrane separated the worlds from each other . . .

He could be next.

Nobody ever said it was going to be easy, he told himself.

But he hadn't even left a note. Nobody knew he was here. Ned might guess, but the whole idea of this place actually being real was so far off the wall, he doubted that even Ned—experiencing the flashes as he had—would be able to accept its existence as possible, let alone true.

Until Jack's corpse appeared back in the real world, in the same place that correlated to wherever he bought it here. Popping in out of nowhere. With the skin burned away . . .

Maybe then someone would take it seriously. They sure as hell wouldn't otherwise—not without some proof that Jack didn't know how to go about collecting.

Nobody'd believe?

Maybe not.

But they all had to go to sleep sometime. And he

knew that Ned at least was going to show up here the next time his head hit the pillow.

The weight in his right hand helped him decide. He looked down at the .38, then, holding it back down by his leg, muzzle pointed at the buckling asphalt, he trotted quietly across the street. There was a tall brick apartment building there on the corner of Elgin and Waverly. Its windows were all blown out. The side facing Waverly had a hole in it the size of a Volkswagen, bricks and crap lying like rubble around it. The side facing Elgin was a bewildering collage of graffiti. All violent. Threatening. A rat darted out of sight, into the hole, at Jack's approach. The music was coming from Elgin Court, the little basement-level plaza just north of the building.

Jack thought of the stores there. Couldn't be more than four. The ice-cream place. A hairdresser's. A Mexican restaurant. Shake Records, where Anna bought all her blues and import albums . . .

He approached the corner slowly, bobbed his head around once, then ducked back, adding up what he'd seen. Dick-all. He repeated the motions with the same results. Rubbing his face with his free hand, he took a deep breath, then stepped around the corner, gun hand pointing straight, left hand grasping his right wrist for support.

Nothing to see. The glass windows of the stores had all been trashed. There was more graffiti. A litter in front of the record store. Records and CDs pulled out of their packages, cassettes with all the tape pulled from them in long brown streamers. Newspapers and magazines glued together in abstract papier-mâché shapes by the weather.

The music was coming from inside the record store.

Someone had pulled the neon *S* and *H* from the sign so that it read AKE RECORDS.

Cute.

Jack moved down the short incline, eschewing the stairs farther along to walk down the slope of dirt and dead grass beside the apartment building. Gun held out. Pointed at the store.

He had a moment's confusion as he looked at it. The store seemed twice as big as he remembered it, as though it had swallowed whatever had been next door. Then he remembered Anna telling him that they'd expanded a month or so ago. Twice the room. The place looked so clean and bright, she'd said.

She should see it now.

Christ, no. Don't let her ever see this place like it is. In this world.

He jumped down from the incline where it ended in a short stone wall. His boots clunked. The music never faltered. Three quick steps and he was at the door, gun moving back and forth, covering all the angles, slowing to a stop and holding as something moved in a nest of garbage.

The Smith and Wesson Centennial didn't have the usual safety. It couldn't be fired unless it was held in the proper grip. You had to squeeze the handle as well as the trigger.

Jack's fingers started to squeeze as a head appeared out of the refuse, then they loosened.

Garbage dropped away from the figure, revealing an old rubbie in shapeless trousers and sport jacket, no shirt. His shoe tops were cut away at the toes to show dirty socks. He had a straw hat on, the brim gone. A bottle of Jack Daniel's in one hand, half gone. Primo booze for a bum. His face was a road map of every hole and dive he'd crashed in over the past twenty years. Stringy hair crawled out from under the hat. He was unshaven, the stubble dark against the exaggerated pallor of his skin. Eyes no more than dark hollows.

Jack kept the muzzle of the .38 pointed at the bum. His gaze darted around the man, looking for the source of the music. He spotted the cassette deck at the same time as the bum reached for it. Jack started to squeeze the handle and trigger again at the movement, but the man was only pushing the stop button.

The music died in mid-note. The continuous rasp that had rubbed against his spinal column, stroking each nerve into a shriek, was abruptly gone.

The silence almost hurt.

"You look a little wound up," the bum said. He offered up the Jack Daniel's. "Have yourself a swig, stranger."

## 7

ANNA MADE HERSELF a promise while she was out shopping: no more lectures, no more unsolicited advice. Support, sure. Beth needed the support. What she didn't need was a mother hen hovering around her like she was liable to shatter at the slightest jostle. That was *not* the way to build up somebody's confidence, though God knew it sometimes seemed that it took only one wrong word to reduce Beth from what she could be, back into what the ugliness of her past had shaped her to be.

But that wasn't Beth's fault.

She *wasn't* a loser.

Two hours at the Rideau Center, a downtown shopping center that Anna was sure had more shoe stores per square foot than Parliament Hill had MPs, was about all she could take. All she had to show for her effort was a new T-shirt that had been on sale at Fairweather's. Cathy, on the other hand, was loaded down with a pair of sandals, a blouse, three dresses—one so slinky that Anna *still* couldn't believe her friend had bought it—and a jean jacket that had been on sale at the Bay, a department store that was all that remained in the eighties of the Hudson Bay Company, which had been responsible for most of Canada's first explorations when it was still considered to be the New World.

"Think about it," Cathy said as they left the Bay. "We're the only country founded by a department store. That makes it our duty, as good citizens, to shop till we drop."

"Well, I'm ready to drop," Anna said.

"Me too. I'm going to go home and just collapse for a few hours. But you can't fool me. You're going to go home and probably clean the house, put in a couple of hours on your sculpture, write a book, and do God knows what else—all before dinner. I don't know how you do it."

Anna grinned. "Clean living, toots."

"Are you staying in tonight?"

"Probably."

"Maybe I'll come by later. I was supposed to go out with Janice, but she's probably still in bed with her bejeaned dreamboat."

"So *that's* why you bought the jacket."

"Oh, please."

They took separate buses. The #1 bus deposited Anna just a block or so from her house. She started off whistling as she walked, then remembered Chad Baker as she looked down Chesley. She got a chill looking at his house and quickly stepped up her pace until she was home. She flung the bag with her day's one purchase onto the neat stack of Jack's bedding and called a cheery "Hello" but got no response.

Beth must have already gone off to work, she thought.

She started for the kitchen to make some tea, then paused to look back at the front door. It hadn't been locked. She'd just walked right in. That was odd. Beth never went out without locking up behind her.

All of a sudden the house had a funny feel about it. Anna's head filled with a tumbling rush of all the strange things that had happened in the last little while. The horrible discoveries at Chad Baker's house. Last night's dreams. Jack acting so funny. Beth getting weirded out this morning.

She went quickly up the stairs, calling Beth's name as she went.

There was no reply.

Anna shivered as she went into Beth's room. The bed was unmade, Beth's nightie thrown on top of the rumpled comforter. That wasn't like Beth, either. Then Anna spied her housemate's purse, sitting on the chair by the window. The room took on a sudden closeness, and she found it hard to breathe. She went over to the chair and picked up the purse. Rifling through it, she found Beth's keys, and her wallet with all its ID.

Something was very wrong.

It took Anna ten minutes to go through the house from top to bottom, but there was no sign of Beth. No sign of a struggle. Nothing. She looked behind the stack of stereo and appliance boxes in the basement, in back of the furnace, under the beds, in every closet. Still nothing. It was as though Beth simply had walked out in whatever she was wearing, leaving her purse behind, her bed unmade, the door unlocked.

That was *not* Beth.

She called Mexicali Rosa's, but Beth wasn't there, either.

You're making too much of this, she told herself, but by now she had the heebie-jeebies so bad that she was expecting the worst.

She called Jack, at home and at his answering service, then at home again. No answer. The answering service hadn't heard from him all day. Periodically, as the afternoon dragged on, she tried Jack's number. Mexicali's again.

Nothing.

She sat in the living room, in the easy chair by the window, and stared out at the street.

You're just letting yourself get spooked, she thought, berating herself. You're making a fool of yourself. What could happen in the middle of the day?

But she thought of Chad Baker. Everybody had liked him and the odd, weird feeling she'd gotten from him; she had just put that down to his wanting to get something going with her. Everybody thought he was just a normal guy. Except all the time he was completely wacked out.

Last night's dream.

Jack acting so odd.

Beth going so strange this morning when they were talking about the dreams. She could almost hear Beth now, the wanting in her voice.

I *was the one in control there. I felt like nobody could hurt me—nobody could even touch me.*

Oh, Beth. You're scaring the shit out of me.

She tried Jack's number again. Mexicali's—Beth was late for work by now. Finally she dragged out a phone book and tried to get Ned Meehan at the police station. Gone home. She pulled out her personal phone directory, looked up his number, and dialed it.

She heard it ring at the other end. And ring.

*Please* be home, Ned.

The phone continued to ring.

# 8

JACK SHOOK HIS HEAD at the bottle of whiskey that the bum was offering to him. Mind games, he thought. The place was spitting up mind games just to mess up his head.

Was the bum real? Was he another dreamer, crossed over from the world where Ottawa was still a thriving metropolis, the Nation's Capital, not this dead place? Or was he some part of the angel, lying there in the trash, playing her music? The gun never wavered in his hand, muzzle sighted on the bum.

"Who are you?" Jack asked.

"Nobody special. Just another dead guy looking to get by."

He took a swig from the Jack Daniel's, set the bottle by his knee where it wouldn't tip, and brought out the makings for a cigarette.

"Name's Buddy Dempsey—least it was," he added

as he shook dry tobacco out of a pouch into the crease of the cigarette paper. He rolled the smoke one-handedly and stuck it in the corner of his mouth, patting his pockets for a light. "You're new here, I guess. Got a match?"

Jack shook his head slowly. He wasn't sure he was ready for this conversation.

Buddy Dempsey.

*Just another dead guy looking to get by. . . .*

"Are you saying you're dead?" he asked.

"I like to think of it as an alternative life-style." Dempsey pawed around in the trash as he spoke and came up with a Bic lighter. He lit his cigarette, blowing out a wreath of grey-blue smoke. "Good booze and a smoke," he said. "What the hell else do you need?"

"There's this woman," Jack began.

Dempsey shook his head. "Too late for women now, pal. I'm too old and too dead—haw haw."

Jack lowered the .38 finally, holding it down by the side of his leg instead of holstering it. "Look," he said. "I need to know—"

"You'll find two kinds of people here," Dempsey interrupted. "Those that're dreaming and those that're dead. Me, well, I fell asleep in an alley back of here one night last winter. When I woke up, everybody was gone and the city looked pretty much like it does right now."

"There's no one else around?" Jack asked. He felt like he was in the middle of one of those European films that Anna liked to go see—the kind where nothing seemed to happen and nothing seemed to make any sense.

"Don't really know how it works," Dempsey said. "I see people from time to time—most of them are dreaming, you know? You see them walking down the middle of the street, all fucked up 'cause there's nothing around, and then bang!" He snapped his fingers. "They just disappear. Those're the ones that are dreaming. The dead ones . . . they're only here for a while and then they go on."

"Go on where?"

"Damned if I know, and I'm not about to follow them to find out. Old Buddy Dempsey, he likes things just fine the way they are. Don't need to eat. Got my booze, got my smokes. Get to walk around in stores and places I couldn't get in the front door of when I was alive. So I like it just fine."

"What do you mean, 'they go on'?"

Dempsey touched his chest. "You get a feeling in here—a kind of pulling that makes you want to get up and go. And they all do just that. Me, I just kind of deaden it with the booze. Gets so I hardly ever feel it anymore."

"That music you were playing . . . ?"

"That helps too." Dempsey popped the cassette out of the machine and read the label. "This here's an old Willie Nelson—back when he was still an outlaw kind of a guy."

He tossed the tape over. Jack caught it with his left hand and looked down. "This is what you were just listening to?" he asked. The label was one of the old red CBS ones. *The Red-Haired Stranger,* by Willie Nelson.

"Where the hell are you *from* that they haven't got Willie Nelson?" Dempsey wanted to know.

Jack shook his head. "What I heard . . ."

Was different music.

Put together in Chad Baker's studio.

Voices instead of instruments.

Pain in every note.

The graffiti-smeared walls of the record store wavered.

Flicker.

And Jack was in the dead plains. The music burned through him, so loud that it made his eyes tear.

Flicker.

The store was back and the old bum was looking at him strangely. Jack ran a hand across his face. He could still hear an echo of the music, like an afterimage of light when a room's plunged into sudden darkness. Dempsey took a quick pull from his bottle.

"That's how they go," he said. "Just like that. Eyes get all glassy and they do a slow fade until you can see right through them."

"What are you talking about?" Jack asked.

"The way the dead ones go. There's like a crackle in the air—a kind of humming—and then they just sort of start to fade away. Not like the dreamers. They just disappear. The dead ones take longer. First they get kind of hazy to look at—just like you were—and then they fade away."

"There's this empty plain—" Jack began, but Dempsey shook a hand back and forth.

"Don't tell me nothing about it—I don't want to know."

Jack wasn't prepared to let it go. "What is this place?" he demanded.

Dempsey didn't answer. He seemed to be listening. And then Jack could hear it too.

There was a buzz in the air—had been for a while, he realized. It had just taken him some time to pick up on it. He glanced around the store but couldn't pinpoint its source. He could hear the music again—just a faint breath of sound under the buzzing. He remembered—

(movement in Janet Rowe's eye sockets)

—the last time he'd—

(her upper torso splitting open with a sound like tearing cloth)

—dreamed himself into—

(the stream of insects flying out to cloud the air)

—this place.

He looked at the bum, the .38 lifting in his hand. But he didn't fire. There was just a corpse lying there in the trash now, maggots crawling under the skin. Sightless eyes stared at him. A slash of mouth appeared to be grinning. The bottle of Jack Daniel's had fallen to one side, amber liquid pouring out. A cigarette still smoldered between the corpse's fingers.

"Jesus," Jack murmured.

He took a step back, started to turn.

"You shouldn't ask so much where we are," a voice said from behind him, "as when."

Jack completed his turn so quickly, he almost fell. The .38 wavered, then its muzzle settled on the woman standing in the doorway.

It was the angel he'd seen come floating out the side of Baker's house—not Janet Rowe. Her voice licked at his ears like a honeycomb with a razor blade hidden in the wax. The showgirl's body was barely covered with a filmy floor-length robe that clung to every curve. Her nipples were hard and dark behind the fabric. There were marks on her arms and legs and torso. Tattoos, he thought at first, then memories flickered inside him. Of the walls in Anna's living room. On all the buildings in this dead place. Not tattoos—graffiti. Her long blond hair streamed down to her waist. Dark eyes regarded him unblinkingly in that angel face.

"Keep your distance," Jack said, making a warning motion with the gun.

Sultry lips shaped a perfect smile, but Jack could only remember—

(a cloud of insects . . . music that was pain. . . .)

"We are locked in a moment of time," the angel said. "You and I."

The buzzing grew louder, riding the music, which also had increased in volume.

"This moment became my world . . ."

The stink of decaying meat thickened in the air. Buddy Dempsey, Jack thought. Rotting away.

". . . when I died. A moment I hold forever."

She *was* Janet Rowe, Jack thought. No matter what she looked like, that had to be what she was talking about. The things that had happened to her in Baker's basement had changed her, letting her break loose. Whatever she'd become had made this place. The world gave her a raw deal, so now she was giving it one back. A piece at a time. Until the real world looked just like this place did.

"Listen, Janet," he said. "There are people who wanted to help you. Just because—"

She wasn't listening. "All time becomes one time," she said.

The music bit at his mind, making it hard to think clearly. His eyes were still stinging from whatever was in the air here. The stink of Dempsey's corpse clogged in his nostrils.

"A killing time," she said.

Her mouth opened wide. Wider than was physically possible. A nest of tongues wriggled like snakes in the back of her throat. She took a step toward him, and he fired.

The bullet hit her in the shoulder, half turning her around, but she recovered almost immediately. As Jack started to fire again, a rotted hand came from behind him and struck his gun hand. The .38 hit the floor in a shower of maggots that included a rotted finger. The gun skittered across the floor. The maggots squirmed toward the finger.

The music whined in his ears.

Flies filled the air.

Dempsey's corpse gripped him from behind.

The monstrous jaws of the horror that had been the angel opened wider, and Jack saw his death in that throat. Her dark eyes regarded him without mercy. Her breath was warm. Growing warmer. Hot.

Now Jack knew just how Baker had died.

(*you're* going to die)

It was just a dream, he tried to tell himself.

(a killing time)

People didn't die in dreams.

(Ron Coffey did)

As she let loose with her fiery breath, Jack lunged to one side, dragging the corpse at his back around. The corpse lost its grip on him and stumbled drunkenly, striking the creature. The stink of cooking meat exploded in the air as her breath fried the corpse. She tossed it aside and turned to Jack.

(you're going to die)

Jack scrabbled for his gun.

# 9

IT WASN'T THAT Ned didn't trust Jack. They'd been friends before they joined the force, and when you work with a guy long enough, especially in the close-knit confines of a partnership as they had, there weren't many surprises he could hand you. He'd seen that Jack was ready to quit, before Jack knew it himself. But trusting Jack as he did, it wasn't until Ned was asleep and dreaming, walking the streets of the dead city, that his last doubts about its reality fled.

He'd wasted no time at all when he first woke up in the ruin of his apartment. He'd been exhausted when he got home and had just lain down on the bed, not even bothering to undress. The first thing he saw was a scrawl of graffiti across the ceiling. Blood-red letters.

OPF—ANNA FUCKED 'EM ALL.

Sure. The whole Ottawa Police Force. He tired to ignore it—it was just there to piss him off. But even knowing that, he couldn't stop the dull rage that was starting up in his chest.

He got out of bed, glad that he was still dressed. But when he searched for his revolver, he couldn't find it. He'd left it on the dresser with his sport jacket when he'd lain down. There was nothing there now. The dresser was in pieces. Somebody'd crapped on the rubble.

Was this how it had been for Ron Coffey? Waking up—dressed in just his skivvies, or maybe sleeping nude? Putting on some of the rags he found lying around his place and then going outside, trying to figure out just what the fuck was going on?

As if any of them knew. Though maybe Jack . . .

He remembered what Jack had been saying about this place back in the squad room. It was—

*Someplace that lies side by side with our own world, only we just can't see it.*

Except when you're dreaming.

*What did you dream last night, Ned?*

He got out of the apartment and hit the streets. The city was just as Jack had described it. Empty. Dead. It wasn't just the unnatural silence. The ruined buildings. The sky above looking like somebody'd thrown up their scrambled eggs. There was something lying under it all, a feeling of desolation, as if this were a place that was never meant to have people in it. Never meant to have any happiness at all. Nothing but an empty ache.

He took his time, walking downtown from his apartment on Renfrew Avenue in the Glebe. The farther he went from home, the more the sense of isolation settled in him. Finally he just turned and retraced his steps.

Go home, he told himself. Wake the fuck up before whatever took out Baker and Coffey catches on that you're here and takes you down as well.

He had nothing to protect himself with. No gun. No backup to call. He was just begging for trouble out here on the streets by himself. These streets. In this place.

When he got back to his house, he saw what he'd missed on his way out. There was a caricature of Anna's face drawn on the side of the building—the way he could tell it was supposed to be her was mostly from the way the hair was drawn. Black bangs coming down to the eyes, the rest of the hair shoulder length. Her lips were painted around a window, and a telephone pole had been thrust in through the broken glass, making it look like she was giving it a blow job. The words COP SUCKER were written on the pole.

Ned clenched his fists, looking at it. That's what this place wanted to do, he realized. It took whatever meant the most to you, then crapped on it. It wanted to bring everything down to its own foul level.

He walked over to the pole and worked at getting it loose. He got a splinter in one hand for the effort but finally managed to drag it free enough that it fell from the window. He looked up and down the street. Nothing moved except for refuse, stirring in the wind.

"Fuck you too," he muttered as he went inside.

He was on the landing just by the front door to his apartment when he heard a phone ring. Its sudden clangor lifted him almost a foot off the ground. Prickles of uneasiness went skittering up and down his spine as he walked into the apartment, following the sound to where his phone lay in the moldering ruin of his couch. He picked up the entire instrument and gave the cord a tug. The end of the cord was just a fray of wires, as though someone had pulled it from the wall.

It continued to ring.

His palm was sweaty as he reached for the receiver. When he pulled it free, he had a sudden moment of vertigo. The apartment flickered. The ruin was gone. The apartment was back to how it had been before he fell asleep. The end of the lond cord ran into the wall socket. Then he looked at his hand. It still hurt from where the telephone pole's splinter had stabbed him. The skin was still broken. He walked over to the window and looked out on Renfrew Avenue. Everything was like it should be.

Faintly, as if from a great distance, he could hear a voice calling to him. Then he realized it was coming from the phone. He lifted the receiver to his ear.

"Yeah?"

"Ned—is that you?"

Slowly Ned sat down on the couch. "Yeah, it's me, Anna."

(ANNA FUCKED 'EM ALL)

He wondered about the dead city. Had he become suggestible to dreaming about it only because Jack had talked about it earlier? He'd like to believe that. Except his shoulders still ached from the effort expended in moving the telephone pole. And the skin of his hand was still broken from the splinter.

"Are you all right?" Anna asked.

(COP SUCKER)

That was a cute play on words, wasn't it just? When he caught the fucker who was playing these mind games, he'd—

"Ned?"

He forced himself to concentrate on the moment at hand. One thing at a time.

"I'm here," he said. "I'm just a little groggy."

"Oh, jeez. I woke you up, didn't I?"

"It's okay. I was getting up, anyway. What's up?"

"It's just . . . God, I feel so stupid now."

"One thing you'll never be, Anna, and that's stupid."

"Fat lot you know." Her tone was light, but Ned could sense the tension in her voice.

"I'm always here for you," he said. "You know that. Talk to me."

"I know, Ned. It's just that everything's been a bit off today. I've been trying to get hold of Jack, but I haven't been able to all day—not even through his answering service. They haven't heard from him, either. He was acting weird—because of that business last night. And Beth's disappeared. She left without locking up or taking her purse and never showed up at work. And we all had these weird dreams this morning—God, I just feel so mixed up and worried. . . ."

"Dreams?"

Anna gave a nervous laugh. "I guess I'm sounding a little flaky."

"What kind of dreams? And who was having them?"

"Well, Cathy stayed over last night—you remember her, right? She had them. And so did Beth and I. We all had the same one. It was like something had happened to everybody in the city, and we'd be just wandering these empty streets . . ."

"Did you talk to Jack about them?"

"No. Why should—"

"Where are you calling from, Anna?"

"Home. But, Ned—"

"Stay there. I'll be right over."

"Ned, you're beginning to scare me."

"I'm sorry. It's just— Look, I'll tell you all about it when I see you. Just stay where you are. And, Anna, don't go to sleep."

"Ned, you're—"

"Ten minutes, Anna."

He hung up and dialed his partner's number, carrying the phone to the bedroom as it rang on the other end. He put it down on the dresser and shrugged into his sport jacket. Ernie Grier came on the phone as he was clipping his .38 onto his belt. Left side front, for quick access, instead of on the right, as he usually did.

"Ernie? It's Ned."

"This better be good, partner, because I am *not* having a good day. Judy's acting like I've got AIDS or something, my kid comes home and she won't even talk to me, and I'm lying here trying to rest but scared to sleep because of all this shit you've been laying on me. . . . I tell you, I'm not having a good time."

"Yeah, well, it's getting worse. You remember where Jack's sister lives?"

"Anna? Sure. Right near that Baker guy's place."

"Meet me there as soon as you can, okay?"

"What's this about, Ned?"

"Just be there."

He hung up before Grier could answer. From under his socks he grabbed a box of extra bullets and headed out the door. He was on the stairs when the phone began to ring back in the apartment, but he didn't stop to answer it. If it was Anna or Ernie, he'd be talking to them soon. If it was anyone else, he just didn't have the time for them right now.

## 10

JACK GOT TO his gun before the creature let loose with a second fiery breath. He turned and fired point-blank, aiming for the torso, emptying the weapon of its four remaining shots. Every bullet hit, driving the creature back, but she didn't go down. She swayed in the center of the store, wheezing for air. The wall behind her was sprayed with blood from the exiting bullets. Not waiting to see if she was breathing her last or just getting her wind back, Jack headed for the door and ran headlong into someone.

It took three seconds for Jack to place him.

John Paige. The uniform from Traffic that he'd met in Baker's kitchen.

Paige recovered first. "What the hell's—"

Jack gave him a push with his shoulder. "Get out of here!"

Two more seconds went by. Jack was fumbling bullets from his jacket and reloading his gun. The music trilled painfully, high notes as sharp as razors, cutting at his eardrums.

"This place . . ." Paige said.

"Move it!" Jack cried.

He could feel her coming up behind him. Her approach made the skin crawl up his back. Another three seconds had gone by. Paige's features went slack, the blood draining from his skin. The music whined like amplified feedback. Jack bent low, dropping to one side while trying to push Paige out of the way.

Too late.

The blast caught Paige straight in the face, burning away the flesh from his head and shoulders. He made a grotesque figure, arms waving, legs buckling—dead on his feet, although the lower part of his body wasn't aware of it yet. Then he started to fall.

As his fleshless skull neared the ground, gray matter pouring out of the eyeholes and from under his jaw, the corpse began to disappear. It was as though it were falling out of sight around a corner, except there was no corner here.

The corpse was returning to the world from which it had come.

Bringing a nightmare to a quiet Ottawa street.

Jack didn't stay to watch the last of the corpse disappear. He bolted up the stairs leading from the recessed shops, making it to Elgin Street. Having only had time to reload three bullets, he turned at the top of the stairs and fired at the creature again. Three times. Point-blank. Not one miss.

Again she stood there, swaying and wheezing. Jack took to his heels, reloading as he ran. Counting the seconds. It had taken her eleven to recover the last time. From four body shots. This time he'd hit her twice in the chest, and once straight in the face.

Three seconds were already gone.

He chanced a glance behind him. Her head lifted, half the face blown away from his last shot. The flesh of one cheek hung in bloody tatters. Tongues wriggled out the hole of her cheek now, as well as from her mouth. Her dark eyes settled their gaze on him.

Two more seconds gone.

The music screamed in Jack's ears, like fingernails on a chalkboard, magnified a thousand times.

She stepped up onto Elgin Street.

*I need my own frigging flamethrower,* Jack thought.

The seconds sped by.

Jack finished reloading. The creature was floating down the street after him. He turned in the middle of the street to make his stand, assuming the Academy stance. Legs apart. Gun arm straight, supported at the wrist by his left hand.

He knew he didn't have a hope in hell, but he meant to go down trying.

# 11

I DON'T NEED THIS, Cathy thought.

She'd fallen asleep on her couch after getting home from shopping at the Rideau Center with Anna, only to wake up back in the same dream she'd had this morning. Except this time it was her own apartment that was trashed, not Anna's.

The place looked as though it had been vandalized while she was sleeping. No, she thought as she got up quickly from the couch. There were too many rotting smells and old refuse for the mess to be recent. She brushed at her clothes where moldering bits of the couch had stuck from where she was lying on it. This was what her place would look like if George Romero had decided to film something in her apartment, set a few years after they dropped the big ones.

Graffiti on the wall caught her eye. A crudely drawn male figure with a meat cleaver was standing over the severed remains of an equally crudely drawn woman. Underneath it were the words: YOUR GONNA DIE SCREAMING.

You get an *F* for spelling, she thought, trying to keep her mood light. But crudely drawn or not, the graffiti disturbed her, bringing a sour taste up into her throat. It seemed to be too much of a . . . promise.

Time to wake up, she told herself.

Time to get out of here.

She closed her eyes and concentrated on waking, but it didn't help. When she opened them again, everything was the same. Except the smell was worse. She tried pinching herself and succeeded only in raising a bruise.

What did she have to do to get out of here?

She couldn't find an answer, so she left the apartment. There was worse graffiti in the hallways and the stairwell going down. Her high heels clicked hollowly on the stairs. Her short skirt was too tight. Not exactly exploring gear, she thought.

Outside, she hugged herself, staring at the desolation around her. The streets were torn up. The church across the street had every vulgarity one could think of spray-painted across its walls. The skies were heavy with sickly yellow clouds, hanging down almost to the top floor of Le Marquis, her apartment building. It was so silent, she found herself straining to hear something. Anything. If only there were somebody else around. . . .

Maybe that was the wrong thing to hope for, she thought, considering the graffiti.

She started to walk. By the time she was across Pretoria Bridge, a few blocks north of her apartment building, and walking by the police station on Elgin, she decided to go to Janice's apartment. Janice had the bottom floor of a two-story redbrick on Gilmour Street, just a block and a half east of Elgin. When she reached the building, she stood and stared at it for long moments. The porch was sagging. All the windows were smashed out. Someone had cut down the big oak tree on the front lawn—the grass all dead there now—and it had fallen lengthwise in front of the house. Half on the street, half on the lawn.

Janice wasn't going to be in there. So what was she doing here? The house—the entire street—looked as though it hadn't had a person on it in years. But she circled around the fallen oak all the same, and walked up onto the porch. Her heel caught in a loose board but thankfully didn't snap. She was careful where she put her feet then. Pushing open the sagging front door, she walked into Janice's apartment.

It wasn't as bad as her own place had been. In fact, it looked as though someone had been straightening it up. The floors were fairly free of refuse. A table and two chairs had been set by the window, a vase with plastic roses in it on the table. The graffiti on the walls had a faded look about them—as though someone had been trying to scrub them off.

She heard a faint noise and turned from the living room to look down the hallway that led to the kitchen, bedroom, and bathroom.

"Janice?" she called softly.

The sound had been close—probably in the bathroom. A scraping kind of a sound. She took a step down the hall.

"Is that you, Janice?"

There was no reply. No repetition of the sound. The silence was a little unnerving. Just the house settling, Cathy thought. Maybe . . . maybe a rat?

That thought made her shiver, but she moved toward the bathroom all the same. When she reached the door, she called out softly again, then gave the door a push. It opened on an empty bathroom. Fairly clean—like the rest of the apartment had been. The shower curtain, which Janice had added to the old-fashioned claw-footed bathtub, was drawn closed.

No way I'm looking behind that, Cathy told herself.

But she took a step closer. Reached out a hand to draw aside the heavy plastic with its flowered pattern. Tugged it open.

The scream that came up her throat got lost in her

frantic attempt to back out of the bathroom. She hit the wall behind her, lost her balance on her high heels, and slid down to the floor. By then she was shaking so badly that she couldn't get up. All she could do was stare.

At the corpse.

A nude corpse, the flesh white as alabaster, hanging from the opposite curtain rod by a rope made from a jean jacket torn into strips.

The belly cut open, entrails spilling out of the ghastly slit.

The dried blood pooled in the bottom of the tub.

The swollen features puffed almost beyond recognition.

But not enough.

She could still see Janice in those bloated features. The dead eyes staring down at her. The blue-black tongue thrusting out from between the swollen lips.

It was when the arm twitched that Cathy moved. The arm rose to point at her. A noise came from between those horrible lips.

". . . ah . . . thee . . ."

Her name. It was calling her name.

She found the strength to stumble to her feet and flee the apartment. She lost one shoe in the living room, the other on the porch. It didn't matter. She ran in her stockings down the street, oblivious to the bruising that her feet were taking on the uneven asphalt.

The sound seemed to chase her—

(. . . ah . . . thee . . .)

—filling her head—

(. . . wahn . . . yhou . . .)

—with its ghastly slurring syllables. Until another sound overrode it. Music. Synthesized music. But it had voices in it too. Cries of pain and fear. An aching, painful sound. Mixed in with it were sharp popping retorts—like the backfiring of a car.

Please God, she prayed as she ran. I won't ever be bad again. I'll—

Suddenly she was on Elgin Street. There was a man in the middle of the street—

(Jack!)

—aiming a gun down toward . . . When she saw the monstrous creature bearing down on Jack, she skidded to a halt, only to fall headlong in the rubble, a scream like a siren ripping her throat raw. Jack turned toward her.

And so did the creature.

# 12

NED LEANED ON the doorbell twice before Anna answered it. He was shocked at her haggard appearance when she opened the door to the limit of its security chain. She seemed smaller than usual—a bundle of tightly wound nerves. Worry had etched unfamiliar lines in her face and underscored her eyes with dark circles. She gave him a weak smile, then closed the door to unlatch the security chain. When it opened again, she stepped into his arms, pushing her face against his shoulder. Ned enfolded her in an embrace.

"You must think I'm a real shit," she said, her voice slightly muffled by his sport jacket.

That it took a bad time like this to put her in his arms? Ned thought. Maybe. But not likely. The press of her body against his, breasts soft against his chest, felt too right.

"You know how I feel," he said.

She nodded against his shoulder. "But that's just it," she said as she stepped back. Taking his hand, she drew him into the house, then closed and locked the door. "I do know how you feel. And that's why I feel so rotten. We haven't seen each other for months. It has to take me feeling so lost to call you. It's not fair."

"I wouldn't have wanted you to call anybody else."

"You're too nice, Ned."

She led the way into the living room and had him sit on the couch, keeping his hand in her own.

"Yeah," Ned said, keeping his tone light. "I hear that all the time when I'm busting some jerk. 'Officer, you're so nice.' " His pulse started doing a time-and-a-half rhythm as she leaned closer to him. "Nobody tells me they feel harassed. They know I hate to hear talk like that—I lie awake nights just thinking about it."

That tugged a small smile from her lips. "It must be so hard," she said as the smile faded, "having everybody hate you."

"It's not fun," Ned replied seriously. "The only people who seem to care about the law are those who've got something to lose. Everybody else just . . . You know Andy Coe?"

Anna nodded. Coe had been both Ned and Jack's Staff Sergeant when Jack was still on the force.

"Some days I think he's dead-on with his little bit of cop philosophy. He says there's only three kinds of people in the world: cops, civilians, and assholes. And that's the thing I don't like about the job. Everybody's got to be on one side or another. When you're wearing the uniform, everybody's walking tippy-toe around you. When you're in plainclothes and somebody finds out you're a cop, right away everything tenses up. It's no wonder we stick to ourselves. But when that gets in the way of . . . well, you and me, for instance . . ."

"It's just not fair."

Ned nodded.

"*I've* not been fair," Anna added.

"It's not just you. I haven't exactly warmed to your friends, either."

"But that's mostly because of the way *they* treat *you*—once they find out you're a policeman."

"Nothing's that simple," Ned said. "They just bugged me—I've got to admit it. It's like, they've got all these real strong feelings about causes—saving whales, helping starving people in Africa, raising money for AIDS research—but they don't do anything about it. It's just talk. Most of them wouldn't help a bum lying on the sidewalk in front of their own apartment building."

"Most people are a little mixed up about their priorities, Ned—not like you. But at least most of them mean well. At least they've got some concerns."

It was going all wrong, Ned thought. He didn't want to get into just another rehash of all the shit that kept them apart.

"Listen," he said. "Maybe we should just forget—"

Anna laid a finger against his lips. "Just a sec, Ned. I need to tell you this. When I first started worrying this afternoon, I called Jack right away. I think of Jack first, because ever since I can remember, he's been there to help me out. You know what it's like between us. It's not just brother and sister—we're real friends."

Ned nodded.

"But when I couldn't get hold of him, the next person I thought of calling was you. That doesn't mean I care about you less than Jack—it's just different. I felt bad about it, though, because with the way things are going for us, I didn't want to phone you just when I needed something."

"Anna, you know I'd never—"

"But when you answered the phone, I got a real lump in my throat. I know it sounds corny, but I realized right then that we're both being stupid. Sure, we've got problems—but it's not like we can't work them out. Not if we both really care—about the relationship, about how the other one feels. I'm not saying you should give up being a cop or that I should stop what I'm doing. I just think we should make room in there—we *have* to make room in there—for the relationship as well."

"Are you saying what I think you're saying?"

Anna put her hand behind his head and drew his mouth down to hers. When they finally came up for air, they both drew back for a moment. Her eyes were shiny as her gaze met his. There was a thickness in Ned's throat, a tightness in his chest, a foolish grin on his face.

"God, I love you," he said. "Always have."

"I know." She put her arms around him and laid her head against his chest. "I love you too."

Ned didn't want the moment ever to end—he'd been waiting for it too long. Okay, there were going to be tough spots, but he knew as sure as he was sitting there holding her that if they could make the commitment, they could work them all out. Trouble was, there were some immediate concerns that needed to be seen to first.

He gave her a squeeze, then took her lightly by the shoulders and held her at arm's length.

"We've got to talk about Jack," he said. "And Beth."

Anna nodded. Worry took hold of her again, washing the softness from her features.

"I've got such a bad feeling, Ned," she said. "That's why I had to tell you this before . . . before something happens to us too."

"We don't know that anything's happened to either of them."

Anna pressed a hand against her chest. "I know. But it doesn't stop me from feeling this way."

Ned took her hand to maintain contact with what they'd just shared, but he put on his cop face and led her through a quick rundown of what was bothering her. The dream that the three women had shared. The odd phone call with Jack this morning and his subsequent unavailability. Beth's disappearance.

He knew some of Beth's history—but not the things Anna was telling him now. About how Beth had been a victim since her early childhood—her father abusing her, the foster homes, the bad marriage. About the basement that her ex had kept her jailed in for weeks. About his threats to find her and take her back.

"You got this guy's address?" he asked.

Anna nodded.

"Well, we'll go check him out—as soon as Ernie gets here."

"You're taking it seriously, then?"

"With the background you've given me, what else *can* I do? Christ, that poor woman."

"What about Jack?"

"We can take a turn by his place on the way to this Hawkins guy's house. Knowing Jack, he might've just unplugged the phone. Last night . . . he just saw that as a personal failure. He was taking it pretty hard."

"He always does."

Anna rubbed at her face, making Ned smile. Just like Jack.

"When I called you earlier," Anna said suddenly, "you were asking me about dreams. You told me not to go to sleep. What was all that about, Ned?"

He shifted uncomfortably on the couch. The whole idea of that dream world being real—never mind his own experiences in it—was something he couldn't talk about easily. He was a nuts-and-bolts type of man. Spacey things like this were for nut cases. Except when he remembered the dream that Anna's call had woken him from—

Flicker.

For one moment the orderly present was gone, and Ned was back in that world. Anna's apartment trashed. Graffiti sprayed on the walls. Artwork vandalized. Front window broken, the glass shards sprayed around his feet. And beside him, on the rotting couch, a heap of bones where Anna had been sitting, her skull lying on its side. . . .

Flicker.

He shuddered as the room returned to what it was supposed to be. Anna there beside him. Alive.

"Ned?"

He gave her a sickly look. "Did . . . did anything happen to you just now?"

"Happen? What do you mean?"

Maybe you only went there when you dreamed, he thought. Maybe these flashes were just like looking in through a window. You weren't real there—yet. But you would be. . . .

"Ned?"

The concern in her voice, in her eyes, gave him the strength to lay it all out for her. What had happened in Baker's basement. The things he and Jack had seen. Coffey's unexplained appearance in the middle of the gun range. Jack's theories. His own experience just before she'd phoned him.

Her eyes grew wide—more with horror than with disbelief. "It . . . it's *real*?" she said in a strained voice.

"It's impossible," Ned replied. "But I've *been* there. And nothing else ties it all together."

"But . . ."

"Like I said, it's impossible."

She sat back in the couch, staring out at the lengthening shadows in the living room, trying to digest it all.

"It's horrible," she said softly. "God . . ." She turned suddenly to Ned. "You don't think . . . Jack and Beth . . ."

"Christ, I never stopped to think that maybe—"

The doorbell rang, interrupting them.

"That'll be Ernie," Ned said, standing up to get the door.

"The shit's really hitting the fan," his partner said when he opened the door. Grier looked from Ned to Anna, who had come up behind Ned.

"What're you talking about?" When Grier gave Anna a glance, Ned added, "It's okay—she knows about it."

"Knows about what? That we're all losing our minds?"

Ned laid a hand on his partner's arm. Grier looked really shook up. "What's happening, Ernie?"

"What isn't? Benny Dwyer's wife found him dead in his bed this afternoon—same MO as Baker and Coffey. Petrin from the ID Unit's in intensive care at the Civic. He's in some kind of coma. Inspector Fournier was found butchered in his office. And then, while I'm driving down here, I hear Dispatch saying on the radio that there're stiffs popping up on Elgin Street. This is getting way out of hand, Ned. The body count just keeps rising. When I think . . . Christ, I don't know. It's like some frigging nightmare, except it's . . . Christ . . ."

"Take it easy, Ernie."

"Take it easy? We're on the list, Ned! Everybody who's bought it so far was *there*—you understand what I'm saying?"

Anna was standing close to Ned now, clutching his arm. Grier's panic was infectious. Ned could feel Anna trembling against him. There was a sick feeling in the pit of his own stomach.

"Okay," he said, taking charge. "We'll go to Elgin Street. Have they already called in some backup?"

Ernie nodded.

Ned turned to Anna. "I've got to go. But I'll put in a call to Dispatch and have them send a couple of uniforms around to where Beth's ex lives en route. Can you get me the address?" As she went to get it, Ned added to Grier: "You go on ahead, Ernie. I'll be right behind you."

"Sure. But, Ned, what the hell can we do?"

"Our job. That's all. Stop in at the station and pick up some riot gear. I want a shotgun with lots of spare rounds."

"They've already called in the Tactical Squad. The place is in an uproar."

"Just get going," Ned said. "I'll be right behind you."

"Here's the address," Anna said as Grier went down the walk to his car.

She was wearing a jean jacket over the black T-shirt and blue tie-dyed skirt she'd had on when Ned had arrived. Hightops on her feet. Shoulder bag in hand.

"Where are you going?"

"I can't stay here," she said. "Not alone. If Jack or Beth are there . . ."

"This is craziness, Anna."

"Ned, *please*."

Craziness? he thought. Well, why the hell not? Nothing was making sense right now. And at least this way he could keep an eye on her. If anything happened to her now . . .

"Okay," he said. "Let's go."

He set off at a quick jog for his own car. In her sneakers and loose skirt, Anna had no trouble keeping up with him. Once inside, he set the cherry on the dashboard. The light spun, throwing red patterns in the growing dusk. He floored the Buick, leaving rubber behind as he pulled away. The sound of his siren preceded them as they sped downtown.

Beside him, Anna braced her hands against the dashboard. He tried to give her a quick smile, but it came out like a grimace. Grabbing the radio mike, he called in their position, remembering to ask that a car be sent out to Hawkins's house.

# 13

Out on the street, Hardass leaned against the wall of Julie's building for a long moment, trying to stop the world from spinning around on him. Being with her hadn't helped. Maybe nothing was going to help him now.

That dream . . .

Julie making out like he'd disappeared from her bedroom—like he'd *really* been there, for chrissake. . . .

But that was what it had felt like, hadn't it? Like he'd really gone someplace else. To a dead city. To the place where all his old ghosts were waiting for him.

Humping away at Julie, he'd kept seeing her features change. Face after face appeared there on her shoulders—the same parade, over and over again. All those people he'd screwed over . . .

He pushed himself away from the wall.

Screw it. He was going to get a drink, that was what he was going to do. He was going to get so shit-eyed drunk that he couldn't see his own hands held out in front of him, let alone hallucinate.

Trailing a hand along the wall of the building as though he were already drunk, he headed for the nearest bar.

# 14

WHEN THE CREATURE started to turn toward Cathy, Jack saw Janet Rowe's features in its ravaged face. Cathy, her scream still burning up her throat, saw Beth Green. The music pierced their eardrums, a shrieking wail that stopped them where they stood. The creature floated up from the street. Airborne, it swept down at Cathy, breathing its fire.

The blast lifted Cathy to her feet, cutting off her scream. For one long, horrifying moment Jack stared at her, the flesh burning from her face. A skull screamed silently atop her flaming body, then she crumpled and fell to the pavement.

(too late)

Jack ran toward the creature, his .38 leveled.

(always too fucking late)

He emptied the weapon into the creature. As it staggered, then fell under the onslaught, he threw the empty weapon aside and grabbed a loose piece of pavement. The creature turned toward him, the tongues in its throat writhing. Jack brought the pavement down against its skull. Bone shattered under the blow. He leapt on top of the creature and continued to batter away, until he'd made pulp of its head. Then he began to work on the body. The chunk of pavement rising in the air, smashing down. Rising again.

The music died as he continued to batter the creature. He was splattered with its blood and gore. He thought about Janet Rowe. About Cathy . . .

(too late)

He brought his makeshift weapon down again and again, until it finally shattered against the stone under the creature's body. Bent over it, he gulped in lungfuls of air, his stomach churning at the rancid stench that rose from the creature's battered remains. The stink of burning flesh was still strong in the air.

Wearily he lifted his head to look at Cathy's corpse, but it was gone. Back to the real world. Just like Coffey's and Paige's and . . . Christ . . .

(too late)

He heard the humming buzz of insects and looked down at the creature's body. It was turning into bugs. Cockroaches skittered away. Flies arose in swarms. Every bit of flesh was transformed into an insect and fleeing. In moments there was only the smear of blood on the pavement—all that remained of the monstrous thing he'd killed.

Slowly he pushed himself to his feet. Janet Rowe, some hellish angel—whatever it had been, it was finally dead. He walked over to where he'd thrown his gun and replaced it in its shoulder holster. There was a dent in the barrel—it was going to need some work. He looked over to where Cathy's corpse had lain. Unlike the blood smear showing where the creature had been, there was no remnant of her left at all.

A bleakness settled inside him—as complete as the desolation of the ruined city around him.

Go home, he told himself. Go home and wake up.

He turned, and it was there again.

The angel.

No, she was a fury now, wasn't she?

Untouched by bullets or the battering he'd given it. The flesh perfect. Showgirl's body and angel's face. As he gazed at her, he watched graffiti in the shape of tattoos appear on her skin.

"Jesus . . ."

His voice was a hoarse whisper. His gun was empty. Probably wasn't even functional from the fall it had taken when he'd thrown it aside. He didn't even bother to try to pick up another slab of pavement. The bleakness inside him had scraped away everything he cared about. This time he was really—

(too late)

"All that's left," the creature said, "is a killing time."

The transformation from angel to monstrosity was almost instantaneous this time. He stared at the tongues wriggling up from the back of its throat. Listened to the music build.

(too late)

As the fiery blast hit him, only one thing rose to mind. One care he could never lose. He prayed to a God that he'd forgotten since he'd attended Sunday School as a toddler that the fury wouldn't take Anna too.

## 15

WALT HAWKINS HAD just finished a solitary dinner when the two uniformed policemen came to his door. He heard them out; told them, sure, if Beth was to come back to him, he'd take her in, no questions asked, but he'd learned his lesson about trying to force her to come back; asked them, did they want to look around?

Calling what they supposed was his bluff, they had a quick look around the one-story bungalow, checked the basement, then left with apologies "for disturbing your evening, Mr. Hawkins. Thanks for your cooperation."

*You stupid fucks,* he wanted to tell them as he closed the door. *You think I'd be sitting here with the little wifey, just waiting for you to show up?*

He watched them leave through the picture window, then got on the phone and dialed the number of the cottage out near Ashton where Ted was baby-sitting the cause of all this official concern.

"So what's up?" Ted wanted to know.

"The Man was here."

"And?"

"And nothing. I let them in, showed them around. They just left, calling me Mr. Hawkins and apologizing for bothering me."

"Toldja."

"Yeah. You did all right by me, Ted. How's the little lady?"

"Just like she was when we dropped you off. Does whatcha tell her, sits like a lump unless you give her something to do. I think she fell asleep a little while ago."

"I'm coming up."

"You sure that's such a good—"

"Hey. They've been and gone—right? Why would they come back?"

"Okay. People next door showed up, though. Probably just for the night."

"So I'll drive up, sleep there, and be ready to start her on her lessons first thing in the morning."

"Okey-dokey, Walt. You're the boss. Bring some beer, wouldja? I'm just about out."

"What're you drinking?"

"Nothing foreign. I'm going to lock her in the back room and catch me some shut-eye. I'll leave the door unlocked for you."

"If she gets away . . ."

"Where's she gonna go, Walt?"

"You said there were people next door—"

"Hey, I'm *locking* her in the back room, okay? Lighten the fuck up. And don't forget the beer."

He hung up before Walt could say anything else. Lighten up. Right. Easy to say when it wasn't his wife playing him for a fool.

Wife. The little whore.

He smacked a fist against a palm. There was going to be some serious disciplining, come tomorrow morning, he thought as he fetched a windbreaker and the car keys. He got a hard-on just thinking about it.

# FOUR

## 1

BETH HADN'T PROTESTED when her ex took her from the house and led her out to Ted Rimmer's van. She got in the back like he told her to and took his perfunctory slaps—hard enough to rock her head and leave red marks on her cheeks—with a dull-eyed acceptance. When the back door was locked and Walt joined his friend in the front, she huddled in a corner of the van, knees pulled up to her chest, arms wrapped tightly around her legs. There was just no fight left in her.

What was the point?

Nothing changed. Every time she started to believe that there really might be a way out of the misery that was her life, things just got worse instead.

From Daddy to Mr. Gregoire.

To Jody and Kirk.

To Walt.

Walt was the end of the road—she could see that now. No matter how far she might try to run, he'd always be there to take her back—

(to that dark place filled with pain)

Walt, who took a perverse pleasure in hurting her—

(his leather belt slashing across her chest)

—and in the scars left by wounds that others had inflicted upon her. Daddy burning her with his cigarettes.

("I don't want to hurt you, honey, but you can't tell me you're going to talk to Mommy about our special times. It just makes me mad. You don't want your daddy to be mad, now do you?")

No. She wanted him dead.

Mommy pretending she couldn't see the bruises and burns.

Dead.

Mr. Gregoire's grinning face, his hand clamped across her mouth as he grunted and thrust between her legs.

Dead.

She wanted to burn away their features so that there was no trace of them left to haunt her. To hurt her.

Jody and Kirk. The looks she got in school from the other kids, the knowing smirks. And Cassie . . .

She wanted them all dead. She wanted the power she'd felt in her dream to be real. She wanted to be able to float in the air, to fly away from the pain. She wanted to pay them all back for everything they'd done to her. For everything that anyone had ever done to others just like her. Everybody had to pay.

Except she didn't have any power.

Instead of being in control, she was locked in a tiny cottage bedroom, out in the country somewhere. Watched over by one of her ex-husband's greasy friends. Feeling the pain. Waiting for Walt. Waiting for the pain that was still to come. For the return—

(to that dark place)

—of everything she thought she had escaped.

Through waves of misery she looked around, every motion setting up a new flare of pain.

The window of her prison was tiny and set high up in the wall. Too high for her to look through. The walls were paneled with fake wood. There was a bed with a lumpy mattress. A night table with a Bible and a *Reader's Digest* collection on it. A bare bulb hanging from the ceiling, the switch by the door. The locked door. Beyond it, the little man who'd tricked her into opening the door so that Walt could grab her.

"I'll be back," Walt had said as he'd pushed her into the room.

She fell to the floor and lay limp, but that wasn't enough for him. It had never been enough.

He stepped into the room after her and kicked her where she lay.

I won't cry out, she promised herself. I won't give him that much.

But her silence infuriated him. As it always did. He kicked her again, then dragged her up into a sitting position against the wall and rained blows against her face and chest until she couldn't stop herself from moaning.

Finally satisfied, he stepped back and let her slide limply to the floor.

"Go ahead," he told her. "Play your little feel-sorry-for-me game. But there's no one coming to help you now. All that's coming is a little lesson in what happens to whores who try to run out on their husbands. To have and to hold, baby. Till death do us part. Think about it."

The thin walls of the room shook as he slammed the door.

Through the ocean of her pain, she heard him talk

to his friend, then heard him drive off. But he'd be back. Walt Hawkins always kept his promises.

"How do you stop this, Anna?" she breathed into the mattress. It hurt to talk, hurt even to move. "How do you stop being a victim when that's all you really are?"

All she'd ever wanted was to stop being hurt. Was that too much to ask for? If she could get away, if she was in—

(that Other Place)

—she'd stop them from hurting her. From hurting anyone.

Except that place wasn't real. It was just a dream.

*This* place was real.

Walt was real.

Pain was real.

When she heard the door unlock, all she could do was lie there and stare. Through swollen eyes she saw Walt's friend open the door a crack to look in on her, then he closed it again. Locked it. She continued to lie there. She let her eyes close. She tried to pretend that she was just lying down to go to sleep. That none of this was happening. That it couldn't be real. That she was somewhere else, just having a bad dream—

(about that dark place filled with pain)

—until the pain took her away into something very much like sleep, where she could dream.

She was changed when she became aware of her surroundings. She was strong when she stood up from the moldering bed, the pain gone, the bruises and swelling vanished. She looked around. The wood paneling was cracked and peeling. She pushed at the door and the rotted wood gave away.

The cottage was empty. Deserted. A ruin. She paced

slowly through the refuse until she was outside. Under the yellow skies, she looked around. There were the remains of other cottages—ramshackle buildings falling in on themselves. Miles of dead forest surrounded them. There was a lake behind her, thick with algae and rotted plants. Dead fish, floating with their white bellies up, lay thick around the shoreline. The swampy smells in the air were tinged with something metallic.

Beth spread her arms wide. She was back. Here she could do anything. She could fly. She could be in control.

She let herself rise and drifted slowly through the thick air.

*I can do anything,* she thought.

In this place she really could.

She could stop the pain forever.

She floated in a slow circle around the cottage. And then she heard something from the building. She let herself sink until her feet touched the yellowed grass. Her footsteps were silent as she closed the distance between herself and the cottage. She could feel a thickness in her throat. Her jaws ached and seemed to to be swelling.

She stepped into the doorway and saw Walt's friend standing there in the middle of the cottage. His eyes bulged in their sockets when he caught sight of her. He slowly backed away until a wall rose up behind him and there was nowhere else to go.

He was part of the pain, she thought as she stepped over the threshold. A festering sore.

A flash of memory touched her—her mother lancing a boil. Heating up the needle with fire. To cleanse it.

Fire.

Cleansing fire.

She could feel a heat in her chest. There was something moving in her throat. Wriggling. Power building up, crackling along her nerve endings. A fire in her lungs.

Fire.

Walt's greasy friend was holding out his hands to fend off her approach.

I did that, she thought. Lots of times. I begged and pleaded, but no one ever stopped.

The heat was almost painful now. If she didn't let it loose, it was going to consume her. But she wasn't the one who needed its scouring touch.

Fire.

She felt her jaws widen still farther, farther than should have been possible, but she was beyond reasoning out what could be real in this place and what not.

All she knew was that she was finally in control.

She could stop the pain.

She stepped right up to him, until there was nowhere he could go. The man beat at her chest, but she couldn't feel the blows. They were futile. As so many times her own had been. But she didn't feel the sense of pleasure that was always there in—

(her daddy's, Mr. Gregoire's, Jody's and Kirk's, Walt's)

—their eyes. She was lancing a boil, that was all. Healing a hurt.

She gripped him, one strong hand on each of his shoulders. A sense of kinship arose inside her, and she felt as though all the victims that ever had been were sitting in her mind. Looking through her eyes. Readying the heat in her chest that burned hot as a furnace.

Leaning in close, she—

(they all)

—breathed on the man—
(a cleansing fire)
—and watched him burn.

## 2

THE BARTENDER in the Lafayette watched Hardass Boucher drink, and shook his head. Whiskey and beer chasers—enough to put a man down forever, never mind for the afternoon.

Any other customer and he'd have tossed the guy out a long time ago. But this was a cop, and you didn't go throwing out cops, no matter how drunk they got, no matter how abusive. Not if you wanted to stay in business without being hassled by him and his buddies from now until hell froze over.

At least he'd quieted down now. He'd stopped shouting at the other customers—driving half of them away—and was sitting in the corner, watching the TV but not seeing it, head drooping until it lay on his arms.

Yeah, you just go to sleep, the bartender thought. Have yourself a little nappy-poo.

He shook his head again. Hardass Boucher, the man called himself. More like Asshole Boucher, if you asked him.

He went to pull a draft for another customer. When he next looked over to the corner where Boucher had been sleeping, the man was gone.

Hit the can to take a leak, the bartender thought, but Boucher never came out.

After a while the bartender went to check the washroom, just to make sure the asshole hadn't passed out in a urinal, but the small room was empty. Must have left the bar under his own steam.

As he went back to cleaning glasses the bartender wished that all his problems could be solved as easily.

## 3

HARDASS BOUCHER'S PROBLEMS were just beginning.

He'd nodded off in the bar but snapped awake just moments later. Trouble was, when he woke, the bar was gone. Or at least the bar he'd fallen asleep in was gone. The place he was sitting in now wasn't fit for a wino.

He remembered being so drunk that he couldn't stand, but he was sober now.

All too sober.

Rising from his seat, he crossed the deserted bar and stepped out onto an equally deserted street.

Man, oh man, what the fuck was going on, anyway?

Where the hell *was* he?

He recognized the Market street he was looking down, but the place looked like it was a war zone. Graffiti was sprayed on the walls of the buildings that still stood. The rusted hulks of delivery trucks and cars littered the street. The sky was the color of yellow vomit. There was an acidic sting in the air that hurt his lungs.

He needed some help, was what it was, Hardass realized. He'd stepped over the line—*way* over the line—and he needed someone to help bring him back. Because this was insanity. This. Just. Couldn't. Exist.

He caught a flicker of movement in the corner of his eye and turned quickly in that direction.

"Hey!" he shouted. "You, there, in that building!"

There was no response, except that what he'd thought was the moaning of the wind coming through the buildings around him was really a kind of music. He drew his gun from its holster under his jacket.

"Police!" he cried, taking a few steps toward the building. "Come on out of there—hands in the air where I can see them."

Still no response.

Where the hell was that music coming from? It grated on his nerves worse than the crap the kids had pounding out of their frigging boom boxes.

Gun held out before him, he approached the building into which he'd seen the figure dart. With his free hand he wiped the sweat from his brow.

Fear.

That unfamiliar emotion was back again, had him by the balls and wasn't letting go.

But he'd put that away long ago, hadn't he? When his old man used to beat him, when the thing in the closet used to stare out at him from between his hanging clothes, when the kids used to gang up on him in the school yard . . .

He'd shown them all, hadn't he? He'd shown them who could be tough. He'd shown them he wasn't afraid of anything. He was a fucking hardass, wasn't he? That's what the guys called him, because they *knew* he was a man. He wasn't some limp-wristed little fuck looking for a handout from the world. He wanted something, he took it. It was just that easy. He wasn't—

(Jesus fuck, he was—)

White with fear. So scared, his goddamned hand shook like he had palsy.

"You . . . you get out of there!" he called out to the building, shocked at how his voice cracked.

"Hardass."

The response, when it finally came, lifted the hairs at the nape of his neck.

Because it came from behind him.

He turned slowly, gun held out before him, to find himself ringed in by a half circle of ghostly pale women and teenagers. They didn't seem quite real—more like semitransparent images superimposed on the film of the street they were standing on. He could almost see right through them.

"Who . . . ?"

But he didn't have to ask who they were. He recognized a face here, a face there, finally realized he recognized them all.

"You took pieces from us, Hardass."

The unearthly music continued to whisper all around him, a maddening grating sound.

"That's all we are."

Hardass looked at the woman who spoke and remembered her. A welfare case. Her husband used to beat on her until she finally got up the nerve to call the cops and got him delivered to her doorstep instead. It was so easy to play on her fear. So easy to scare her into doing anything he wanted, into not saying a thing or he'd be back, and she didn't want him back, now did she?

"The pieces you took from us."

A young girl—fifteen, tops—spoke this time. And Hardass remembered her as well. Bunch of kids got her drugged up and gang-banged her. By the time he got to her, she didn't know up from down, so he had a little fun himself before he brought her in.

"Now we're going to take—"

A child of eight was speaking—he remembered laughing off her claim that her father was abusing her.

"—pieces from you."

A boy of twelve was speaking—he remembered telling him that if his uncle was screwing him, well, it was because he was a fag, wasn't he, so didn't he deserve what he got?

The music continued to whine in his ears.

The half circle closed in on him, backing him against the building.

"Look, I . . ."

He waved his gun at them, but it didn't slow them down for a moment.

"I . . . I'm just dreaming."

The voices whispered around him.

"Just dreaming."

"Bad dreams."

"You make your own bad dreams."

A thirteen-year-old girl stepped forward, her forearms mottled with bruises.

"Isn't that what you told me?" she asked. "That I make my own bad dreams?"

She pulled open her blouse to show a thin chest. There were more bruises here, larger ones that ran into each other and were scarred with cigarette burns.

"This is what my bad dreams did to me after you went away and left me with him."

"I . . . I didn't mean . . ."

The music soared, painfully shrill.

"Hardass."

The word hissed from their lips as they closed in, riding the whining chords of the music.

He leveled his gun at point-blank range. "B-back off. . . ."

They merely came nearer.

He fired, round after round, until the weapon was empty.

It didn't stop their advance.

When their cool hands touched him, the gun fell from his fingers. He screamed as they tore at his clothes. They were all over him. Chewing at his fingers, his face.

And they weren't real. He goddamned *knew* they weren't real. They were just garbage that he'd been carrying around inside him, that he'd brought with him to this place—whatever this place was. They weren't real.

But they were killing him all the same.

Howling, he fought them until he felt something inside himself just let go. A shrill pain traveled up his left arm. His chest closed in on itself. His mouth opened and closed convulsively.

Dying, his body crossed over from the dead city to the living one. Shoppers in the Market screamed as he appeared in their midst, clutching his chest. He staggered, his suit in tatters, bleeding from a hundred small wounds, then dropped to the pavement, striking his head on the curb. But he never felt a thing.

He was dead before the impact.

There were those who'd say he'd been dead a long time before that.

# 4

JACK WAS DEAD.

Anna sat in a corner of the General Assignment squad room, oblivious to her surroundings. Her sense of balance was gone. She couldn't have stood if she'd wanted to. She could barely keep her seat in the chair. Her mind was numb. Her hands wouldn't stop shaking. Her nerves were shot, her body limp.

Voices rose and fell around her as the detectives discussed the case. Dimly she realized that she wasn't just here on sufferance—because she was Jack's sister, Ned's friend. She was here for her own protection. Or so they thought. Only how they expected to protect her when she fell asleep and crossed over . . .

Jack was dead.

No one understood where the bodies had come from, popping out in the middle of Elgin Street, charred beyond recognition. But the ID Unit lifted prints and quickly identified the two men. It was Anna who'd recognized what was left of Cathy. Cathy. Still wearing the same clothes that she had when they were shopping. Dead now. The flesh of her face and upper torso burned away to the bone. Just like Constable Paige. And Jack . . .

"It's spreading like a disease," Ned had said, but only she and his partner had understood what he meant at the time. But that's exactly what it was. A virus. Giving you an awareness of that other place. Giving you the ability to cross over to it when you slept.

A curse.

Ned was still in conference with the brass, trying to explain it to them, while Anna sat in the squad room waiting for him. It felt like he'd been gone forever. Knowing what he'd be trying to explain, forever might come and go long before he got anyone to understand. She needed him right now.

". . . right here in the station," one of the detectives was saying.

"Just like Coffey."

"Poor fucker."

"They're trying to track down Shouldice now."

"It got Alec too?"

"And Hardass. Word just came in from the Market patrol."

"Burned?"

"No, but he popped in out of nowhere, all cut to shit."

"No big loss."

"Yeah? And when you're next?"

"What the fuck's going on—that's what I want to know."

Jack was dead.

Anna couldn't imagine a world without Jack in it. He'd always been there. The big brother. Her best friend. He was there to share the good times. To help her when things got rough. The bleakness that lay inside her, knowing he was gone, grew into a bottomless pit, dragging her down.

Her head sagged against her chest. She stared at the floor between her legs. There was a buzz in the back of her head.

Flicker.

The clean carpeting changed as she stared at it. Now

it was blue with mold. There was a rotting smell in the room. The air was too close. The silence absolute. She looked up to find herself alone in the squad room. The walls were defaced with graffiti and smeared excrement. The desks and chairs were broken like kindling, heaped in one corner. A skeleton lay on the floor beside it—black, charred bones splayed across the rotted carpet.

Anna's eyes widened. A sick taste rose in her throat.

Flicker.

The squad room was back the way it should be. The sudden return of conversation and ambient sound was almost deafening. Anna hugged herself tightly.

That other place. It was so close. The membrane separating them from it so fragile. Was Beth still there? They hadn't found her yet, but she might have reappeared anywhere.

Then Anna remembered last night. Beth. The figure floating out of her house. Drifting down the street. Her chasing it. Finding herself in yet another place. The dead plains. Where there was nothing at all, not even the ruined remnants of the city.

The empty feeling inside her reached out to that memory as though greeting an old friend. Those plains. Where despair ruled.

Cathy was dead.

Jack was dead.

Beth was gone.

The world she'd always embraced with delight had become an empty, inhospitable place. Bleak as the dead plains. Despair ruling here as well. She trembled in her seat, wishing Ned would return.

# 5

THEY WOULDN'T TAKE him seriously, and Ned couldn't blame them. He'd tried to keep it simple, but no matter how it came out, it sounded like he was a primo candidate to eat his gun. It just wasn't something you could explain—you had to be there. You had to feel that other place flickering at the edges of your mind, consciousness only barely keeping it at bay. How the fuck did you explain something like that? When you barely understood it yourself. When the guy who used to be your partner and was still one of your best friends lay dead in the street. When you had his sister with you, freaking as the positive ID was made. When the world was falling to pieces around you.

But nobody laughed.

No matter how wacked out it sounded, nobody could deny that something was happening. Something that couldn't be explained. The growing death count couldn't be put aside. Nor the dozens of eyewitness reports swearing to how the bodies just fell in out of nowhere.

The brass wasn't ready to accept his explanation, but they weren't ruling it out completely, either. *That's* how freaked they were. They'd brought in everyone connected to the case—even the coroner—and were temporarily putting them up in the gym. They let Ned warn the various officers about falling asleep, and then they convened this meeting. Now all they had to do was figure out what the fuck was going on. And how to stop it.

Ned listened to them argue. Everybody was here in the briefing room. The chief. The deputy chiefs. The Staff Superintendents. Inspectors from Police Intelligence, the ID Unit, the Tactical Squad, and Staff Operations. Ernie shifted uncomfortably beside him, and Ned knew just how he was feeling.

"Look," he said suddenly when a break came in the conversation. Like his partner, he felt intimidated, confronting all the brass like this, but he knew there was no more time to stall. "I've got a simple way to prove this."

Everyone waited for the chief to speak. Bernard Gauthier fixed Ned with a considering look.

"What's that, Sergeant?" he asked.

"Put me in one of the interrogation rooms with a cot and something to help me get to sleep. You watch me through the glass. Simple."

"Not alone," Grier said.

The chief shook his head. "I appreciate the strain you've been under, Sergeant, but I don't think—"

"What've you got to lose? We can talk about this forever, but it's getting dick-all done. Put me in the room and watch me. You can keep discussing it all you want while you wait, but if we don't do something soon, the shit's really going to hit the fan."

"You're out of line, Meehan."

Ned turned to John Bohay, Deputy Chief of Operations, who was ultimately in charge of Ned's section.

"I don't think so, sir. If we don't—"

"I said you're out of—"

"Gentlemen!"

All heads turned to the chief. He studied Ned carefully, his fingers tapping the files in front of him.

"You're convinced of the validity of your argument, Sergeant?" he asked.

"Yes, sir. I am."

The chief looked up and down the long table, then came to a decision.

"Go see to it," he said.

Grier stood quickly with Ned. "Sir . . ." he began.

"Both of you," the chief said. "Get whatever you need from the Quartermaster and have someone call us as soon as you're ready."

As they closed the door to the briefing room behind them, they heard voices raised in sudden argument. Ned gave his partner a wan smile.

"It's time for us to put up or shut up, Ernie," he said.

Grier nodded. Returning to the squad room, they sent out men to get the cots. Ned asked for two shotguns and extra shells for the standard-issue .38s. While Grier saw about getting something to help them get to sleep, Ned brought a chair over to where Anna was sitting.

"How're you holding up?" he asked softly.

Anna took his hand. "Not . . . not very good. It . . . How did it go in there?"

"About like we expected."

Christ, it hurt him to see her like this. Every bit of color and vitality had been drawn out of her features. She sat white and pale in the chair, almost a stranger. Her hand trembled in his grip.

"What happens now, Ned?"

He didn't want to tell her, but he didn't see how he could keep it from her. Not and be fair. He explained briefly.

"You can't!" she cried, fingers tightening around his.

"Someone's got to do it, Anna. We know the danger's real. Now we've got to prove that we know what it is so that we can do something about it. And we'll be careful. We'll be ready for . . . whatever's in there."

"Don't you . . . don't you think . . . Jack was ready?"

Ned remembered what they'd found on Jack's corpse. Canteen. Compass. Hunting knife. Unregistered gun. Beef jerky. Jack had gone in hunting bear. Trouble was, the bear found him first.

"We'll be ready," he repeated quietly. "It's got to be done."

"If I lose you too . . ."

"Anna, listen to me. We're not doing this to show how macho we are or anything. It's our job. Do you want more people to . . . to be hurt?"

"No. But—"

"Maybe we'll find Beth. . . ."

Anna looked at him.

For that one moment she was the woman he'd always known. There was strength in her gaze. In her grip. Understanding.

"Promise me you'll come back," she said.

"I promise I'll do my damnedest, Anna."

She nodded and slumped back into the chair, drawing into herself again. Ned wanted just to hold her, to take her away from here to someplace safe, but there was no place safe that he knew of, and then Ernie was back and it was time to go. He leaned forward and kissed her cheek. She raised a hand to touch his face.

"I love you," she said as he drew away.

Ned nodded, his throat constricted with emotion. "I love you too," he said, his voice husky.

When he stood up to go, Anna's head slumped back

against her chest. Ned turned at the door to look at her. He stood there unmoving until Ernie finally touched his arm, then he took the shotgun his partner held out to him and followed Ernie down the hall.

## 6

WALT'S OLD CHEVY shuddered at every pothole it hit on the narrow dirt road leading into the cottage from the highway. The place belonged to a friend of Ted's who was still away in Florida—a guy named Charlie Thornton. Ted liked to make out that Charlie was into some heavy deals in Miami, part of the Quebec crowd that did half their business down in the land of sun, but Walt knew better. Charlie was just a cheap thug who made a good buck doing a bodyguard gig with the Pellier family in Montreal. When the Pelliers went south, Charlie went with them. No big deal.

The Chevy hit a monster pothole that tilted the car in toward the close-hanging trees on the left until Walt dragged it back on course with a quick twist of the wheel.

Christ, Walt thought. The shit a guy'd go through for his woman.

The thing of it was, Walt knew that Beth didn't want to get away from him. That was just her Lesbian friends talking. Women's rights. Jesus. All they were was a bunch of dykes who couldn't get it on with a man if they wanted to. Not the way they looked. Oh, they had some hot little numbers, sure. Dumb little sluts like Beth who got sucked into their game. But when you stripped all the good-looking babes away, all you had was a bunch of ugly broads looking to get back at something—anything!—for the bum deal the world had laid on them. Dog faces and bodies like men.

A good-looking woman needed a good-looking man. Like Beth needed him. Without him she was nothing. No surprise there. So she needed a few smacks to keep her in line. It wasn't like he'd really hurt her or anything.

A menace to society.

That's what her hotshot lawyer had called him. Not just a danger to Beth but a fucking menace to society. "Would you give me a break?" he'd told the court. He didn't hit the streets beating on women. He just wanted to keep his own wife in line. That was all. No big deal. To have and to hold. Goddamned vows meant something to him.

Ted's van loomed up and he pulled in beside it. The lake looked nice behind the cottage. Waters calm. Sun going down behind the trees across it. There were lights already on next door. A nice shiny Volvo wagon parked in close to the building. In front of him, Charlie Thornton's cottage was dark.

He killed the engine. Dropping the keys into his shirt pocket, he hefted the case of twenty-four he'd picked up at Brewer's Retail before leaving town. Molsen's Ex—a good Canadian brew. Suit you, Ted?

The sound of the car door closing was loud in the quiet. Ted was probably sleeping, the lazy fuck. With the case of beer under his arm, Walt went up to the door and tried the knob. It turned easily. There was a funny smell in the air inside the cottage, but it was too dark to see much. He felt around by the side of the door until he found a light switch and flicked it on.

It seemed as though the ground gave a little jolt underfoot. Walt swayed against the doorjamb and stared at what lay on the floor against the far wall of the cottage. His mouth hung open, and a numb feeling went through his body. He started to get the shakes and put the case of beer down on the floor before he dropped it.

"J-jesus Ker-ist," he breathed.

He took a slow step forward. The corpse lay sprawled, looking like someone had taken a blowtorch to it. Staring at it gave Walt a sick feeling.

Ted. What was left of him.

Walt looked around quickly. Holding his hands up to his nose and breathing shallowly through his mouth, he went to try the door to the back bedroom. The knob was locked, the key still in the lock. He turned the key, then swung the door open, sure of what he was going to find.

Beth lying there dead. His little Beth, fucked over by some maniac.

But the room was empty.

As he backed away from the door he remembered something he'd heard on the radio driving up to the cottage. Dead people. On Elgin Street. Popping in out of nowhere, all burned up like someone had doused them with gasoline and then flicked their Bic at them.

His gaze went to Ted's corpse.

Burned up.

Get the fuck out of here, he told himself.

But Beth. Maybe she—

Fuck Beth.

What about "till death do us part," huh?

He continued to back out of the cottage. He wanted to call Beth's name, but his throat was too constricted to let out more than a croak. As he reached the front door he realized that he couldn't go. Not without checking out the rest of the place. If Beth was lying somewhere, hurting . . . She'd need him.

"To have and to hold. In sickness and in health."

He started for the other bedroom, and then he heard it. Something like moaning and a weird kind of music all mixed up together. Some kind of hippie shit like you heard from those Hairy Krishner guys, who were usually bald, so why the fuck did they call themselves Hairy. . . .

The sound got louder. It rasped up his spine like nails on glass.

"B-Beth . . . ?" he called.

He took another step and then—

Flicker.

The cottage changed. It had already smelled bad from Ted's corpse, lying there waiting for the maggots to feed. Now it was like standing in the city dump. A raw sewage smell. Everything was mildewed and moldy. The paneling hanging from the walls in strips. The lights were off, shadows growing long. Furniture looked like someone'd driven a sixteen-wheeler over it.

The music grew louder, and he could hear a buzzing sound under it. Like flies. Hundreds of flies. Whining in his head.

He shook his head suddenly, trying to dislodge the sounds.

Flicker.

The lights came back on. There was Ted, lying against the wall. Nothing broken up. Everything in place. Except the music was still there. And the buzzing.

"Fuck this," Walt said, and got out of there fast.

He was in the Chevy, the engine started, the car turned around and heading back down the narrow road in a blur that seemed all part of one unbroken motion. The car shook as he hit the potholes too fast. He had to fight the wheel to keep control.

What kind of a guy leaves his wife behind at a time like this? a part of him asked.

A sane guy, he told that voice. Now get the fuck out of my head.

Except he didn't feel sane. Not wheeling down this road at this speed. He lost his muffler at the next big pothole. It came off with a grinding shriek of tearing metal. When he reached the highway, he put the gas pedal to the floor. The drone of the engine with the muffler gone sounded too much like the buzz he'd heard at the cottage. Only amplified.

And following him.

What was left of Ted rose up in his mind's eye.

He glanced in the rearview mirror and thought he saw something pale floating above the highway behind him.

Following him.

He kept the pedal to the floor, knuckles whitening as he clenched the steering wheel in an ever-tightening grip. The pale shape he could see in the rearview mirror kept pace.

Still following him.

## 7

IT WAS AN odd feeling for Ned, lying on a cot in the interrogation room, knowing the brass was out there looking in at him through the two-way mirror as he tried to fall asleep. Alone with Ernie but with the attention of those watching eyes upon them. The weight of the shotgun was heavy on his chest. He had one hand on the wooden grip, the other on its cold metal barrel. He could feel the press of that other place against his eyelids every time he closed his eyes. The dead city, leaning up against his mind. It felt more real than the intent gazes he knew were invisibly fixed on them through the two-way mirror.

What were they going to find when they crossed over?

His grip tightened on the shotgun. The pair of sleeping pills he'd taken soothed his jangled nerves. The exhaustion he'd been holding at bay came riding up through his body.

"You think we'll both show up in the same place?" Ernie asked quietly from the cot beside him.

Ned turned his head so that he could look at his partner. "Yeah."

"What if we don't? We're not going to both fall asleep at the same time."

"Whoever gets there first," Ned said, "doesn't do a thing. He just waits for the other guy to show up."

"And if nothing happens?"

"Then we let Bohay call in the shrinks for us."

Ned turned his head again so that he could stare up at the ceiling. The ceiling tiles were perforated with hundreds of holes. He could remember being bored in high school and counting the dots on the same kinds of tiles there. You worked out how many there were on one tile. Multiplied it by the number of tiles in the classroom. Multiplied that times the rooms in the school. Figured in the hallways, the library, the gym, the offices . . .

He could feel himself drifting away.

Ernie's breathing was slow and regular beside him. He shouldn't have let Ernie come. He had a wife. A kid. Yeah, Ned thought. And they'd both caught the creeps from the virus that was touching Ernie. The virus that had touched everybody who was involved with the Baker case. Spreading like a cancer.

This thing had to be stopped now. Before it got out of hand.

He laughed silently. Out of hand? What the hell did you call what was going down now? But then he thought about this thing spreading. Ottawa first. Across the country, maybe. Goddamn world already felt like it was going down the tubes. It didn't need this kind of shit to give it that final push over the edge.

He could remember the way everyone had backed away from the pair of them when they'd come into the briefing room. It wasn't a physical withdrawal so much as a repugnance that lay there, plain in their eyes. He'd been feeling it all day, from everyone. Except from Anna. But then she'd caught the virus too.

Virus. Whatever the fuck it was.

Ernie's breathing had evened out. Stop thinking, Ned told himself, or you're never going to cross over. He went back to counting the dots in the ceiling tiles, eyelids fluttering. Getting heavy. Drooping. He realized that he couldn't hear Ernie's breathing anymore, but then he was drifting off himself.

Crossing over.

He wondered if he'd ever feel comfortable going to sleep again.

Get through this first, he told himself.

A rush of images flickered through his mind, flipping past like the faces of playing cards manipulated by a gambler's hands. Images of corpses. Ravaged by fire. All the dead. The last card was the joker. Untouched by fire. It had his own face under the cap and bells. Then, like the pinpoint of fire that comes from the sun channeled through a magnifying glass onto paper, the face started to burn.

Get through this first, he repeated.

Then sleep finally claimed him.

# 8

"JESUS CHRIST," Chief Gauthier said softly on the other side of the two-way mirror.

The bodies of the two detectives had just faded away, as though erased by the hand of an invisible artist. There, then gone. Not even the cots remained.

"I didn't see that," Deputy Chief Bohay said beside him. Sweat stood out on his brow. "It's just not possible."

Gauthier nodded to one of the detectives standing with them. The man left their vantage point to enter the room. He walked through the space that had been occupied by the cots, moving slowly, brushing his hands back and forth through the air. He looked up at the window and shook his head.

"I want somebody watching this room—around the clock," Gauthier said.

"It's got to be some kind of a trick," Bohay said.

"If it's a trick," Gauthier said, "then it's a very effective one. Gentlemen, we have work to do."

"The press . . . ?" someone began.

"Are just going to have to wait. We have two men in a critical situation. I want weapons issued to every officer at the station. Those men are going to need backup."

"We're sending people . . . after them?" Bohay asked, plainly unable to accept what his own eyes had shown him.

"If possible," Gauthier replied.

He was thinking about what Detective Meehan had said in the briefing. About the ability to cross over spreading like a virus. How those initially involved in the investigation were more susceptible to the virus.

"Let's see if we can get some volunteers," he added.

Without waiting for a reply he set off for the gym, where all the rest of those connected with the case were being kept together in hopes of protecting them against whatever it was that was decimating their ranks.

"This is nuts," Bohay muttered as he followed.

Gauthier nodded in agreement and simply kept on walking. He agreed wholeheartedly with Bohay, but he didn't see that they had any other choice. Politics be damned. He'd rather be lambasted as a fool for setting into motion such unorthodox procedures than lose any more men.

"Is there anyone already involved in the case who's also a member of the Tactical Squad?" he asked Bohay, who hurried to catch up when the Chief spoke.

## 9

NED'S PARTNER WAS standing by the door, looking out into the hall, when Ned opened his eyes. Grier started when Ned called out softly to him.

"Jesus," Grier said, turning from the door. The shotgun had swung around to cover Ned. Grier lowered its muzzle point down to the floor. "You scared the shit out of me."

"Been here long?"

"A couple of minutes."

Ned sat up slowly, cradling his own shotgun. No matter how much he'd been expecting it, it was still a shock to be back here again. Really here. With his partner.

The room stank. Paint was peeling from the walls. The carpeting underfoot was moldy. There was trash lying around, graffiti spray-painted on the walls. In other places it had been applied with excrement, which had dried to a dull brown. A man sucking on a revolver. A woman with a cobra coming out of her vagina. She held a bloody heart in her hand. EAT YOUR GUN, it said below the first. BE MY VALENTINE, read the other. Another showed two men, one getting bumfucked by the other. PARTNERS DO IT BEST, it read under that one.

"Is this place real?" Grier asked as Ned got to his feet.

"What do you mean?"

Grier shrugged uncomfortably. "I can't help thinking I'm just really fucked up," he said. "If I'm dreaming . . . how do I know I'm not just dreaming that you're here with me?"

"People die here," Ned said, "then their bodies get dumped back in the world that they came from. How much more real than that can you get?"

"I guess. What do we do now? We proved our point, right?"

Ned thought of the brass standing behind the two-way mirror, watching the two of them disappear. They'd believe him now.

"So do we go back now?" Grier asked.

"How do we wake up?"

"How do we . . . ? Jesus. You mean, we're stuck here until . . . *when,* Ned?"

"Take it easy, Ernie. We're here. We proved our point. So we've got to wait around awhile. We might as well check things out."

He wasn't feeling nearly as calm as the tone of his voice made him sound, but the matter-of-fact setting-forth of the situation did its job. He could see Ernie relaxing, shifting from just being fucked up to being a cop again. The change in his partner helped Ned bring his own fears under control.

"Where do you want to—"

Ned held up a hand, stopping Grier in mid-sentence. Grier cocked his head, listening, then he heard it too. Someone out in the hallway. Trying to be quiet. Moving very carefully.

"Showtime," Ned whispered.

The two men moved toward the doorway, shotguns leveled, fingers taking up the slack on their triggers.

## 10

DETECTIVE STAN LYNCH had it all figured out.

He sat in the General Assignment squad room, looking at Jack Keller's little sister. She was nodding where she sat, all drawn in on herself. Part of him was just enjoying the sight of her—even at a time like this—though he felt bad for what she was going through. Still, Meehan was a lucky stiff to have hooked up with her. But another part of him was getting some weird feelings from her. She was a looker, all right, but there was something kind of creepy about her at the same time.

He looked away and went back to chewing on the problem at hand.

He figured it for a scam.

Ottawa, being the nation's capital, was an embassy city. It had representatives from most countries in it—including most of the wacked-out places. He wouldn't put it past one of them to be running a number. Bunch of terrorists wiping out people, making it look spooky. He hadn't quite figured out how they were doing it, but it was the only thing that made sense.

You hit a city where it hurt. Take out the guys that kept it in line and all you had left were civilians and assholes. With the force all tied up, trying to get a handle on what was going down, they'd just move into the next phase. Scare people enough and even a quiet place like Ottawa could explode. Riots and violence. Some jerk-ass group taking credit for it. Making demands.

Christ, when you came right down to it, it didn't even have to be some backwater Third World country running the scam. Not when you had Uncle Sam right next door. The President had just been in town for a visit and they'd been kept busy with the security, but they'd been fielding a lot of complaints too. Civilians getting hassled by U.S. Secret Service agents in the fucking hotel—that kind of thing. Guys thought they owned the frigging world. With the trade talks floundering and ill will building up between their governments, who knew just what the President's boys might try to pull off.

A little warning, like.

Don't fuck with us, Canada. We're big-time.

Could be, he thought. He read about that kind of thing in Ludlum's books and the like. No way it was all bullshit. And when you thought of Nixon and Iranscam, you had to know that you couldn't trust any of those—

"They're gone!"

Lynch blinked, looking up to see Any Coe standing in the doorway.

Coe snapped his fingers. "Just like that. Ernie first, then Ned."

"You're shitting us," said one of the other detectives in the squad room.

He had to be shitting them, Lynch thought. There was no way that . . .

His gaze had drifted over to the corner where Keller's sister was sitting, and his jaw went slack. The corner was empty. Even the frigging chair was gone. He looked around the room, expecting to see her standing somewhere else, maybe having dragged the chair over to another part of the room, but she was definitely gone.

"Keller's sister," he said hoarsely. "Did . . . did anyone see her leave?"

He pointed to the corner where she'd been sitting. One by one the other detectives looked over.

"She never left the room," one of them said. "She never *walked* out of the room. . . ."

Lynch felt a sick feeling start up in his stomach. "Then how the hell . . . ?"

"I'd better tell the chief," Coe said.

He turned and sprinted down the hall. Behind him, the detectives shifted uncomfortably in the squad room, looking at each other, no one quite making eye contact. There was only one thought in their minds right then.

Which one of them was next?

## 11

BETH WAS ONLY one of a host, riding in the creature's body, but she was the one who recognized her ex-husband.

After the fire cleansed Ted Rimmer, the creature had returned to sail the dead plains, gliding like a manta ray through the thick, smog-laden air, coasting on a wind that carried a metallic tang in its teeth as it nipped the brittle vegetation and woke swirling dust devils in their wake. Beth rode with it, the wasteland unwinding below them.

There was peace to be found in the empty reaches, a peace that could only be found in its desolation. Music followed the creature—

(Beth)

—in its flight. The agony of the synthesized voices lent an edge to its—

(her)

—indolent mood, giving it a bright blade of strength. A promise of peace.

The death left behind in Charlie Thornton's cottage lay forgotten under the sweep of sound, body moving with the wind, hair streaming behind. It was only Walt Hawkins's arrival at the cottage that shook the creature—

(Beth)

—from its—

(her)

—peaceful mood.

Movement ceased. The creature drifted to the ground, sand squeezing up between its toes, dry plants crushed underfoot. The plains faded and they were back in the ruined cabin, peering through the thin membrane that separated the world they were in from the one Beth had left behind when she'd fallen asleep. A part of, apart from, the creature, Beth watched through its eyes as Walt came in through the cottage door.

She was only dimly aware that a murder had been committed, that she had been a party to Ted Rimmer's death. She remembered only that he'd been cleansed. In her mind it was akin to taking a shower and washing the day's dirt from the pores of one's skin. When she saw the corpse lying where it had fallen, uncertainty stole up through the calm layers that the creature and the music had erected inside her to block her from her memories of the past. Of the pain. The hurting.

The creature plucked at the membrane separating the worlds, long nails tearing at its invisible fabric, reaching for Walt. In the creature's mind Beth saw what it meant to do with him. He was to be cleansed. As the other man had been. The furnace breath burning away his skin, flesh bubbling, charring . . .

Beth gagged.

She drew back from her joining with the creature, fighting its influence on her. As Walt fled the cottage, the creature sent images cascading through Beth's mind.

It let her know that if they let Walt live, all Beth would ever know was the pain he had waiting for her.

It filled her with an image of—

(that dark place filled with pain)

—Walt dragging her down the stairs, throwing her on the mattress he kept there, drawing the leather belt from its loops in his jeans.

"No," she said.

She would know pain forever, the fury let her know. She would always be in—

(that dark place)

—there.

And then they were no longer joined.

A woman, beautiful as an angel, held Beth. All around them was the ruin and stink of the cottage. The angel smelled of apple blossoms and lilacs. Beth leaned closer to her, resting her head on the angel's ample bosom. She closed her eyes to hide the ruin surrounding them. She burrowed her face in the angel's hair, breathed in deeply the sweet scents.

*Stay with us, little sister,* a voice said, riding the music.

Then there was a chorus of voices speaking all at once.

*Stay with us . . . stay with us. . . .*

Beth looked up into the angel's eyes, and in her mind's eye she could see the speakers. Bruised and battered women. Boys and girls wearing the scars of their abuse. Infants not even out of their cradles.

Victims.

*Stay with us. . . .*

All of them victims.

*Stay with us. . . .*

She could stay with them and know peace or return to—

(that dark place)

—a world that gave her only pain.

"What . . . what is it that we become?" she asked.

*Strong,* came the answer, not in words, but she understood all the same. In control. Free from hurt. Strangers to pain.

"I . . ."

The angel drew her close. The voices murmured and caressed her with their sound. They were the same voices that made the unearthly music, but the torment was drained from their tones.

"I don't want to be hurt anymore," Beth whispered.

And then she was back, a part of the host once more, riding in the angel's body as it rose to follow her fleeing ex-husband. They rode the winds of the dead lands, flickering between the worlds where the membrane was thinnest.

Following him.

And she was no longer alone.

Strong now. In this company. Free from pain.

No one would ever trouble her again, she was promised as the winds bore them on. Her time had finally come. . . .

## 12

ANNA WASN'T EVEN aware of falling asleep. It wasn't until she looked up to find herself back in the ruined squad room, the minutes passing by without the flicker that would return her to the waking world, that she realized what had happened.

Just stay here, she told herself. Don't move. You'll wake up soon enough.

But the sense of confinement pressed in close around her. The graffitied walls were too close. The stink was too strong. A foul wind blew in from the hallway, fluttering a sheaf of papers against her feet. Some were flat, others loosely crumpled into unevenly sized balls. There was something familiar about the handwriting on them, so she leaned over to pick one up.

Lined three-holed foolscap, the holes ripped as though it had been torn from a binder. A phrase of three words was repeated over and over again, covering the surface of the paper.

. . . *stop hurting me* . . . *stop hurting me* . . .

It was Beth's handwriting.

Anna bent down and picked up more of the sheets. They were all the same. The same phrase covering each sheet. Thousands of times. Rising slowly from the chair, Anna walked over to the door and peered down the hall. The paper rustled underfoot. She wanted to call Beth's name, but something held her back. She had a sense of being watched, that there was danger near. A warning prickle at the back of her neck.

She wiped her damp palms on her skirt and retreated back into the room. Wherever she stepped, paper crinkled underfoot. There was far more of it on the floor than there had been only moments ago. It seemed to be growing like drifts of snow, only each big flake was exactly the same. Lined paper. Torn from a binder. Drifting around her feet. The same words covering each sheet.

*. . . stop hurting me . . .*

Anna thought of Beth—God, was it just this morning?—and what she'd been saying.

"You don't know what it's like being me. Or somebody like me. Everybody's always hitting on me, using me."

And she didn't know, did she? Not *really.* How could she?

*. . . stop hurting me . . .*

But in Beth's dream . . . Here. In this place.

"I was the one in control," she'd said. "I felt like nobody could hurt me—nobody could even touch me."

And in her own dream. She'd seen Beth come floating out from beside their house, drifting down the street, then leading them both into that wasteland. That Beth had been strong. In control.

The paper was up to her ankles now, loosely crumpled balls of foolscap. She couldn't move without setting up a teeth-gritting sound as the stiff edges rubbed against each other. Where was it all coming from? She uncurled a couple more of them, but the message was still the same. She let them fall from her hand.

What did it matter, anyway? What did anything matter? With Jack dead—

She turned at a sudden sound. Paper rustled, then slowly fell still as she stood without moving, looking into a corner of the room. The sound was repeated there. A rustling. Under the growing drifts of paper. Anna had a sudden flash of rats coming for her, invisible under the drifts, the only clue to their presence being the sound they made as they moved through the ever-increasing sea of paper.

She grabbed a thick handful of sheets that weren't crumpled and, using them as a makeshift broom, began to sweep away the paper in the direction of the corner from which the sound was coming. She thought she heard a faint voice as she worked her way closer. A voice calling her name.

Goose bumps raced up her arms. She hesitated just a few feet away from the source of the sound.

"Ah-nuh . . ."

Definitely her name. Muffled by the paper. The sound of the faint voice was familiar in a way that was too horrible to contemplate.

"Ah-nuh . . ."

I can't move, she thought. I can't go on.

But her hand moved of its own volition, sweeping away paper, parting the sea of crumpled sheets, drawing her on toward the source of that faint voice. A last sweep and then she could see what it was. A face rising from the floor.

It looked like one of the fabric-mâché masks that hung in her workroom—as though someone had stolen one and laid it here on the floor. Except this face grew right out of the carpet. The skin of the brow, the cheeks, and the chin flowed seamlessly into the rotting fabric. The flesh was a dead white, almost translucent. The eyes were cloudy but they still focused on her. The lips moved, still calling her name.

"Anna."

Clearly now. No longer muffled.

"You shouldn't be here, Anna."

All the strength left her, and she fell back onto her haunches, hands limp on her lap as she stared at the thing. Her head whined with a sudden headache. Her stomach roiled sourly. Slowly she reached out a trembling hand to touch one cold cheek.

"J-Jack . . . ?" she said in a low, shaky voice. "Is . . . is that you?"

"There're only two kinds of people in this place," the face with Jack's features said, echoing the words of the old bum Jack had run into himself, just before he died. "Those that're dreaming and those that're dead. I'm going on, Anna. I can feel the pull of that other place, but I knew you were coming. When I saw Cathy, I knew you and Beth would be coming, so I stayed to warn you. Get out of here, Anna."

"You . . . you're dead," Anna said.

"When you step into this place," the face continued, ignoring her, "it doesn't matter whether you're guilty or not. The goddamned fury burns you all the same."

"Jack—"

"There's only one kind of time here, you see. A killing time. That Baker guy—he opened up some kind of a door to this place with what he was doing. This is where the victims wait to get even, Anna, and they don't give a shit whether you were one of the ones dumping on them or not. You step in here and all they want to do is burn you."

Tears were streaming down Anna's cheeks. "Oh, God, Jack. . . ."

"The thing is, you bring your own pain in here with you, and it changes things too. Calls up your private demons. Makes it personal. But things don't work the same here as they do in our own world. Here it's the weak that're strong. It's their place to get back at everything that ever hurt them, Anna."

"Jack, you never hurt any—"

"Everybody's done some shitty stuff, Anna. Everybody's carrying a bit of guilt. You, me—Christ, even the victims. So you've got to get out of here."

"I don't know how."

"You got to close that door that Baker opened or it's just going to keep on getting worse."

"Jack. I—"

"I can't hang on any longer, Sis. Just get out of here."

"Don't leave me, Jack!"

The face looked as though it were deflating, disappearing back into the rug. Anna lunged forward. She put a hand on either side of its cheeks, her lips against its cold lips. Something moved against her skin. Wriggled. She pushed herself back and saw that the oval where the face had been was now a writhing mass of white maggots.

A scream started up her throat but drowned in vomit. She emptied the contents of her stomach, wiping desperately at her mouth. Stumbling to her feet, she bolted for the door. The crumpled paper was now up to her knees in places.

She burst out into the hallway and turned to her left. Manlike shadows appeared suddenly from another doorway. There was a gleam of metal in the hands of the foremost. A shotgun. The scream that finally loosed itself from Anna's throat was drowned in the booming thunder of the weapon's discharge in the narrow confines of the hall.

## 13

THE TABLOIDS that Walt picked up every week at the supermarket were full of stories not so different from what Walt, himself, was experiencing right now. Strange deaths. Lights in the sky. UFOs. Weird cults. Animal mutilations. Babies giving birth to kids of their own.

Weird shit.

The glowing shape was still following him as he reached the city limits. He looked away from the rear-view mirror. He didn't need no frigging close encounter, thanks all the same. The old Chevy shuddered under him. Tires humming on the asphalt. Sounding like a tank with the muffler gone.

Walt kept remembering what was left of Ted—the burned shape lying against the wall, charred skull grinning up at him from the ruin of its body. It didn't take a whole lot of thought to put two and two together. Whatever was chasing him was the same thing that had stolen Beth and done in Ted. And now it wanted him.

The dusky streets outside the Chevy kept flickering in his vision. Half the time he was fighting light traffic, cutting in from lane to lane, just trying to put distance behind him. Streetlights and the glowing windows of the houses and fast-food outlets whipping past. Then everything would go dark except for the Chevy's headlights, and it was like he was barreling through a ghost town. Swerving around dead cars and mounds of rubble. Nobody out except for him and whatever the hell it was that was following him.

Ever since he'd discovered Ted's body, the weirdness didn't really surprise him. Whole fucking world was going down the tubes—no question about it.

Or maybe he was just losing it.

A glance in the rearview mirror showed him that the bobbing light was still on his tail. Floating there above the streets, keeping pace.

What the fuck do you want with me?

But all he had to do was think of Ted again, and there was no question as to what it wanted. Knowing what it was going to do when it caught up with him didn't explain dick-all, but right now Walt wasn't about to stop and ask twenty questions.

Flicker.

The dead city was back. The parking lot of Billings Bridge Shopping Centre on his right went black as the lights winked out. He swerved around a stalled delivery truck in the right lane, wheels screaming on the pavement as he went around it. His headlights picked out a shopping cart in the middle of the left lane. It came up too suddenly to avoid. The left front end of the Chevy gave it a whack as he went by, sending it onto the grass verge where it rolled over three times before it came to a halt. The impact took out the left headlight. He gripped the wheel tighter and kept his foot on the gas.

Bank Street came up then. He made a decision and tromped on the brake. The car skidded sideways into the intersection. When he booted the gas again, it shot up Bank, heading across the bridge over the Rideau River toward downtown.

Where'm I going? he thought suddenly.

He looked in the rearview mirror. The light behind him was still on his ass, hanging steady.

He'd go someplace safe, he'd thought when he fled the cottage. Where there were lots of people. But the whole frigging city seemed to be in the middle of a blackout. Nothing looked right. His lone headlight continued to pick out dead cars and buses, buildings with holes gaping in their walls, rubble pooling under them. The air coming in from the Chevy's vents had a bitter, metallic sting to it.

He caught a billboard as it flashed by. It read, NOWHERE LEFT TO GO, and there was an old beat-up Chevy under the letters, driving down a deserted street. What the—

As he turned to look back at it an intersection loomed up, a stalled car right in the middle of it. He hit the brakes, swerving around it. The Chevy started to slide across the pavement. It scraped against the other car with a whine of screeching metal. He fought the wheel, straightening the tires until he was aiming north again.

His whole body shook as he continued up Bank, and it was all he could do to keep going.

Going where?

It was still on his tail. The goddamned UFO, or whatever the hell it was. The whole frigging city was gone. Ted was dead. Probably Beth too. And the goddamned Martians were after his ass now. Where the hell was a cop when you needed one?

He was past Gladstone Avenue now, still heading north, the nose of the Chevy pointed straight at Parliament Hill. Where the *hell* was he going to go? Then, a block past Gladstone, the car just gave out. The one headlight continued to pierce the gloom, but the engine sputtered, then died. The car continued to coast for another block, finally coming to a halt just past the corner of Waverly and Bank, right in front of Arthur's Comics and Used Records Store.

He tried the ignition, then saw the gas indicator sitting on empty. Jesus. He turned and looked out the back window. The frigging Martians were coming up fast.

He jumped out of the car and started to run up the block, but the sidewalk in front of Arthur's was strewn with moldering comic books. He slid and fell, scrambled to his feet. He could see what the glowing shape was now. Some kind of flying woman. Blond hair streaming behind her. Thin nightgown kind of a thing not doing a whole hell of a lot to hide a body that just wouldn't stop.

He backed away until he was up against the storefront of Randall Paints, two stores up from Arthur's. The plate-glass windows were gone, so he could step over the ledge and get inside. Here the stink of paint drowned out the metallic smell outside. He crept toward the rear of the store, his gaze locked on the front. When the woman came floating in through the window, he ducked around behind a broken counter.

His heart drummed a wild staccato in his chest. He had to grip his knees to stop his hands from shaking. It didn't do much good. He peered about in the gloom behind the counter and found a length of wood with some nails sticking out one end.

Okay, he thought. Fuck this shit.

He stood up from behind the counter, his makeshift

club raised over his shoulder. The woman was in the middle of the store, just floating in the air. The glow that came from her laid a soft white light throughout the room. He could see her face now. She had the perfect, airbrushed features of one of those *Playboy* centerfolds, with a body to match.

"Listen, lady," he began. "I don't know what you . . ."

His voice trailed off as the face began to change. Her lower jaw dropped, the mouth widening. The smooth, pale flesh took on a mummified look. Incisors sprouted from under her upper lips. He could see things wriggling in the back of her throat. The fingernails of each hand merged with the fingers to become claws. The hands lifted, one claw beckoning to him.

Walt took a step back, shaking the length of wood menacingly.

"You just . . . you just keep back. . . ."

He was losing it totally, he realized. This kind of thing couldn't possibly exist. The way the city was, everything was just too insane. He could feel heat building up in the room. He kept the length of wood between them as he continued to back up.

"I . . . I mean it. . . ."

"Walter."

The voice was oddly familiar. He stared at the creature, and suddenly he could see something of his ex-wife in those hellish features.

"B-Beth . . . ?"

"To have and to hold," the fury said. "For better or for worse . . . isn't that what you always told me, Walter?"

He shook his head, the length of wood vibrating in

his trembling hands. He was up against the back wall of the store now, with no place left to go.

Losing it.

Lost it.

"Nuh . . . nuh . . ."

"To have and to hold. Don't you want to hold me, Walter?"

"Nuh . . ."

"Don't you want to have me anymore?"

The jaws opened wide and something died in Walt when he saw the wriggling mass of snake heads that came lifting out of the back of the creature's throat.

The creature floated closer.

Walt heard a woman scream, then realized that it was his own voice he was hearing, his own scream ripping his throat raw as the creature breathed fire on him. All around the store, the paint burned with him. The creature's final words buzzed in his head, whining above the pain.

"To have and to hold, Walter . . ."

## 14

THERE WAS a gloomy cast to the hallway outside the interrogation room, making it too dark for either Ned or his partner to really make out what it was that was coming out of the squad room a few doors down. Both men were on edge, expecting anything. Expecting the worst. But as Grier began to fire, Ned recognized Anna in time to throw himself against his partner.

The shotgun discharged into the wall, blowing a hole

three feet wide into the plaster. Pellets ricocheted down the hall. Anna's wail merged with the blast of the shotgun, hanging on through its booming echoes.

"Are you nuts?" Ned yelled, pushing past Grier.

"Jesus, Ned. I never even thought . . ."

But Ned wasn't listening. He reached Anna and caught her where she stood swaying against the doorjamb, pulling her close with his one free arm.

Grier came up behind him. "Ned, I . . ."

"Take it easy," Ned was whispering into Anna's ear. "Everything's going to be just fine." He turned to look over his shoulder at his partner.

"Ned . . ."

"It's okay, Ernie. Nobody got hurt."

"Yeah, but . . ." Grier wiped the sweat from his brow with a sleeve, his shotgun hanging loose in his other hand, muzzle pointed to the floor. "I'm so goddamned wired. . . ."

"The whole situation's fucked, partner."

"That's no excuse. Christ, I could've killed her."

Ned held Anna closer. Just the thought of her being hurt gave him a sick feeling. First Jack and now . . .

"The . . . the face . . . ," Anna mumbled against his shoulder. "Jack's face in the floor . . ."

Ned and Grier exchanged glances.

"I'll check it out," Grier said.

He moved around the pair into the doorway and stared at the ocean of paper that covered the squadroom floor. It wasn't too bad around the door, but just a few steps in it came up to mid-thigh on him.

"Look at this," he said quietly to his partner. "There could be anything under this shit," he added as Ned looked into the room.

"What happened?" Ned asked Anna.

She took a shaky breath and stepped away from him to lean against the wall.

"I . . . I fell asleep," she said. "In the squad room. And then . . ." She rubbed at her face. "Then I was here with all that paper . . . and it just kept getting deeper."

Grier bent down to pick up a sheet. He held it up so that Ned could see it as well. The foolscap was covered with writing, the same phrase repeated over and over again.

. . . *stop hurting me* . . .

"It . . . it's Beth's handwriting," Anna said.

"You said something about Jack—about his face being . . . in the floor?"

Anna nodded dully and pointed to one corner of the room. "You're going to think I'm crazy."

"After crossing over to this place?" Ned said. "Not a chance."

Anna wrapped her arms around herself and took another long breath, let it out slowly. She was starting to get over whatever had spooked her, Ned saw. The scare was still sitting there in her eyes, giving her the shakes, but she was pulling through. She was tough. Just like her brother.

"Jack was in there," she said. "His face . . . it was just coming out of the carpet. Like it was growing there. Nothing but his face."

Ned wanted to hold her again but held back. She had to get this out first, on her own. Her fingers were going white where they gripped her arms, but otherwise she was still holding up.

"He . . . he talked to me, Ned. Said he was waiting here for me to warn me. He told me to get out of here."

She went on and related what the face in the carpet

had told her. Her voice grew firmer the longer she spoke. When she was done, she gave them a look that Ned knew was just begging for them to say, "It's okay. It's just a dream. Nothing's real here."

But they couldn't do it.

People died here.

Died for real.

"I guess we've got two choices," Ned said finally. "We stay here and wait to wake up, or we go looking for whatever it is that's running this show."

Anna straightened up from the wall. "I'm not waiting here," she said.

Grier nodded in agreement.

Ned didn't even think of protesting Anna's decision. There was no way he wanted to leave her alone in this place. Even if they just waited here, who was to say which of them would wake up first? It could happen to any of them. He and Ernie might just wake up, end up abandoning Anna here. But it was Anna's brother who'd died here. She deserved a shot at whoever it was that had taken Jack down.

"Do you know how to use this?" he asked, holding out his revolver.

Anna nodded, but she wouldn't take the weapon.

"The rules are all different here," Ned said. "We can't play it the same way we would in our own world."

Anna took the sheet of foolscap that Grier was still holding and showed it to Ned.

*. . . stop hurting me . . .*

"Remember what Jack said? This is where the victims wait to get even."

"We're victims too."

Anna shook her head. "If we go out, just looking to get even, then we're no better than the people who created this place. Read what it says here, Ned. 'Stop hurting me.' That's a plea for help—not an attack."

"People are *dying* here," Grier said. "People like your brother, who never hurt anybody."

"He's right, Anna," Ned added.

"Jack said that the weak were strong here," Anna said. "Do you understand what that means? Force won't work."

Her gaze left his face to look at his partner. Her hands rose to rub her face again. The familiar gesture awakened an ache in Ned. It was still so hard to imagine that Jack was gone.

Anna folded the foolscap she was holding and put it in a pocket of her skirt.

"We should be thinking of helping whoever we find here," she said.

"Even when they killed your brother?" Grier asked.

Anna swallowed thickly, then nodded. "Even . . . even then," she said quietly.

"So we just wait for them to come and take us down too?" Grier looked from her to his partner.

"No," Anna said. "We go looking for them."

"And when we find them?"

When Anna didn't answer, Ned took over. "Let's find them first," he said.

He wasn't sure he agreed with Anna's forgive-and-help ideas—not right now, not here in this place—but he was at least willing to wait and see what they found. He led the way out of the building.

The elevators were dead, so they took the stairs down to the main lobby. Refuse lay underfoot, so thick in places that they had to skirt it. Outside, the smoggy skies had darkened into night. The air still held its metallic sting, broken by occasional wafts of rotting smells driven toward them by the wind.

The streets appeared deserted, though each of them had the sensation of being watched. There seemed to be motion in the glassless windows of the buildings around them. Pale faces ducking out of view. Feral bodies moving across doorways, disappearing from sight when one of them looked in their direction.

"Any ideas where we start?" Grier asked.

Ned and Anna both looked northeast. There was a dull glow in the sky there, enough to set off the plumes of smoke that spiraled above it. The smoke was thick and black, visible even against the dark night skies. A gust of foul wind from that direction brought the smell of the fire to them.

"Looks like someone's left us a calling card," Ned said.

Each of them thought of the burned corpses that had appeared in their own world.

"Pick it up and burn," Grier muttered.

"Do we need to take a vote?" Ned asked.

Anna glanced at him. "Do we have another option?"

Ned shook his head. Hefting their weapons, the two men set off in the direction of the fire with Anna walking in between them.

## 15

THEY WATCHED him burn.

Inside the creature, the host held to a judgmental silence. Beth could feel their presence surrounding her—

no longer warm, no longer comforting. They were too intent on the sentence brought down upon the tormentor of one of their own to offer solace. Strength was still present. Sharp, bright as silver. The agonized voices cried their bitter music. Their peace had shattered, and they watched Walt Hawkins burn through the creature's bleak eyes, following the simple logic of its thoughts.

He was a bug.

They had stepped on him.

He was a tormentor.

They had turned his torments back upon him.

He was evil.

They had cleansed him of that evil.

The fire rose crackling and pure around the creature, feeding on more than its victim. Fumes ignited and burned. The cans of turpentine and paint exploded from the heat, splattering their contents in flaming sheets throughout the store. The fire was a rainbow of colors. Hot. Fierce. Cleansing. Hawkins had danced his pain in its flames, skin bubbling and popping, before his charred figure was entirely consumed.

The fire had no effect on the creature.

It cut Beth to her very soul.

When Walt died, it wasn't her ex-husband she saw burning. It wasn't relief from—

(that dark place)

—his torments that the flames took from her. She saw only the painful death of another human being.

No one deserved such torment. For all the hurt he had given her, for all the pain that the world had let her experience, she couldn't have wished this on anyone.

She struggled to break the connection that joined her to the rest of the host inside the creature.

But if she left the protection of the host, she would die.

When she continued to struggle, the fury gave her a taste of what lay beyond the protection of their shared body. A momentary taste—that was all. The sheets of flame and heat drove her back as effectively as any of Walt's disciplines ever had.

"This is wrong!" she cried.

The fury was an elemental force—it had no need to explain its existence. But the other souls that shared its body with Beth replied.

*This is justice,* they said.

"It's . . . inhumane. . . ."

*He—and those like him—they taught us inhumanity. All we do is show them how well we learned the lessons they taught us.*

"It's wrong," Beth said.

Her voice lost some of its conviction as the others with which she shared the host washed her with their chorusing voices—women's voices, children's voices, babies' cries—all upholding the same argument.

"It . . . it can't be right . . . ," Beth said.

*In this place there is no wrong, no right. Only our will.*

The music whined, shrieking chords underlying the words.

*Our will,* the voices echoed.

Through the rush of the flames, sheets of heat that leapt in a solid blaze from floor to ceiling, she caught a glimpse of the dead plains. That unending vista of wasteland, rolling emptily to every horizon, spoke to her as the voices couldn't. She remembered floating above it. The peace of that flight. The escape it offered from all hurts and pain. From decisions.

*That will always be ours,* the voices told her. *Only the need for justice calls us back. We visit here—nothing more.*

Beth was too used to letting others have their way with her to fight the creature or the host for long. Instead she concentrated on the peace she'd known in that wasteland and drank it in, letting it wash away the more immediate memories of how Walt had died. Tried to forget his pain.

*We draw the guilty to this mid-ground and visit them with justice,* the voices said. *And then we return.*

Their chorusing voices soothed her.

*We always return. . . .*

The view of the wasteland was lost in the flames once more, but its memory shone bright inside her. She was barely aware of the creature lifting its head, like a hound catching a scent. The painful music returned. The tongues in the creature's throat hissed like a nest of snakes.

Part of the host, Beth knew what it sensed. More were coming. There were always more. . . .

As they glided toward the front of the burning building a skeletal hand, bones charred black, gripped its ankle. Walt's skull lifted from the floor, eye sockets empty, fleshless mouth shaping a death's-head grin.

"To have and to hold, babe," it said, its voice ringing clearly above the roar of the flames.

Through the creature's eyes Beth stared at the monstrous thing. Terror rose whining up through her nerves.

The creature shook its ankle until the bones of the hand fell apart and the skeleton collapsed back into the rubble. But that moment had been enough to shatter the druglike mood that was holding Beth. She screamed—a shrill wail of fear that went on and on, echoing into infinity.

The host shifted restlessly inside the creature, disturbed by that sound. Then Beth's voice was drawn into the unholy music that was still growing in volume. The host settled once more as the creature continued its interrupted journey toward the front of the store.

# 16

POLICE CHIEF Bernard Gauthier stood with Staff Sergeant Andy Coe and Deputy Chief John Bohay, looking into the interrogation room where three more volunteers lay on new cots that had been brought up from the quartermaster's storeroom. The volunteers wore the vests and helmets of the Tactical Squad, shotguns laid across their chests as they tried to sleep.

Gauthier looked at his watch. "It's been fifty-five minutes," he said. "Why isn't anything *happening*?"

"The men are trying, sir," Coe said. "It's just hard to get to sleep when your adrenaline's got you all wired up."

"I don't trust any of this," Bohay said. "There's something off about every one of these men." He glanced at the chief. "Can't you feel it?"

Gauthier nodded. "But I've read the files, John—just as you have. These are all good men, no matter how . . . uncomfortable they make us feel."

"Ned said something about that," Coe said, "and

I'm beginning to feel it too. People getting hostile for no good reason. Just a bad feeling whenever someone looks my way. I don't know, it's—"

"Unless you've got something constructive to offer, Sergeant," Bohay interrupted, "I suggest you keep your—"

"John!"

Bohay glared at Coe, then slowly looked at his commanding officer. "Sir?"

"Think about what Sergeant Coe has just told us—and then consider your own reaction to him."

Bohay got a sullen look on his face, but he kept quiet.

And God help me, Gauthier added to himself, I'm feeling it too. I just want to get as far as possible from Coe and the men behind the glass here. But they're all we've got. If we don't give them the support they need . . .

"Sir?"

Gauthier turned to the duty sergeant who had approached him. "What is it, Sergeant?"

"You asked to be kept informed of any unusual occurrences, sir?"

"What have you got?"

"There's a major fire out of control in a paint shop on Bank Street, between Lewis and Waverly. We've got men on the scene with the firefighters, and the initial reports are that there was no explanation for how it started."

Gauthier rubbed his temples. He thought of charred corpses appearing out of nowhere in the gun range downstairs and in the middle of Elgin Street. No question about it, it was escalating right out of control.

"Thank you, Sergeant," he said. He turned to Coe.

"Keep watch here and let me know the moment something changes."

He left without waiting for a reply. It was time to get back to the mayor again.

# FIVE

## 1

THE FIRE WASN'T far from the police station on Elgin Street. The three of them took their time approaching it, starting at shadows, at the rustle of old papers whipped by a sudden gust of wind. Rats watched them from the refuse. The night was filled with a mixture of rotting smells, a metallic tang, and smoke. There was a sound in the air that started off like the drone of insects and grew into a kind of music. Faint and vague, dark with menace, the sound of it settled inside them, making them walk closer together.

The walls of the buildings they passed were covered with graffiti. Most of it just variations on what they'd already seen. Violent. Of a sexual nature. But here and there, in paint that looked so fresh that it had to have been applied recently, was that simple phrase repeated from the foolscap in the squad room.

. . . *stop hurting me* . . .

"Why now?" Grier said suddenly as they paused near the corner of Gladstone and Bank.

They were a half mile or so from the station, just a couple of blocks down from the fire. They could see the blaze clearly now. Its glare lit up the dark column of smoke that rose from the burning building beside it.

"What makes now so different?" Grier went on. "This fucking place looks like it's been here forever. How come it took until now for everything to bust loose?"

"It ties into Baker," Ned replied. "Something he was doing—not just what he did to the girl—something more than that opened things up."

"The music," Anna said.

As they were approaching the fire it had been increasing in volume. Synthesized voices caught in a moment of agony, trapped into a music that echoed every pain, every hurt that men and women had visited upon each other. Now that they were stopped at the street corner, the music still continued to build.

Anna thought about Jack, gone forever, drawn into that web of sound, and then vomited on Elgin Street, a burned ruin. She thought about Baker and what Jack had told her had been found in that secret room in his basement. How many times had she been down in his studio—just one wall away from that hidden room? Had there been victims trapped in its darkness, begging for any kind of release from their pain, while she leaned into a mike one room away, singing backup on somebody's demo?

She shuddered and took Ned's left hand, gripping his fingers tightly.

"How're you holding up?" he asked her quietly.

"I . . . I'm okay. I was thinking. Remember the first kid Jack lost?"

Ned nodded. Jack had been hunting down a runaway, who'd later turned up as a floater in the river. It was the worst Jack had ever seen. Anna had called him and Ned had gone from bar to bar, looking for her brother until he'd finally found him drinking out his brains in a little dive out in Vanier.

"I thought he was going to lose it all the way that time," he said.

"He almost did," Anna said. "But then he realized that he had to go on. For all the ones he lost, there were going to be so many more that he still could help. If he'd quit then, they might've ended up just the same as that one."

"I remember," Ned said.

"That's what's keeping me going. Knowing that something we might do now could stop what happened to Jack from happening to anybody else."

Listening to them, Grier licked his lips nervously and looked up the street. "You really think we can make a difference?" he asked.

He wasn't about to fold on them. This was his job—weirder than fuck right now, but it was still his job. He was being paid by the city to look after its citizens, but it wasn't just money that kept him and every other cop worth his badge on the job. It was the commitment. To help. To protect. Sure, you got tired. Or fed up. Or scared. But you went ahead and did your job all the same. Because you made a difference. Not always. But enough.

The only thing that could stop Grier dead in his tracks was if that changed. If he couldn't make a difference anymore. No matter how small.

"Every time we take a stand," Ned said quietly, "we make a difference. Even if we go down trying."

"Then let's do it."

They looked from one to the other. Anna gave Ned's

hand another squeeze, then they set off up Bank Street toward the fire.

She walked in the middle again, the two men flanking her on either side. The air was thick with the smell of the fire now. By the next block they could feel the heat being thrown off from the building. The glare hurt their eyes.

"Jesus," Grier murmured.

They all felt the strangeness of staring at that huge, two-story building going up in flames. They'd almost gotten used to the emptiness of the city. But here, where the night should have been busy with fire fighters, flashing lights, crowds of bystanders looking for a quick thrill, the alienness seemed more pronounced.

They moved closer. A half block away they had to stop because of the heat. A section of roof fell in, and they all started, moving back a couple of steps in unison. They kept a careful watch on the buildings around them, looking up and down the streets, but the fire kept drawing their gaze.

Like moths to a flame, Anna thought. This is what they feel like. This is why there're always people drawn to disasters. They weren't necessarily ghoulish. It was a reminder that there, but for the grace of God . . .

Grier turned away and made another quick sweep of the streets.

"There's no one around," he said softly. "No sign of the perp, but I got a feeling."

Ned and Anna nodded. They did too. Whatever was responsible for the deaths, for this blaze, was very close. They continued to scan the buildings and streets. When movement finally came, none of them was prepared for its source.

She came floating out of the flames, pale and ghostly.

Her long, bleached hair streamed down her shoulders. Her robes shimmered in the heat. Her face drew their gazes like magnets. Her beauty stilled their breaths. For one long moment they all saw her in the same form—Jack's angel, heartbreakingly lovely—but then her features changed and—

Ned saw the bruised and battered face of the little girl he'd found going in on a routine domestic on his first year as a rookie.

The parents had been beating on the kid for so long that her bruises had become her natural coloring. Broken nose. A busted arm that had never been properly set. Five fucking years old and her parents used her for a whipping post.

He'd hit the father—had just started beating on him when his partner had pulled him off. Then he was all set to go after the mother. His partner had covered for him—the man had been resisting arrest, they told their sergeant. With the way the kid looked, Ned hadn't been charged himself, but he never forgot that poor kid's face. She never got off. The scars she had, physical as well as those you couldn't see, were going to be with her forever.

Seeing her face now, older but still recognizable on the shoulders of the angel, all that old frustration and empathy came rushing back so hard that his eyes teared and his chest hurt. Because in her eyes he saw that same dumb misery that had been there when he'd found her all those years ago. It was like nothing had changed.

He wanted to have her father back in front of him again. Here, in this place. With no one to stop him as he finished the job on him, hitting the fucker until he was just as helpless as the poor kid he'd been beating on, and then hitting him some more. . . .

But piggybacking that rage was a sense of shame. Because at the same time as the righteous anger filled him he was also remembering all the times he'd been on the giving end of misery. Nothing major—just all the minor hurt that people dumped on each other.

Making fun of some nerd in high school.

Standing up a date because she didn't match up to some new flame—and being tactless enough to tell her so.

Roughing up some longhair for being too lippy.

Little things. But if you got it all your life, they added up to a lot of pain. . . .

Ernie Grier saw the face of Wendy Kerr.

She was a kid in his senior class in high school. A real looker. A little wild. She liked to hitchhike, and one time she caught the wrong ride and ended up dead in a ditch. Ernie was the one who found her, riding by on his ten-speed, catching a flash of color by the side of the road as he went by. He grabbed the brakes and turned around. When he saw her—the bruised face, the head hanging at an impossible angle, the nude body that awakened no lust in him because of its pathetic situation—he knelt in the dirt beside the road and threw up, dry heaving long after he'd lost the contents of his stomach.

That was the moment when he realized he had to be a cop, to do what he could to stop this kind of thing. And if he couldn't stop it, then he wanted to make sure the fuckers responsible got theirs.

Wendy Kerr. She looked a little older, and the color

of the angel's hair wasn't the same as her own auburn ponytail, but he knew her all the same.

He held the shotgun with whitening knuckles. Left hand tense on the slide handle, finger tightening on the trigger. If he'd had the fucker who'd hurt her in his sights right now . . .

The anger had never died. It was as alive now as it had been then. But, like Ned, he knew shame too.

Nobody was perfect. And he'd dumped on his share of people who hadn't deserved it. . . .

Anna felt the same guilt that her companions did. Faces rose in her mind's eye—the faces of all those that she'd ever hurt in one way or another. Confronted by their accusing features, she was ashamed. But then the memories blurred. The angel's features appeared for a moment, blurred again, became Beth. . . .

Anna had first met Beth while doing volunteer work at a home for battered women, and she'd taken her under her wing, the way she always did with strays, with anyone who needed help. But there was something different about Beth right from the start. It wasn't just that life had been so very hard on her—there were too many other women in exactly that same situation. It wasn't that she felt more pity for Beth than for the other women in the home. It was that she could see that Beth could really be something special, but she needed more help than the home could give her to attain her potential.

The women who ran the home were too overworked to be able to give her that extra attention. But Anna wasn't. Especially because it wasn't pity that drove her but a true sense of kinship with the lost soul that Beth had been at the time. A strange sense of déjà vu—they had been friends before, in other lives, and would be friends again. It was something she never could have explained clearly to anyone, and she'd never bothered to try. So she'd simply devoted her time to Beth.

Sometimes Anna was tough on her. Sometimes she got so frustrated at the way Beth just let life hand her what scraps it would without question that she wanted to shake her friend silly. But more and more often, as good memories built up to at least ease, if not erase, the past, Beth's potential began to shine through.

But this . . . Beth's features in that face. Beth floating from the flames in the angel's body.

The shock of recognition paralyzed Anna.

Not Beth.

It couldn't have been Beth who killed all those men—

(killed Jack!)

—so brutally.

*I was the one in control there. I felt like nobody could hurt me—nobody could even touch me.*

Not you, Beth, Anna said. You didn't kill Jack. Please tell me you didn't. Jack never hurt you—he never hurt anyone. How . . . how could you do it?

*You don't know what it's like being me. Everybody always hitting on me, using me. . . .*

A bitter numbness spread through Anna. If she'd never taken Beth in, then Jack would still be alive.

. . . *stop hurting me* . . .

I only wanted to help you.

. . . *stop hurting me* . . .

The music was still building—Baker's music. His concerto dedicated to pain. To suffering.

. . . *stop hurting me* . . .

Anna could almost understand the need for Baker's death. The suffering he had caused. But Jack . . .

. . . *stop hurting me* . . .

The anger that fell like a red cloud across Anna's eyes was an alien thing to her. The need to take Ned's revolver and empty it into the woman was as unfamiliar. But Anna's hand twitched at her side, longing for the weapon all the same. Because when she thought of Jack . . .

. . . *stop hurting me* . . .

All she wanted to do was erase Beth from the face of the earth.

It was then that the angel's features began to change. The skin peeled away, fangs protruded, her nose disappeared, leaving a hole in the middle of that once perfect face. The mouth opened wide, jaws unhinging like a snake's. Dozens of tongues writhed in that dark maw.

No angel now, but a fury.

The music rose to a crescendo. Anna could sense the men on either side of her tensing, raising their weapons. Her fingers continued to twitch, wanting a weapon of their own. But then she saw something else.

Behind the creature's monstrous features she saw a flicker of faces, going by so fast that there was barely time to make one out from the other. But she recognized them all the same.

Victims.

Battered women, abused children.

They were faces she'd seen in photos in the newspaper, and in that home for battered women. Faces from the snapshots that Jack carried when he was on a case—the kids he was looking for.

Victims.

Their faces going by in a blur. So many of them.

Hundreds.

That wasn't Beth, she realized. She could hear Jack's voice, whispering under the whine of the music.

*This is where the victims wait to get even, Anna.*

This fury wasn't *just* Beth. It was all of them. All of the hurt people that no one has time to help.

*The thing is, you bring your own pain in here with you, and it changes things too.*

The sound of the slide handles pumping shells into the firing chambers of the shotguns on either side of her was loud—even with the roar of the fire and the music.

My pain is Jack's death, Anna thought. I brought that with me here. Just like Ned and Ernie have brought their own pains. Their own injustices. Here we just want to get even. We want to act, to be strong. To have our own justice.

*Here it's the weak that are strong. It's their place to get back at everything that ever hurt them.*

But it's not our place. If we bring our anger to it, our need for justice, we're just calling that thing down on us.

The creature floated away from the flames, moving toward them. On either side of her, Ned and Grier raised their weapons.

"No!" Anna cried.

She put out her hands, to the left and right, pushing the barrels of the shotguns away from their target.

"Throw them away," she said. "All your weapons—throw them away!"

"Jesus Christ, Anna!" Ned cried. "What the fuck do you think you're—"

The creature had drifted closer. It was hard to look

into the horror of its features and think of victims. Of not striking back. Oh, God, if she was wrong—

(Jack!)

She turned on Ned. "Do it, please God, just do it, *do it*!"

Then she faced the creature and took a step closer to it. She held her hands out open in front of her and composed her features to show no anger, no fear. Her stomach churned. The music made her head ache with its ugly tones. She took a couple more steps.

"Beth . . . ?" she said.

"Anna!" Ned cried.

"Trust me in this," she called back to him without turning. "Please, Ned."

She moved closer still to the advancing creature.

"I know you're in there, Beth. It's Anna. I want to help."

## 2

THROUGH THE CREATURE'S eyes Beth could see her.

Anna.

Her best friend. Her only friend.

What was she doing here?

In the voices of the host that shared the fury's body with her, she heard the answer. She came to die.

The music moaned and wailed, a shrieking chorus.

*To die . . . to die . . .*

It bit at Beth's thoughts, worrying and tearing at them like animals feeding on a kill. But seeing Anna freed Beth of her fear. The horror of Walt's corpse fled.

The power that the creature held over her drained away.

She *could* be strong, she realized. In control. It required taking a stand and sticking to it. It was so simple. So impossible. It meant losing the promised comfort of the wasteland. The endless, peaceful flight. It meant going back to the real world and the possibility of finding herself in—

(that dark place)

—the role of a victim again.

But everything had a price, didn't it? Helping Anna meant losing the promise of peace. Retaining the promise meant Anna had to die.

There was no question which she had to choose.

Anna never hurt anyone, she told the fury and its host.

*She came here with anger in her heart,* the voices cried. *They came with weapons with which they meant to hurt us.*

They . . . they're just scared, Beth replied.

The thought surprised her, but she realized it was true.

They're just like us, she said.

*Only the guilty are drawn to this mid-ground,* the voices told her.

*Only the guilty,* the music echoed.

*So we visit them with justice,* the voices said.

The elemental force that was the fury said nothing, allowing the host to answer for it.

But everyone's got something to feel guilty about inside them, Beth said. That doesn't mean they're bad people. Look at them. You *know* they're not evil. Don't tell me you can't see that.

Through the creature's eyes Beth watched Anna approach, hands held open before her. Behind her, the two men hesitated. She recognized Ned.

He was the first to throw his shotgun off to the side. He drew his handgun and threw that away as well, then stood his ground, hands pulling open his jacket to show that he had no other weapons. Moments later the other man did the same.

"Beth, please," Anna was saying.

*She considers herself better than you,* the voices said. *She always set herself above you.*

No, Beth replied. All she ever wanted to do was help.

The music whined, the host chorused a hundred pains, but still the fury remained silent.

"I know it's hard," Anna said. "I know it hurts. I know about pain, Beth. Jack's dead—don't tell me I don't know about pain."

Jack was dead?

Beth felt sick. Had she been a part of his death too?

"But being here doesn't solve anything," Anna went on. "You never like to hear this, but it's true. Running away never solved anything. There's good things in the world, too, Beth. Think of the times we've had—you and me. Think of what can be."

*Pain,* the voices said to Beth. *More suffering. More hurt.*

"I . . . I need you, Beth."

Looking at her now, Beth had never seen Anna look so disconsolate.

"I need a friend, Beth."

*Who protected you from your Walt Hawkins?* the host demanded. *Was* she *there for you?*

But the music wasn't so fierce now. It still tore at Beth's thoughts, trying to keep her from thinking straight, but she was becoming stronger than it.

Ever since we met, Beth said, she's been there for me. Let her go. Let them all go.

*This is the killing time,* the voices replied.

I won't let you do it.

*How can you stop us?*

Beth swallowed thickly. Maybe . . . maybe I can't . . . but you'll have to kill me first.

*We can't harm you—you're one of us. You're a part of us.*

Then let them go.

*You'll never be able to return.*

I don't want to return. Close the door that the music opened and let us all go.

*There are other doors.*

Beth nodded. She could feel the press of the host around her, begging her to remain. She could feel the fury, touching her thoughts like the angel she could be, reminding her of all she would lose. The peace of the wasteland. The freedom from hurt. But none of that was worth the price. None of it was worth becoming the same as the people that made you a victim in the first place.

There'll always be other doors, she said softly, so long as people treat each other the way that they do. Just close this one. Let us go.

The music was just a faint hum, ticking the back of her thoughts now. The host touched her—hundreds of hands, brushing her with a feathery lightness, fading one by one, until only the presence of the angel was left.

*I pray the world treats you more gently than it has, little sister,* the angel said. *But I fear it won't.*

Then she let Beth go.

# 3

WE'RE STANDING in hell, Ned thought as he watched Anna pleading with the creature. The burning building made an apt backdrop.

He'd finally thrown his weapons away, not so much because he thought Anna was going to convince the creature to spare them as he knew they weren't going to be effective, anyway. Not against something that could start up a blaze like that. Not against something that totaled people the way the corpses had been fried. Not against a monstrosity like that.

He wasn't ready to go down without a fight, but he figured it was Anna's play, she was carrying the ball, and he'd let her run it her way. If that meant tossing away the guns, fine. They were tossed. But he still had his hands, and when that creature came to fry him, he was going to take his fist and ram it right down that fucking boa-constrictor mouth. Just watch him.

They were nuts to have crossed over in the first place. What the fuck had he thought they were going to accomplish? And Anna . . . Jesus, Anna dying here. . . . Just thinking of that creature frying her had him ready to go pick up the shotgun and give the goddamned thing a couple of loads straight in the head, anyway.

It was just then that he noticed the quiet.

The building was still burning; the sound of the flames as they ate the air hadn't diminished one bit. But the music was gone. And the creature . . .

The fury was gone.

It was a woman again. A shining woman. A frigging angel.

Her chest was swelling—no, she was drawing back and something was falling out of her. . . .

Slack-jawed, he watched Anna's roommate tumble from the floating angel. She drifted to the ground, landing on her knees, gaze fixed on Anna's face, while behind her, the angel rose higher into the smoky air. Higher still. He craned his neck to watch her go, a shining image against the black smoke.

Then she was gone.

He looked at his partner. Grier had as stunned an expression on his face as Ned knew was on his own.

"Does . . ." Grier paused, cleared his throat. "Does this mean we won?"

Anna knelt on the ground and reached for Beth, holding her tightly. Tears brimmed in Anna's eyes, then she burrowed her face in Beth's shoulder and wept. Beth wrapped her arms around her friend and held her in a protective embrace. The sensation of being needed was unfamiliar to her, but it was the best validation that Beth could have had to tell her that she'd done the right thing.

"Is it over?" Ned asked her.

When Beth turned her battered face toward him, he saw in her features the faces of a hundred domestics he'd caught—all those bruised women carrying the unhappy wounds of their painful liaisons. But there was a strength in this woman's face that belied the pain she had to be feeling. By all rights, hurt as she was, she shouldn't have been able to move, let alone hold and comfort Anna, but she was doing both.

Ned's heart went out to her courage.

When she nodded in response to his question, he let

out a sigh. His partner collected their weapons while Ned stood beside her and Anna.

It was over. That was all he needed to know for now. He didn't know what had happened, or how they'd pulled it off, but at least it was over. He could find out the hows and whys later.

He was just starting to wonder how they were going to get back when he felt a familiar sensation.

Flicker.

For one long moment it was like they hadn't gone anywhere. The fire still raged. The air was thick with its smoke. But then Ned realized he was right up near a huge fire truck with a man in a turnout coat and helmet staring pop-eyed at him. Red lights swept the buildings in circular sweeps. Crowds pressed against barricades, trying to get close to the excitement.

"What the . . . ?" the fireman began.

Ned just grinned at him. They were back. All four of them. He helped Anna and Beth to their feet.

"How the hell are we going to explain any of this?" Grier asked.

Before Ned could answer, a pair of uniforms came running up, drawing their weapons.

"Police," Grier told them.

He carefully laid the handful of weapons on the pavement and fished for his ID. Beside him, Ned put one arm around around Anna's shoulders, the other around Beth's.

"We're going to make it," he told them. "We'll help each other."

"Starting right now," Grier added, turning toward them as one of the uniformed policemen took his ID.

"I'll handle things here, Ned. Why don't you see about calling an ambulance?"

Ned nodded his thanks, then led Beth and Anna to the nearest patrol car to make the call.